CLASSES IN KIDNAPPING

CONTENTS

SAFECRACKING FOR STUDENTS

CONTENTS

MASTER CROOK'S

CRIME ACADEMY

CLASSES IN KIDNAPPING and
SAFE-CRACKING FOR STUDENTS

TERRY DEARY

SCHOLASTIC

Scholastic Children's Books,
Euston House, 24 Eversholt Street,
London NW1 1DB, UK

A division of Scholastic Ltd
London ~ New York ~ Toronto ~ Sydney ~ Auckland
Mexico City ~ New Delhi ~ Hong Kong

Classes in Kidnapping first published by Scholastic Ltd., 2009
Safecracking for Students first published by Scholastic Ltd., 2009
This edition published by Scholastic Ltd., 2019

Text © Terry Deary, 2009
Illustration © John Kelly, 2009

The right of Terry Deary and John Kelly to be identified as the author
and illustrator of this work has been asserted by them.

ISBN 978 1407 19564 3

Printed and bound in the UK by CPI Group Ltd, Croydon, CR0 4YY

2 4 6 8 10 9 7 5 3 1

Th
di
fi

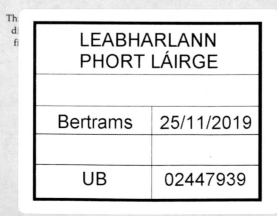

CRIME ACADEMY

CLASSES IN KIDNAPPING

Before word

THE QUEEN IS DEAD. "LONG LIVE THE KING", AS THEY SAY. WHO SAYS? I DON'T KNOW, BUT IT WAS A CLEVER THING TO SAY.

YOU'LL HAVE READ THE REPORTS IN THE NEWSPAPERS. THE OLD QUEEN HAD SOME STRANGE IDEAS...

Saturday 2 February 1901

The Wildpool Daily News

QUEEN: CORPSE TO COFFIN!

THE LATE QUEEN VICTORIA will be buried at Windsor Great Park today. (For our Wildpool readers we should explain that Windsor is near London.)

THE QUEEN said she wanted to be lifted into her coffin by her sons and so she was. Our Wildpool Special Royal reporter explains that she said this before she died.

SHE ALSO SAID (before she died) that she hated black clothes at funerals, so London was decorated in purple and white for the event.

THE MAYOR OF WILDPOOL, Sir Peter Puddle, said that Wildpool should be decorated in purple and white too. Nobody agreed with him so it

Cont.

never happened. As his wife said, "Queen Victoria never came to Wildpool so why should we care?"

THE QUEEN'S CORPSE was dressed in a white wedding dress – not the dress she wore for her wedding to Prince Albert, of course. She had grown much too fat for that.

OUR SPECIAL ROYAL reporter telephoned to say that when she was laid to rest it began to snow.

VICTORIA HAD REIGNED for sixty-three years, seven months and two days – the longest of any British ruler. (Oddly, as she was only five foot tall, she was also the shortest of any British ruler.)

THERE WERE EIGHT attempts to kill her in those sixty-three years. None of them harmed her, though Robert Pate crushed her bonnet when he struck her with his walking cane in 1850. Pate was mad. And the queen wasn't very pleased either.

IN THE END that great assassin "Old Age" got her. She left nine children and forty-two grandchildren – many of whom are kings and queens across Europe.

SHE WILL BE BURIED next to her husband, who died forty years ago, so he'll be a bit mouldy now.

THE CROWN PASSES to Prince Edward, who has only been waiting fifty-nine years to get it.

THE VERY MOMENT OLD QUEEN VICTORIA POPPED HER CLOGS, PRINCE EDWARD BECAME KING EDWARD. SO THE COUNTRY AND THE EMPIRE ARE NEVER WITHOUT A KING OR QUEEN. NOT EVEN FOR A SECOND.

HERE'S A STRANGE THING . . . NO ONE CAN TELL ME WHY.

WHAT USE HAS A KING OR QUEEN EVER BEEN TO US POOR PEOPLE? DOES ANYBODY KNOW? DON'T GET ME STARTED ON THE SUBJECT OF THE RICH AND THE ROTTEN WHO RULE US.

NO, INSTEAD I WANT TO TELL YOU A MORE REMARKABLE STORY. YOU SEE THE MAYOR'S WIFE SAID, "QUEEN VICTORIA NEVER CAME TO WILDPOOL."

THE MAYOR'S WIFE WAS QUITE RIGHT.

BUT THE MAYOR'S WIFE WAS ALSO QUITE WRONG.

I KNOW. I WAS THERE AT THE TIME. THERE IN WILDPOOL BACK IN MARCH 1837. THE STORY HAS BEEN A SECRET FOR ALL THESE YEARS. BUT NOW I AM GOING TO LET YOU IN ON IT.

MR X

18 MARCH 1901

Chapter 1

SHADOWS AND SHEEP-HEADS

Monday 12th March 1837

The girl walked the dim streets of Wildpool. Gas lamps glowed with a silver-green light and made her pale, thin face look sickly. Her worried eyes flickered like butterflies in a bowl.

There was no one on the streets to help her. It was near midnight and even the drinkers from the ale-houses had rolled and reeled, lurched and lumbered, bumbled and blundered, bobbled and hobbled, staggered and stumbled, tottered and tumbled home.

Stray dogs played and cats ratted and bats batted . . .[1]

---

1 at least I think that 's what bats do.

The girl looked round quickly. Something vanished into the shadow of a doorway. It was the shadow of a shadow. She looked up the steep street, Sea Road, and towards Wildpool High Street at the top. Another quarter of a mile and she would be safe.

But anything can happen in a quarter of a mile. They could still catch her and dispatch her. She pulled her shawl over her fair curly hair and hurried up the cobbles, slippery in the damp night air.

The clock on the town hall chimed the three-quarter hour. *Bing-bong, bing-bong, bing-bong...*

It was quarter to midnight. She had fifteen minutes to reach safety. And a lot can happen in fifteen minutes ... some people can eat twenty pork pies in fifteen minutes.

Gas lamps did not glow at all in the dark alleys that ran between the back yards of the rows of houses to her left. She stopped at the corner of the first street and looked into the grim gloom of the alley that ran at the back of Fulwell Street. She heard an eerie creaking sound, a slosh and a panting breath of something huge and hairy...[2]

There was a sharp clink of metal on the cobbles; then it started again.

Creak, slosh, pant, clink.

And the smell. The sour smell of the back house. A fat rat ran out of the alley. Not even a rat could stand that smell.

Creak, slosh, pant, clink.

She looked over her shoulder again. The shadow disappeared into the next dark doorway. Only one shadow. There should have been two.

Creak, slosh, pant, clink.

The sounds from the back alley were coming closer and looming into the light of the gas lamps on the front street.

A large hairy horse appeared first. Then the cart. And finally the two men. The night soil men. They looked up and smiled at her.

---

2 All right, all right! You are right. You can't HEAR if something is hairy. It sounded huge and the girl imagined it would be hairy. In fact I once had a history teacher who breathed like a bull but was quite bald. Bald and ugly. Apart from that she was quite a nice teacher.

One man bent down and lifted the wooden flaps in the back yard walls. *Creak*. The other man thrust a shovel into the gap and scooped out the ashes and the human filth that had been left in the back house.[3]

They loaded the foul mix of human waste and ashes on to the muck cart. *Slosh!*

The horse strained in its shafts to move on to the next back house flap. *Pant!*

It's hooves struck the damp cobbles. *Clink!*

The men reached the last house on the corner and stopped. "Evening, lass," the shorter one said. "Want a stick?"

She looked over her shoulder. There were a hundred shadows on the street but none were moving now. So long as she stayed with the night soil men no one could touch her.

"Why would I want a stick?" she asked.

---

3 You will have a back house at the bottom of your yard, but these days you call it a toilet, don't you? Yours probably is kept clean with flushing water. But in the old days they had a box that you filled with cold ashes from the fires. You sat on a wooden plank with a hole in and did what you had to do into the ashes. Then the night soil men came along at night and emptied it. A nice job ... well, a steady job. YOU'D enjoy it.

The taller soil man shook his head. "Kids these days!" He rested on the horse and said, "You take a long stick. You poke it in the back of our cart, and you get a lot of very smelly stuff on the end."

"I see," the girl said . . . though she didn't.

The shorter night soil man put in, "Then you take the stick up to the posh houses – somewhere like South Drive – and you wipe the stick on the door handles. When the posh folk come home and try to open the door. . ."[4]

"Yes! I understand," the girl said quickly. "But I haven't time for games at the moment. I need to get to the police station on the High Street."

The men nodded. "We'll give you a ride for a hundred yards on the cart!" the little man offered, and he stretched out his hands to lift her up.

---

4 No one has played this game for years. It 's sad the way these old sports die out, isn't it? Of course I wouldn't want you going out and trying this for yourself! Oh, dear, no! After all you may pick on MY door handle! Can you just forget I told you that story of the soil cart and the sticks? Thank you.

"No!" she said quickly ... even in the dim gas-light those hands looked crusted with something unspeakable. "I'd rather walk, thanks."

The men nodded and turned the horse into the steep Sea Road. The horse grunted and heaved at its load. They reached the next back alley and turned into it. "Goodnight, miss," the shorter night soil man said.

The girl looked over her shoulder. The shadow was hiding in the shadow of a lamp post. But at least she was another hundred yards nearer to safety. Only three hundred to go. Suddenly, the sharp clack of running feet could be heard coming along the dark alley. The night soil men looked at one another in horror. "They're on to us!" the shorter one croaked. He let go of the reins of the horse and started to run up the hill.

A police whistle blew. The first set of footsteps had an echo. Another pair of police boots were also coming down the hill. A policeman as thin as a cucumber, with a moustache like a white bootlace, skidded to a halt. He grasped the shorter night soil man by the shoulder. "Pooh!" he cried.

Out of the dark alley came the policeman's partner – a constable as round as the moon with a face as red as Mars. He huffed to a halt.

"I arrest ... you in the name ... of Wildpool ... police service..." he managed to say. It was a chilly evening but the constables were sweating in their navy woollen uniforms. "Put your handcuffs on them, Constable Liddle."

"I don't have my handcuffs, Constable Larch," his thin partner said quietly. He lifted his tall top hat and mopped the sweat on his bony face and thin grey hair. "I left them in the drawer back at the station."

Larch groaned, unsure what to do. He pulled out his printed orders for the night.

WILDPOOL POLICE FORCE

DATE: 12th March 1837

Orders for Night Patrol.

Proceed to Sea Road and Fulwell Street, Wildpool. Patrol the back alleys that run off Sea Road. Be careful not to be seen by anyone.

Seek out and arrest the men who are emptying the night soil boxes.

Lock them in the police station cell. Take them to court tomorrow morning — after you have given them a bath. (And you will probably need a bath yourselves.)

POLICE INSPECTOR BEADLE

Larch glared at him. "Says nothing here about forgetting handcuffs."

The taller night soil man grinned. "You'll just have to let us go then, officer!"

Larch scowled. "We'll just have to hit you over the head with our truncheons and carry you up to the police station in the back of your cart."

"No!" squawked the taller night soil man. "We'll come quietly. Honest!"

"If you were honest you wouldn't be stealing the night soil," Constable Larch grumbled. "Take them to the station, Liddle."

"Me? What about you?" the thin policeman whined.

"I'm arresting the horse and cart." He turned to the horse. "Now, are you going to come quietly too? Or do I have to use my truncheon on you?"

"Neigh," the horse replied.[5]

They all began to march up the steep street towards the police station. The girl trotted alongside them. She was safe now. The shadows couldn't get her while she was with

5 This was meant to be a JOKE. It wasn't a very good joke but Constable Larch was a policeman not a Music Hall comic. He wasn't even a very good policeman. But trust me, he would NEVER use his truncheon on a horse. He would use a Pony Club. Hah! Get it? Maybe not. Just another joke. An even worse one than Constable Larch 's some might say.

the Wildpool police force. Constable Larch held his black wooden truncheon in his fat paw. She smiled.

"What have the night soil men done?" she asked.

"Stolen the night soil," Larch told her as he struggled to lead the awkward horse up the hill.

"It's their job to empty the back houses. How could they steal something worthless?"

"They sell it to the farmers. The farmers spread it on their fields as manure. It's a good trade in the springtime, you know. And spring's not far away now. The real night soil men are very upset that these two have pilfered their poo. But we have cracked the crime and caught the thieves red-handed."

"*Red*-handed?" the girl said, remembering the hand that tried to lift her on the cart.

"You know what I mean," Constable Larch said. "Ah, here we are," he said as they turned at the top of the steep street and into the High Street. The police station stood fifty yards to their left. A gas lamp glowed in a blue glass bowl that had the word *Police* painted on in white.

The girl turned and looked back down Sea Road. The gas lamps made a necklace of light that ran down to join the rows of lights in the shipyards on the river. The furnace at the glass factory made the low, cold clouds glow a dirty red. A boy stood in the middle of Sea Road, staring up at her. He'd come out of the shadows now. Defeated.

The thin girl gave a thinner smile. "Yessss!" she hissed. She looked towards the large house that stood next to the police station.

A sign hung on the gate.

MASTER CROOK'S

CRIME ACADEMY

TUITION FOR THE CHILDREN OF THE POOR TO HELP THEM STAY OUT OF PRISON.

She would step through the gateway, walk ten paces across the garden, past the wind-withered tree, and enter the school. Then she would be safe. Then she would have won.

She turned to the policemen. "Goodnight, officers!" she cried cheerfully.

"Evening all," the policemen cried.

The shorter fake night soil man stopped and turned to her. "You don't know anyone wants to buy this load of night soil, do you?"

She shook her head.

"Oh, just it's a shame to see it go to waste," the man sighed and trudged under the blue light and into the station.

The girl gave one last look over her shoulder. The boy stood, helpless, at the corner of Sea Road and High Street. She wiggled her fingers at him in a cruel wave.

The town hall clock started to chime midnight. *Bing-bong, bing-bong, bing-bong, bing-bong. Donnnng! Donnnng! Donnnng!*

She stepped between the gateposts of Master Crook's Crime Academy ... *Donnnng!* ... and two things happened. She suddenly wondered what happened to the boy's partner.

Donnnng! Why weren't there *two* of them at the street corner?

And then a large, rough sack was thrown over her head.

Donnnng! She breathed in to scream and the dust of the sack choked her. *Donnnng!* Before she could let out a yell, a strong hand clamped over her mouth and pressed the rough sack over her face.

Donnnng! She struggled but she knew it was useless.

The dust of the sack soaked up her tears.

Donnnng!

They weren't tears of fear or pity. They were tears of rage. Rage at knowing they'd got the sack from the sheep-head shop on Harrow Lane ... she could tell by the smell.

Donnnng! But most of all, rage at knowing they had tricked her.

Donnnng! She was a very bad loser.

Donnnng!

Chapter 2

WOOFS AND WATERLOO

Tuesday 13th March 1837

T he poster had been printed in a hurry and the ink had run a little bit. But the people of Wildpool crowded round it.

PUBLIC MEETING

THERE WILL BE A MEETING IN THE TOWN HALL
ON TUESDAY 13TH MARCH AT TEN A.M.
MAYOR OSWALD TWISTLE WILL MAKE SOME IMPORTANT
ANNOUNCEMENTS
ABOUT THE FUTURE OF WILDPOOL TOWN
AND A SECRET ROYAL VISIT

The beggar (who usually sat on the corner of the High Street) sighed and said, "I bet it means trouble for us."

The woman who owned the hat shop squinted at him. "How can you read that notice? You're supposed to be blind. I give you pennies to feed your poor little guide dog – the one with the waggly tail!"

The beggar shrugged. "This is one of my good days. I can see quite well on my good days."

"Oh! I hope my money goes to buy food for your poor little dog," she snapped.

"I buy it the best meat the butcher has in his shop and I cook it till it's perfect," the beggar said, licking his lips.

"And does your little woofy-woofy with the waggly tail like it?"

"No, but I do."

"You?"

"Yes, I eat it."

"What does the woofy with the waggly tail eat?"

"Nothing. It's a *toy* dog, you see," the beggar said and lifted it up for the hat-seller to see. The black button eyes stared at her like windows in an empty house. The shiny black nose was painted wood. The cute red tongue was felt and the teeth had once belonged to a dinosaur.[6]

The hat-seller shook her head and her big bonnet waggled like a dog's waggly tail. "I was sure the little woofy wagged its tail every time it saw me!"

"That's because of the bit of string," the beggar explained, "fastened to my ear. I waggled my ear and the tail wagged. My ears always waggled because I was pleased to see you, of course."

"Because you admire my fair face and golden hair?" she giggled.

"No. Because you always throw a sixpence in my cap."[7]

---

6 Don't worry, the dinosaur was dead and didn't need the teeth. The blind beggar had seen them in a museum and had borrowed them to make his toy guide dog. It was a very small dinosaur and the teeth were a bit grey. The dog now had a very cute smile. Cute but grey.

7 What he really wanted to say was, "Because you are daft as a two-foot brush." And she was. Even YOU would not have been fooled by the dog with the waggly tail. It was the big red wheels on the paws that gave it away.

He looked up. "Now, if I wasn't blind I would say the town hall clock is just about to strike ten and the meeting will be starting soon. Better get along."

He put the dog down and pushed it along on its wheels with one hand while waving a white stick with the other. Sure enough the clock began to strike. *Bing, bong. . .*[8]

The beggar and the hat-seller stepped into the town hall. Mayor Twistle was very proud of his town hall. It looked a little like a Greek temple – and when Mayor Twistle looked in the mirror he saw a Greek god. Not a lot of Greek gods wear gold-rimmed spectacles, as you will know, or fine black suits. And they didn't have neat little beards either. But Mayor Twistle didn't see what the rest of the world saw – a man who was taller than a gnome . . . but only just.[9]

Twistle's temple was fine. Tall columns painted gold held up a ceiling with a painting

8 Oh, I'm sure you know the rest. Just finish it off in your head. The chimes bonged to ten . . . if you are not very good at counting then that is one bong for each finger. Unless you are an earthworm, in which case you have a problem, or a centipede in which case you have an even bigger problem.

9 None of us look in a mirror and see what the rest of the world sees.

of gods having a picnic with lots of colourful fruit. At one end stood a platform where people stood to make speeches – it was quite a high platform because as you know, Mayor Oswald Twistle was a very small man.

The *bings* had finished *bonging* but the mayor had not appeared yet. He liked to keep his people waiting. He liked everyone to be in their places before he and his wife made a grand entrance. He *hated* anyone turning up late.

Behind the fine oak door he practised his speech one last time. "Mimble orrible," he said. "Mimble *orrible*?"

Bing, bong! Bing, bong. . .

The chimes sounded in Master Crook's Crime Academy. The class was restless and didn't notice the time.

At the front of the class stood their teacher, Samuel Dreep, who *did* notice the time. His gooseberry-green eyes seemed to glow. His fingers rippled like raindrops on a window pane when he talked. When he smiled his ivory teeth shone under his thin, dark moustache.

This morning, the class seemed sulky and angry. Mr Dreep was pleased. This was a class that really *cared* about their homework. When they got it *wrong* it only made them stubborn. *Next* time they'd pass the test.

"Now, class, I need to leave you to go to a meeting in the town hall," the teacher said.

A boy with hair as wild as a dandelion, but as dark as the hold of a Wildpool coal ship, spoke up. "Is it about our next crime, Mr Dreep?"

"It may be, Smiff. I think there is a terrible wrong coming to the poor people of Wildpool," the teacher said.

A girl with a face as plain as a bag of white flour spoke up. "And, where there is a wrong, it is Master Crook's job to put it right."

"Correct, Nancy."

Nancy was a large girl with a kind face. Not at all the sort you would expect to find in a school for villains. A thin girl with fair curly hair and a face as fierce as a fox sneered. "Ooooh! *Correct*, Nancy. Well done, Nancy. Teacher's *pet* Nancy!"

Mr Dreep spoke sharply. "I know you are

in one of your bad moods, Alice," he said. "But we do *not* bully our friends in Master Crook's Crime Academy."

"Hah! Who says? You says?" Alice snorted.

Mr Dreep went across to the wall and tapped a sheet of paper that was pinned there. "Rule ten, Alice ... the top rule."

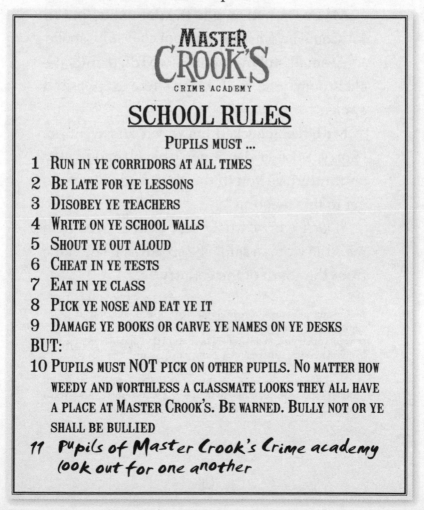

MASTER CROOK'S
CRIME ACADEMY

SCHOOL RULES
PUPILS MUST ...

1 RUN IN YE CORRIDORS AT ALL TIMES
2 BE LATE FOR YE LESSONS
3 DISOBEY YE TEACHERS
4 WRITE ON YE SCHOOL WALLS
5 SHOUT YE OUT ALOUD
6 CHEAT IN YE TESTS
7 EAT IN YE CLASS
8 PICK YE NOSE AND EAT YE IT
9 DAMAGE YE BOOKS OR CARVE YE NAMES ON YE DESKS
BUT:
10 PUPILS MUST NOT PICK ON OTHER PUPILS. NO MATTER HOW WEEDY AND WORTHLESS A CLASSMATE LOOKS THEY ALL HAVE A PLACE AT MASTER CROOK'S. BE WARNED. BULLY NOT OR YE SHALL BE BULLIED
11 Pupils of Master Crook's Crime academy look out for one another

Alice pouted. "If it's the top rule then why is it number ten? Eh?"

Mr Dreep ignored her. "While I am out I will leave you in the care of the greatest expert in kidnapping in this country."

The class snapped to attention. A new guest teacher was always exciting.

Mr Dreep marched to the door and opened it. "Come in, Miss Friday!"

A small, tubby woman waddled into the classroom. She had a face like a polished apple.[10]

Mr Dreep checked his watch and went on. "Sorry, Miss Friday, I don't have time to stay and introduce you to the class. I really *have* to get to this meeting."

"Don't worry, Mr Dreep. Leave them with me," the woman said. She spoke as if she came from the south of the country.[11]

---

10 I mean, of course, a rosy apple. If you said, "Ooooh! A green apple, was it?" then you are either being stupid or awkward. Stop it at once. I am trying to tell a story here and I don't need smarty-socks like you making silly remarks. Now, can I get on? Thank you.

11 Or, if like me you are from the north of our noble country, you could say she spoke as if she came from the sarf uv ahr cantry. You'd be right. She was from the dark and dismal streets of London.

Dreep gave a small bow, pulled on his gloves and wrapped a red-and-white striped scarf around his neck. He left.

Miss Friday looked around the room. "Nice place you have here," she said. And it was true. The ceilings were high and decorated with plaster angels. The large windows looked out over the river and the hills to the north.

Master Crook's Crime Academy was in a house that had once been the home of a grand family. But as the shipyards grew, and the slums spread up the hill from the riverside, the rich moved out. The rich escaped the terrible disease they called cholera when it struck in 1831.[12]

And Master Crook moved in. He had opened his Crime Academy just two months before in January 1837.

"I am Miss Ruby Friday," the woman said. "Tell me who you are."

12 You do not want to know how hideously painful cholera was. How it spread through dirty water, how the victims were sick until they turned blue and died, how the people that nursed them died too. So I won't tell you.

And the students did. There were five of them altogether. As well as large Nancy, wild-haired Smiff and fierce Alice there was a set of thin twins – the Mixley twins, Martin and Millie.

Miss Friday looked at them. "Twins, eh? Does anyone ever Mixley you up?" the woman chuckled.

"No," Alice snapped. "Martin's the boy with the short hair and Millie's the girl with the long curls. Obvious to anyone with a bag of beans for a brain."

Ruby Friday's eyes twinkled and she smiled softly. "Oh dear, Alice. We are in a bad mood this morning. Must be because of what happened last night, is it?"[13]

Alice did not want to talk about last night. "So why are you the greatest expert on kidnapping in this country?" she demanded.

Ruby Friday sat at the desk. "Back in 1815 Britain was at war with France."

13 If you take a beetroot and crush it in a bowl you will get some bright red juice. Paint it on your face and that is the colour Alice turned. Some would call it "beetroot red ". I'd call it "furious red ".

"This is a crime academy," Alice snapped sourly. "We don't need no history lessons."

"I think we *all* need history lessons, Alice," Ruby Friday said quickly. "We learn lessons from the past ... from our mistakes. Have you ever made a mistake, Alice?"

Alice snapped her mouth shut tight as a rabbit trap. Smiff smirked. "Carry on, Miss Friday."

"Britain was faced by the mighty Emperor Napoleon," the new teacher went on. "The French army met the Brits at a village called Waterloo and we all knew who was going to win."

"The British!" Martin Mixley said in his piping voice.

"No. The *French*!" Ruby Friday said. "No one could beat Emperor Napoleon and his mighty French army."

"But we did!" Millie cried.

The teacher raised a finger. "The British leader, the Duke of Wellington, sent for me. I was the British army's only hope!"

"I thought you were a kidnapper," Alice

grumbled. "Now you're telling us you're a general?"

Again Miss Friday raised a finger. "I went to Paris. I kidnapped Napoleon's wife, the Empress Josephine."

The class gasped.

"We sent Napoleon a little message the night before Waterloo. Lose the battle ... or lose your empress."

"And he lost the battle to save Josephine!" Millie Mixley cried. "That's romantic. Ahhhh!"

"See? Kidnapping isn't just for money," Ruby Friday said. "A good kidnapping can change the history of the world. And that's what we plan to do, isn't it?"

The five Master Crook students nodded ... even angry Alice.[14]

---

14 The Duke of Wellington went on to be Prime Minister of Britain and one of the most hated men in Britain – he loved to crush the poor people. Oh yes, he won the battle of Waterloo, of course. But he never told anyone the tale of Ruby Friday and the kidnapped Josephine. Welly was just too ashamed of his sneaky trick.

Chapter 3

RUBY AND RANSOM

"Friends!" Mayor Oswald Twistle cried. The audience looked up to see their mayor standing on the platform in the great hall of the town hall.

Lady Arabella Twistle stood next to him in a dress of finest silks. Today the colour was pink to match her nose. She always wrote her husband's speeches.

"Friends, Wildpoolians, countrymen!" the mayor went on. "Today is a mimble orrible day for Wildpool."

"What?" the crowd gasped.

"Memorable," Arabella hissed. "The word is memorable."

"Today is a memble-rabble day."

The large woman sighed. "It is a day we will never forget."

"Today is a day we will always forget!" Oswald cried. He cleared his throat. Now he had started it got easier ... in fact it was sometimes hard to stop him. But the door at the back opened and a man with a red-and-white striped scarf stepped into the chamber. Late. Mayor Twistle looked at the young man with poison darts.

"Why is it a memorable day?" the blind beggar called out.

"Yes! Get on with it you buffoon," the latecomer shouted from the back. It was Samuel Dreep, the teacher at Master Crook's Crime Academy.[15]

"Last year," Mayor Oswald went on, "the council of Wildpool raised thirteen hundred pounds in order to build a workhouse for the town. As you know it is the fine stone building at the north end of the bridge!"

15 But you knew that from the red-and-white striped scarf, didn't you? You have a sharp mind. Be careful it doesn't cut its way through your skull.

"Yes, built well away from your posh house at the south end of town," Mr Dreep jeered. The mayor ignored him.

"Last month Lady Arabella Twistle ... my wife..."

"My *lovely* wife," her ladyship muttered. "Read what I wrote," she said and sat down.

"...my *lovely* wife, became leader of the workhouse governors. This afternoon the workhouse will open its doors for the first time." He let the speech rest on the table and peered through his glasses at the curious crowd. His voice rose. "Now there is somewhere for the poor of Wildpool to be shut away, out of our sight, so we don't have to suffer their begging, their whining and their horrible smell! We won't have to bear the stinking scent of their unwashed clothes and their unpolished boots, the shame of their seatless trousers and their meatless meals, their bawling babies and shivering shoeless, clueless, useless children; their cold old codgers that can't keep their teeth and the layabout lazers who sleep in their sacks till it's time to come out and rob the rich of our hard-earned gold, and I for one have had *enough*, I say. *Enough!* And that's not all..."

Lady Arabella rose quickly to her feet like a hot air balloon rises over the basket when the hot air fills it. "What my husband *means* to say," she bellowed over the top of him, "is that now there is somewhere for the poor, the sick and the old to be cared for. We want to make sure there is work for everyone and there will be lots of work in the workhouse."

"That's probably why it's called a workhouse then!" the trouble-making Dreep laughed.

Mayor Twistle jumped up and said, "Our new workhouse will be run by the overseers – Mr and Mrs Humble. A fine pair of caring people you will all agree ... if you meet them ... which I hope you don't ... because if you meet them, then that means you've been locked away in the workhouse ... and you wouldn't want that! I suppose, of course, you *could* be a visitor to the workhouse in which case you will *not* be locked away ... and if you visit you WILL get to meet the

Humbles ... and you will see how fine they are ... See?"[16]

Lady Arabella rested a hand on her husband's shoulder and pushed him into his seat. She smiled her pink smile at the puzzled people. "What this means is there is now NO excuse for the poor to clutter up the streets of Wildpool and make it look untidy. No excuse for beggars to bother the rich people like us with their pawing, clawing, grubby hands. Now we have somewhere for them to go."

The blind beggar sighed and looked at his dog. "I knew it. I said it would be bad news for us, didn't I?" The dog didn't answer.

"No one will be *forced* to go into the workhouse, of course," the mayor's wife went on.

"Can I take my dog with me?" the beggar called.

---

16 I did warn you that once the mayor got started he was hard to stop. He was a bit like a dripping tap. Have you ever had one of those? Drives you mad. The more you WANT it to stop the more it annoys you. A dripping tap can sometimes be fixed by a sharp blow from a hammer. So could Mayor Twistle I suppose.

"No you CANNOT."

"Then I won't go," the beggar shrugged.

Lady Arabella's face turned a deeper shade of pink. "Then we will *force* you to go."

"Force me to go into the workhouse where no one will be forced to go?"

"Exactly!" the woman said with a grim grin.

Lady Arabella whispered to Sir Oswald and he scurried off the stage to the door at the side. She waved in the two Wildpool policemen.

"We have here our fine police force," Lady Arabella smiled.

The two men shuffled into line. They bent their knees and bobbed down. "Evening all," they said as one.[17]

Mayor Twistle bounced back on to the stage. "And last night they cracked yet another major crime in our fine town! They arrested

---

17 It was morning. You know that. I know that. The policemen know that. But they hadn't practised "Morning all," so they didn't want to get it wrong and look stupid. Instead they said "Evening all" in the morning ... and looked stupid anyway.

the night soil thieves *and* their horse! They can look forward to a life of hard labour in Darlham Gaol for that!"

Constable Larch lurched forward. "Ahem ... I'm sorry, Sir Oswald, but we have just come from the courtroom. The trial has just ended. A young girl stood up in court as a witness. She said the usual soil men spent all night in the tavern before they set off to empty the privies. She said the fake soil men did a much better job! The judge sentenced them to one month of emptying the soil from the new workhouse without pay. He said Constable Liddle and I should be doing more useful things than nicking a pair of poo pinchers!"

Mayor Twistle's face twisted as if he were chewing a worm. At last he managed to smile. "Quite right – and so you shall! You have a new task. Your job is to sweep the streets of Wildpool. . ."

"Do we have to buy our own brushes?" Constable Liddle asked.

"Sweep it of the poor, the beggars and the orphans, the homeless and the old. You are going to clean up this town," the mayor said.

"But do we have to buy our own brushes?"

Mayor Twistle rolled his eyes. "No, you idiot. I *mean* you take these dreadful people and drag them off to the workhouse. No trials, no judges. Just stick them out of sight."

"No brushes?"

"No brushes."

"That's good."

"Why?"

"Because I haven't got one."

Lady Twistle stepped forward again and her chubby elbow knocked the policemen to the back of the platform. "We need clean streets because at the end of this week Wildpool will have the most important visitor it has ever had in its proud history!"

"Who's that then?" Samuel Dreep shouted.

"Someone so important that it has to be a secret!" Lady Arabella said with a smug smile.

"The king?" a woman with a glass eye and an umbrella cried.[18]

"Don't be daft – King William's too sick to leave London."

"Oh, well, if it's not the king I won't get me flags out," the woman sighed.

"This is a private visit ... arranged by Sir Oswald and myself," Lady Twistle said. "But our guest will travel through the streets and we don't want it cluttered with beggars, do we?"

"Bad news for me," the blind beggar sighed.

Samuel Dreep twirled his curled moustache. "Ah, but a chance for someone to have a little fun, I think."

He chuckled. He chuckled all the way back to Master Crook's Crime Academy.

*

Ruby Friday looked at the class. "Now, Mr Dreep gave you some homework last night. Tell me how you got on."

---

18 I know what you are going to say. You are thinking that she could have worn an eye patch instead of a glass eye. But she didn't have any black material to make an eye patch – she'd used it all up to make the umbrella. She had very little money. But don't weep for the woman – her glass eye never cried for her, so why should you?

Millie Mixley raised her pale hand as if she were in school. "Please, miss, the homework was this: Alice had to walk from the shipyards on the riverside, up the hill up to Master Crook's Crime Academy. Two of us had to kidnap her before she got here ... but Alice didn't know *which* two."

Alice glared at the girl. "I could have guessed it would be sneaky Smiff and tough Nancy Turnip."

Ruby nodded. "And you all failed dreadfully, didn't you, Smiff?"

"No!" the rough-haired boy cried. "I think not! Alice lost. We got her!"

"You cheated," Alice spat.

Smiff raised his nose in the air. "School rule number six. Cheat in tests. I prefer to say we had a clever plan and it worked."

"Tell me," Ruby said softly.

Smiff began. "I hid on the corner of Garth Court because you can see all the streets that lead from the shipyards. I just had to wait for Alice to appear and follow her."

Alice blew out her cheeks and made the

sound of a snorting pig. "I saw you. You were hopeless. You tried to hide in the shadows. But I *saw* you."

Smiff gave that annoying smirk. "You were meant to."

"What?"

"You were *meant* to see me. You tried dodging into back alleys. Then you met the night soil men. The policemen arrested them and you went along with them all the way to the gates of the Crime Academy. All the time you thought you were safe because you could see me."

"And I was," Alice argued.

"But Nancy was waiting behind the gatepost of the Crime Academy. *She* got you!"

"Yeah, with a smelly sack from the sheep-head shop. There was no need for *that*," Alice snarled. "I had to wash my hair to get the smell out."

"First time this year, was it?" Smiff jeered.

Alice made her fists into tight balls and half rose. Ruby Friday spoke quickly, "But you *failed*, Smiff."

Alice froze. "Did he?"

Smiff blinked. "I think not ... er ... did I?"

"Yes! Alice *saw* you."

"That was part of the plan! She was so busy looking at me she never saw Nancy."

The old teacher shook her head. "If this had been a real kidnapping, for money, what would you do next?"

"Please, miss," Martin Mixley put in. "We would write out a ransom note. We tried some in class yesterday." He showed it to Ruby Friday.

DEAR MASTER CROOK,

WE HAVE TAKEN YOUR GIRL, ALICE WHITE, PRISONER. WE WILL NOT HARM HER IF YOU PAY US FIFTY POUNDS IN GOLD.

PUT THE GOLD IN A SACK AND LEAVE IT BEHIND THE OAK TREE WHERE THE GREAT NORTH ROAD CROSSES THE WILDPOOL TO WISHINGTON RAILWAY LINE.

IF YOU DO NOT DO THIS I WILL NOT TELL YOU WHAT WE WILL DO TO ALICE. IT IS SO HORRIBLE YOU WOULD NOT WANT TO KNOW SO I WILL NOT TELL YOU. JUST LEAVE THE GOLD OR ELSE.

A FRIEND

Millie Mixley explained. "The note says what we want in return for the victim. We collect the ransom and we're rich!"

Ruby Friday looked at Alice. "Suppose these kidnappers had sold you back to Master Crook for fifty pounds. . ."

"I'm worth at least a hundred," Alice grumbled.

"Very well, a hundred pounds," Miss Friday said calmly. "They get their hundred pounds. Then they set you free. What would you do, Alice?" the woman asked.

"Get my own back on Smiff!" Alice said with a fierce grin.

"And how would you know it was Smiff to blame?"

Alice frowned. "Cos I *saw* him!"

"Exactly!" Ruby Friday nodded. "Holy crumpets ... excuse my bad language. A kidnapper must *never* let their victim see their face!" She turned to Smiff. "Alice *saw* you. She would tell the police. The police would arrest you and you'd spend the rest of your life in Darlham Gaol – that's if they didn't hang you."

Alice was smiling sweetly now.[19]

"Yeah! I'd come and visit you, Smiffy. Heh! You loser!"

"If you came to visit I'd *beg* them to hang me," he muttered.

Ruby Friday clapped her hands. "So that's our first lesson in kidnapping! We need to work on the art of *disguise*."

The door opened and Mr Dreep stepped in. "Sorry to interrupt your lesson, Miss Friday, but it is lunch time now ... and I need to tell the class about Master Crook's Crime Academy's first school trip."

"Somewhere nice?" the Mixley twins cried.

"The mayor says so," Mr Dreep shrugged.

"But the mayor tells lies," Nancy said quietly. "The mayor tells terrible lies."

*

The March day was cold and gloomy. But not as gloomy as the gloomy room in the

---

19 Well, as sweetly as a bull terrier could ever smile – the sort of smile the terrier has when it is guarding a house and it sees a burglar 's leg appear through a window. A sweet smile ... but not a nice smile.

Wildpool police station. Inspector Beadle sat behind his desk and shook his head. This was a great effort. It was a very large head. It sat on an even larger body. That body wasn't as wide as a rhino or as heavy as a hippo. But you wouldn't want to bump into it when you were running to catch a bus ... or catch a cold ... or whatever else you run to catch.

"It has not been a good day for Wildpool police," Beadle said and his voice rumbled till the gas lamp on the ceiling trembled.

Constables Liddle and Larch trembled too. They twisted their top hats in their hands and looked at the floor.

"The night soil thieves went free," the inspector went on.

"And the horse," Liddle added. "Did you know they didn't even let the horse into the court room? He was properly arrested and everything! Look!" He waved the paper at the inspector.

WILDPOOL POLICE FORCE

CHARGE SHEET

Arresting officer/s: Liddle and Larch

Date of arrest: 13th March 1837

Place of arrest: Fulwell Street

Time of arrest*:   ten minutes past midnight

Accused: Edward (Ned) Carthorse

For the crime of feloniously aiding the filching
of foul filth

Signed   PC Septimus Liddle (PC 01)

PC Archibald Larch (PC 02)

* Note: no person may be held for more than
twenty-four hours without being charged with a
crime. This law goes back to 1215.

Notes: the law goes back to 12:15, but we
arrested this horse five minutes <u>before</u> that,
at 12:10, so it doesn't count. We can keep him
as long as we like, or until we run out of hay.

Inspector Beadle shook his huge head sadly. "Mayor Twistle was not pleased. In fact, Mayor Twistle said he would like *you* to spend a few years in Darlham Gaol."

"It wasn't our fault!" Larch wailed and his chins shook as if he were about to cry. *"You gave us the order."*

Somewhere in the folds of fat, Inspector Beadle's mouth may have smiled. "Yes, I did, didn't I?" He spread his hands, each one as large as a night soil shovel ... only cleaner. "But now you have a chance to make Mayor Twistle a very happy man and save your jobs. All you have to do is fill up his new workhouse on North Bridge Street."

The constables nodded. "How do we do that, sir?"

Inspector Beadle pointed to the Wildpool map on the wall. "Down by the river there is a square of houses. It's called Garth Court."

"Ooooh!" Liddle gasped. "We never go in there! It's dark! Even on a sunny day it's dark and damp."

"And smelly," Larch added.

"And that's where the cholera lives. You turn blue, you know, before you die," Liddle moaned. "I don't want to turn blue!"

"I don't want to die!" his partner added.

Inspector Beadle leaned forward and glared. "You are two old town watchmen. We gave you jobs in the new police force. If we sack you then you will have no jobs. Where will you end up? In the workhouse. You either fill the new workhouse with the poor people of Garth Court or you end up there yourselves."

Larch dared to look up. "Oh, that's not so bad, then! Mayor Twistle said it's a lovely place!"

Inspector Beadle's eyes were cold and hard as winter. "Mayor Twistle lied."

Chapter 4

PENCE AND PAUPERS

Wildpool workhouse was grey. Grey as a tombstone. Grey stone walls, grey stone floors and the cheap, grey-stained glass let in grey light from a grey sky.

A man and a woman looked at the rows of empty seats in the great hall and dreamed. "These seats will soon be full, Angela."

"Amelia."

"What?" the man asked and scratched his thick, dark, greasy hair that sat low on thick eyebrows that met in the middle. His eyes were too close together, his nose too small and his mouth too wide. A mouth full of grey teeth like tombstones. He may have been thirty years old. He may have been thirty thousand.

It's hard to tell the age of someone who shares his face with a cave man.

"My name is Amelia. We agreed."

"I forgot, my sweetness," he sighed.

"You would forget your own name if it wasn't stitched on to the front of your uniform," she smiled. She had a lovely smile, rather like a gorilla with a bunch of bananas. Her face was as rough as the workhouse walls, scarred with old diseases, her sharp eyes like silver beads and her needle nose as dangerous as a dagger.

He looked at the label. "Mr Humble – Overseer."

"That's right. You are Harry Humble and I am Amelia Humble. But, when we are in here, I will call you Mr Humble and you will call me Mrs Humble. Understand, my duckling?"

"Yes, my sweetness."

"Now ... Hengist, I mean Harry, I mean Mr Humble ... what were you saying?"

He scratched his dark hair again, pulled something out and popped it in his mouth where he crunched it with tombstone teeth. "I forget, sweetness."

"You were saying, this room will soon be full of the poor people of Wildpool."

"I just said that!" he cried. "Yes, I did … and the more poor people we have in here the more money we are paid." He chuckled and rubbed his rough hands together.

"We are paid six pence a day for every pauper we have," the woman who called herself Amelia Humble said. "We feed them for three pence a day. The other three pence goes in our pocket, my duckling."

"Twenty-one pence a week for every pauper. A hundred paupers and we have twenty-one hundred pence a week … that's a hundred and seventy-five shillings … that's eight pounds fifteen shillings a week … every week!"

3 pence x 7 days = 21 pence
21 pence x 100 paupers = 2100 pence
2100 pence divided by 12 = 175 shillings
175 shillings divided by 20 = 8 pounds and 15 shillings left over.
Total: 8 pounds and 15 shillings a week
Total every year: 8 pounds and 15 shillings times 52 = a lot!

He scribbled it on some paper with a sharp new pencil.[20]

"We'll be the richest people in Wildpool before the summer comes!" Mrs Humble crowed.

"Ah, my sweetness, we will have to take care of the paupers," her husband warned.

"Why is that my duckling?"

"Well ... if one of them dies we will lose ... erm..." He scribbled again.

3 pence x 7 days = 21 pence
21 pence x 52 weeks = 1092 pence
1092 pence divided by 12 = 91 shillings
91 shillings divided by 20 = 4 pounds and 11 shillings left over.

20 Like many wicked and greedy people the man was not exactly clever. But when it came to money he had a brain like one of those new adding machines. But trust me, in every other way the man who called himself Harry Humble was stupid.

"There you are, Angela..."

"Amelia or Mrs Humble, duckling."

"There you are, *Mrs Humble*. If a pauper dies we lose four pounds and eleven shillings every year!"

The woman's silver eyes glittered. "Oh, no. If a pauper *dies* we keep on taking the six pence a day for them. But we stop paying the three pence for their food – dead paupers eat less... Heh! Heh!"

"Oh, very funny, Mrs Humble."

"Instead of *losing* four pounds and eleven shillings we get *another* four pounds and eleven shillings! A dead pauper makes us nine pounds and two shillings every year!"

"Ah, yes, my sweet, but we have to pay the cost of the funeral. They can cost almost a pound these days," he reminded her.

She shook her head slowly. "No funeral. We are near the bridge. We wrap up the pauper in a sheet with some stones. When the workhouse is asleep we slip out and drop the body off the bridge and into the river. No one will ever know."

"That's good, that is, Mrs Humble," the man said. "I could kiss you on your clever little nose."

"And so you shall, sweetness, after we have finished the menu for the week. Mayor Twistle and his royal guest will want to see it. Here we go, almost finished."

She wrote the last figures in the last day and looked at it proudly.

DIETARY

	THE GENERAL DIETARY								AGED, INFIRM AND SICK DIETARY								
	Breakfast		Dinner				Supper		Breakfast		Dinner				Supper Men	Men & Wom.	Women
	Bread oz.	Gruel pints.	Beef oz.	Soup pints.	Suet Pud oz.	Potatoes lb.	Cheese oz.	Broth pints.	Bread oz.	Gruel pints.	Beef or Mutton	Potatoes lb.	Soup pints.	Rice Pud oz.	Cheese oz.	Broth pints.	
MONDAY	14	1.5	5	~	~	1	~	1.5	10	1.5	5	1	~	~	~	1.5	Tea to be made by the Matron, and one Pint to be given to each person twice a day with Bread & Butter, in Lieu of Gruel or Broth
TUESDAY	14	1.5	~	1.5	~	~	2	~	10	1.5	~	~	1.5	~	2	~	
WEDNESDAY	14	1.5	5	~	~	1	~	1.5	10	1.5	5	1	~	~	~	1.5	
THURSDAY	14	1.5	~	1.5	~	~	2	~	10	1.5	~	~	1.5	~	2	~	
FRIDAY	8	1.5	~	~	14	~	2	~	10	1.5	~	~	~	10	2	~	
SATURDAY	14	1.5	5	~	~	1	~	1.5	10	1.5	5	1	~	~	~	1.5	
SUNDAY	14	1.5	~	1.5	~	~	2	~	10	1.5	~	~	1.5	~	2	~	

"Oh, those lucky, lucky paupers," Mrs Humble sighed.

"And lucky, lucky us!" her husband chuckled. "Who'd have thought we'd get such a good job so soon after coming out of prison, sweetness?"

Her voice turned as sharp as her nose. "Never mention that, duckling. Never. No one must know. No one."

*

In Wildpool police station, Inspector Beadle looked at the card in front of him on the desk. The prison artist had drawn the faces well. They stared out at him as real as if they were alive.[21]

He tapped the card with a finger that was as thick as a sausage. Then he placed it carefully in the drawer of his desk and locked it.

---

21 You have to remember that this was back in 1837 and photographs had not quite been invented. But a good artist can show a face BETTER than a photograph. A villain can hide their wickedness when the camera clicks. But an artist sees the lies behind the eyes and sketches them. Next time you are arrested let them take your photograph – don't let them sketch you! I offer you this priceless tip for free. I am too, too kind.

Samuel Dreep stood in front of the Wildpool workhouse gateway. It was a fine arch with heavy doors painted dark green. The walls were high. There were spikes along the tops of the walls and the gate itself. It would be as hard to escape from here as from Darlham Gaol.

The Mixley twins stood by his side. Millie's hair was now as short as her brother's. They wore the oldest clothes their mother could find – the clothes they had worn when they were penniless and before Master Crook had saved them.

"You know why I chose you?" Dreep asked. He twirled the tip of his moustache. The twins looked so frail he was worried this would be too tough a task. But their bright faces smiled up at him.

"We always do as we're told, sir," Millie said.

"If you sent Alice in here she would start a riot, and that's not what we want, sir," Martin added.

"And if you sent Smiff in here he'd spend all his time in the punishment room in the yellow jacket ... please, sir, what's the yellow jacket?" Millie asked.

"Ah! Workhouse rules. Anyone who makes trouble is forced to wear the yellow jacket so they are easy to spot," Samuel Dreep explained.

The twins nodded. "You'd never see us in the yellow jacket," Millie said.

Dreep leaned forward. "They will work you hard and try to starve you," he said.

"That's all right, sir, we can take it!" Martin laughed. "Last month when we were poor our mother fed us peas for dinner."

"That's good," the teacher said.

"We had one pea each," Millie sighed.

"That's bad," the teacher agreed.

"One evening I got upset," Martin put in. "I thought Millie had *two* peas!"

"But I'd taken mine and cut it in half!" she said and the twins giggled.

Millie shivered suddenly as the March wind blew in from the river. "Oh, I can't get used to having my hair cut short like Martin," she sighed. "Or the trousers."

Samuel Dreep nodded. "You too look so alike now ... and that may help. The plan is for Martin to find out how the workhouse works ... is there a good way to get in and out? Are the Humbles as good as Mayor Twistle says?"

"Mayor Twistle *lies!*" Millie gasped. "Nancy says so and she should know – she used to work for him!"

"Or are the Humbles really the wicked Harpers from Darlham Gaol the way Master Crook says?" Dreep went on. "Now, you have the paper and pencils?"

"Yes, sir," Martin said.

"Wrap a message round a stone and throw it over the gate if you need any help or if you can find a way out to report. Now, are you ready?"

"Yes, sir!"

"Millie, you hide round the corner. Don't let them see you."

Millie nodded and ran off.

Mr Dreep tugged at the rope that hung by the side of the gate and somewhere inside a bell rang. A minute later they heard bolts being pulled back and the new doors creaked on their new hinges. A man with a face like an angry beetle glared out at them.

"What you want then, eh?" he said.

"Mr Humble?"

"Pleased to meet you, Mr Humble," beetle-face said.

"No, no, no," Dreep laughed. "*I'm* not Mr Humble ... *you* are Mr Humble."

"Who says?"

"Mayor Oswald Twistle."

"Oh ... yes! That's right. I'm Humble. Humble by name and humble by nature, Mrs Harp – er – Mrs Humble always says! What can I do for you?"

Dreep handed him a printed card.

"Dreep, eh?"

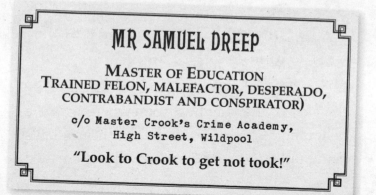

MR SAMUEL DREEP

MASTER OF EDUCATION
TRAINED FELON, MALEFACTOR, DESPERADO,
CONTRABANDIST AND CONSPIRATOR)

c/o Master Crook's Crime Academy,
High Street, Wildpool

"Look to Crook to get not took!"

"This unfortunate child was found on our doorstep this morning."

"Doorstep? What were he doing there?"

"Crying."

"Yes ... I meant. . ."

"He was left with a label around his neck. Here it is!"

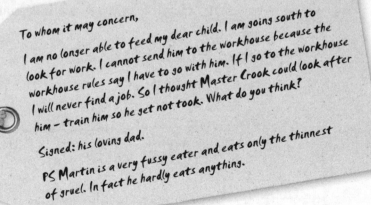

To whom it may concern,

I am no longer able to feed my dear child. I am going south to look for work. I cannot send him to the workhouse because the workhouse rules say I have to go with him. If I go to the workhouse I will never find a job. So I thought Master Crook could look after him – train him so he get not took. What do you think?

Signed: his loving dad.

PS Martin is a very fussy eater and eats only the thinnest of gruel. In fact he hardly eats anything.

"Sadly Master Crook has no room in the academy. I wondered if you could break your rules and take him in without a parent?" Dreep asked.

"Hah! At sixpence a day! I'll say I can."

"Even though it's against the rules?"

"Hah! Rules was meant to be broken," beetle-faced Humble snorted.[22]

"There you are, child! You can go in here and break the rules!"

"No!" Humble squawked. "Not *my* rules! You break *my* rules and I'll beat you like a dog," he said fiercely and spit flew out on bad breath as he raged. He looked up at Samuel Dreep. "Don't worry, Mr Dreep, I'm sure he'll be very happy ... oh, and if you find any more then bring them along. The more the merrier, we always say."

"The child is called—"

"Doesn't matter!" Humble cut in. "From now on he will be a *number* not a name." He

22 I will call him Humble even though YOU know he is really Harper. You don't have to show how clever you are and tell me, "You got his name wrong." Don't try being clever, try being humble – after all, Harper did.

pointed at Martin and said, "You are number one. Welcome to Wildpool's Wonderful Workhouse!"

He slammed the gate and it rang with a boom like doom.

Chapter 5

CARTS AND COPS

Wednesday 14th March 1837

Wildpool High Street was busy and bustling to the point of bursting. The washer-woman had parked her cart on the corner and blocked half of the road while she delivered clean washing and collected the dirty.

Carriages queued and wagons waited, carts collided and barrows tried to barge through. Drivers argued and shoppers smiled to see the sport. The hat-seller came to her shop door and said to the blind beggar, "It's ages since I've seen a good fight."

"I've never seen a good fight!" the blind beggar said.

"You must have done ... sitting there," she cried.

"I'm blind. I see nothing ... that way I don't have to go to court as a witness," he said and he took off the dark spectacles he wore so he could get a better look. Two carters had jumped down to sort out the tangle of their wheels. They were red in the face and shouting while their dogs yapped at one another.

"Call yourself a driver? You shouldn't be allowed out on the roads."

"Call yourself a human being? You look more like a monkey to me except a monkey could drive that thing better. You drove straight into me."

"I think not, my friend."

"I'm not your friend. I don't have monkeys for friends."

"If you've bruised my tomatoes, I'll batter you."

"If you've hurt my toads, I'll splatter you."

"*Toads?* What you carrying *toads* for?"

"The old alchemist shop. He uses lots of

toads in his medicines." The carter pulled one off the back of the cart and waved it under the tomato cart driver's nose. "See?"

"Aaaagggghhhh! Get it away from me. I hate them." He picked up a handful of tomatoes and started to pelt the toad cart driver. Then they started to push one another till they were both rolling in the muddy road.

The hat-seller sighed. "Not much of a fight."

"No," the blind beggar agreed and put his glasses back on. "Just a touch of toad rage."

Constable Liddle and Constable Larch stepped out of the police station and wound their way around the tangle of wagons, dogs and rats, as they read their orders for the day.

WILDPOOL POLICE FORCE

DATE: 14th March 1837

Orders for Evening Patrol:

Proceed through the main streets of Wildpool

Question anyone who is begging or does not appear to be working or is a pauper

Note their name

Accompany the persons to Wildpool workhouse on North Bridge Street

Hand them into the custody of Mr or Mrs Humble

Then proceed to Garth Court and take everyone into custody.

POLICE INSPECTOR BEADLE

They stepped over the two carters who were rolling like slow slugs on the cobbles.

"C-o-p!" the hat-seller said to the beggar.

"Cop?"

"Constables On Patrol ... we call them cops for short, see?"

"I see nothing," the beggar said.

The woman called out, "Here! Constables? Aren't you going to sort out this traffic?"

Constable Larch looked up at Constable Liddle. "Traffic? Is that part of our job?"

Liddle stroked his wispy white moustache. "Here's one of the poems the mayor wrote when he gave us the job..."

CONSTABLES ON PATROL

Go forth my men and fight with crime
Send the villains to do time.
Robbers they will run and flee
When our brave cops they do see.
Beggars bold, pickpockets naughty,
Those shop-lifters, get them caught-y.
Guard the rich and keep us safe,
Lock up paupers, strays and waifs.

"What's a waif?" Liddle muttered.

"A sort of biscuit I think."

"No, that's a wafer." He pushed one of the panting, struggling carters with his boot. "Excuse me, sir, are you a waif?"

The red-faced man looked up. "I don't think so."

Liddle looked at the man he was wrestling with. "What about you? A waif?"

"Yoo-hoo!"

"No, I think he said 'waif' not 'wave'."

"Sorry. No."

The constables nodded. "Thought not. Carry on, gents."

The two men helped one another to their feet and hobbled back to their carts.

"So!" the hat-seller cried. "You're not going to sort out this traffic?"

"That's not a job for policemen!" Liddle said. "Let them sort themselves out."

The woman threw her hands in the air. "The road is blocked. No one can get to my shop. No one can get to this poor blind beggar and his dog. It's costing us money."

Larch shrugged. The cops walked to the corner of the High Street. They stopped. They looked at one another. "Here, Liddle. Did she say what I think she said?"

"Beggar?"

"We need to arrest that man! Take him off to the Wildpool's Wonderful Waxworks."

"I think you mean workhouse, Liddle."

The tall, thin grey policeman looked at his paper. "So I do."

They turned and walked back to the beggar. "Penny for the dog?" the man said in his most pitiful voice.

"Are you begging?"

"I can see you are a clever man, spotting that, Constable. Top marks!" the beggar laughed.

"In that case I arrest you. You will accompany us to the waxworks," Liddle said. "I mean the Work-wax ... where you will be given work to pay for your food and bed."

The man was hauled to his feet. "What about me dog?"

"Can he work?"

"No, but..."

"Then he can't go," Larch said, harshly.

"Don't worry, I'll look after the dear little mutt," the hat-seller said. "He can sleep on my bed every night."[23]

"Thanks, lady!" the beggar managed to cry before he was dragged towards the Wildpool bridge and over to the workhouse.

Mrs Humble answered the bell. "What you want then, eh?" she said.

"We are very happy to deliver this unfortunate beggar to your loving care," Larch said and looked at his paper. "Er ... Mrs Humble."

"The beggar's called *Mrs Humble*? Funny name."

"No," Liddle said. "*You* are called Mrs Humble."

---

23 I 'm pleased about that. I can't stand to see animals badly treated. That lucky dog would have a warm and cosy new home and a loving owner. Of course he'd have to suffer a good bath first – he was as smelly as a sailor 's sock. But afterwards he'd be dried by the fire and brushed. He would be given a name ... dogs like that. And, of course, he would be taken for walks every day and have his wheels oiled with love ... and oil.

"Am I?"

"If you are the workhouse keeper then that's your name," the policeman said with a frown.

"Ah ... oh ... eh ... yes-s-s-s! That's me!" the woman said with a sharp-toothed smile.

"So you'll take this beggar?"

"What? Just *one*? Is that *it*? We can't make a living with just two! We need a hundred. I thought my friend Sir Oswald Twistle told you to sweep the streets!"

"As I told him," Liddle said, "I don't have a brush."

"But is this the best you can do? One miserable beggar?" she raged.

"I offered to bring me dog," the beggar said.

"Dogs don't count. If dogs come here, we cook them and eat them," she snarled.

"Glad I didn't bring him then!" the beggar gasped.

The woman turned her sharp nose on the constables. "We have an important visitor arriving here on Friday. We were promised a hundred paupers by then. If Sir Oswald finds you've failed he really *will* have you sweeping the streets. Sweeping the horse droppings in the High Street. Now push off and do what the mayor said."

She grabbed the beggar by the shirt and pulled him through the door.

"Excuse me!" Constable Liddle said, pulling out his notebook. "But we have to fill in the correct form."

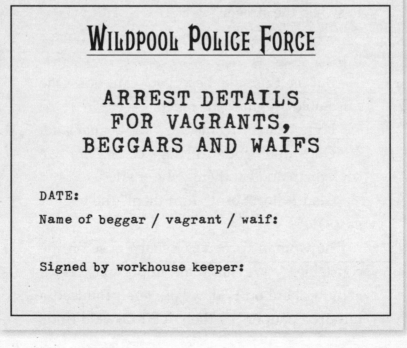

WILDPOOL POLICE FORCE

ARREST DETAILS
FOR VAGRANTS,
BEGGARS AND WAIFS

DATE:

Name of beggar / vagrant / waif:

Signed by workhouse keeper:

He wrote the date then turned to the beggar. "Name?"

"I'm not telling you," the man said in a sulk. "And you can't make me."

"Give it here," Mrs Humble said. The policeman passed the notepad to her along with his pencil.

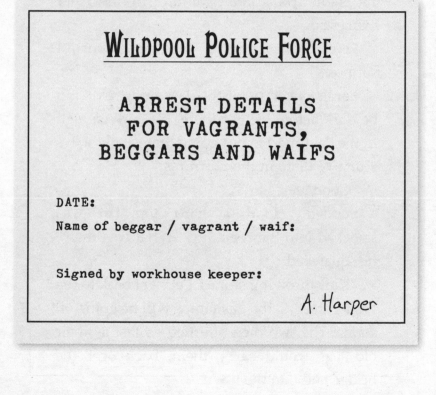

Wildpool Police Force

ARREST DETAILS
FOR VAGRANTS,
BEGGARS AND WAIFS

DATE:

Name of beggar / vagrant / waif:

Signed by workhouse keeper:

A. Harper

She thrust it back at him and reached to close the door. "And don't show your ignorant faces here again till you have ninety-eight more."

She slammed the door.

Constable Larch looked at the form.

"Here, Liddle, that's a funny way to spell 'Humble'," he said.

"She's from the south," his partner explained.

"We'd better get off to Garth Court, I suppose."

Larch looked up at the darkening sky. "It'll be dark before we get there. It's dark enough in the daytime. I'm not going there at night. It's scary. We'll go in the morning."

"Good idea, Larch."

Suddenly Liddle's hard top hat was knocked into the roadway. "What was that?" he squawked.

"Kids throwing stones. Let's get back to the High Street ... the gas lamps will be going on soon." The two men shuffled as fast as their old legs would carry them, back over the bridge and into the town.

A man in an even more battered top hat stepped out from behind the corner of the workhouse. He stepped into the road and picked up the stone that had hit Liddle's hat. A scrap of paper was wrapped around the stone. He hurried back up the hill after the policemen. As they turned into the police station, he turned into Master Crook's Crime Academy.

The four students were sitting at their desks listening to Ruby Friday giving the latest lesson in kidnapping.

"How is Martin?" Nancy asked, anxious.

Mr Dreep unwrapped the paper.

Cold in here. The Humbles feed me cold porridge with more water than oats. They have a fire in their room but won't let me have one. They won't even let me have a candle. I will be fine because I'm only here for a day or so. Don't worry, Millie.

Mrs Humble just took in a new inmate. He is called Two. But we heard her say the mayor wants everyone from Garth Court in here by Friday. And Friday is the day of the visit. Love Martin

Alice said, "So tomorrow we save the families in Garth Court?"

"No, Master Crook didn't order us to save them," Mr Dreep said quietly.

"We'll see about that!" Alice said. She marched to the wall and blew down a tube. A whistle sounded far away in the basement. She placed the tube to her ear and a voice said, "Master Crook here."

"I want a word with you," Alice said and slammed the tube back in its place. Then she stamped out of the door and through another door that led into the basement. Smiff shook his head. "She never changes."

Mr Dreep looked at Ruby Friday. "So Friday is a busy day at the workhouse, Miss Friday ... is that the day you'd choose for the kidnap?"

"Of course!" she said. "We have just been planning it."

A few minutes later Alice slipped back into the room and sat quietly at her desk. "So?" Smiff asked. "What did Master Crook say?"

The girl shook her head. "He said ... he said we have to fight the battles we can win.

There's no point fighting a battle you are going to lose."

Ruby Friday laughed. "The Duke of Wellington said the same ... that's why he never lost!"

"But we're not going to war against the French," Smiff argued. "We're just going to stop two old policemen arresting a hundred poor people. Easy! We've beaten them before. We can do it again."

Samuel Dreep waved his fingers the way he did when he was excited. "Master Crook knows more than you think. If he says Garth Court is a battle we can't win then there is a reason. Something will happen there tomorrow that no one can stop."

"But we should *try*!" Nancy moaned. "Those poor families!"

"We can watch," Dreep said. "Watch and wait. Then make our plans."

"Remember Waterloo," Ruby Friday said. "Fight the battles you can win ... and if you can't win ... then cheat!"

Chapter 6

FEAR AND FIRE

Thursday 15th March 1837

If Wildpool workhouse was tombstone grey then Garth Court was as brown as the soil on a newly turned grave. Grime-brown brick walls round slime-brown earth floors and broken brown shattered doors and rough brown boards over brown holes that were once windows.

The people were brown. Brown rags on skin that was filth-brown and brown shadows round eyes that were empty as the windows. If you cut one in half you would probably find brown bones.

The walls rose three rooms high but there

were crowded attics above them and a cellar where the cess pit held the waste from the toilets. Four walls made a sunless courtyard in the middle where no weeds cared or dared to grow.

From the outside Garth Court looked like a deserted brown brick shell. From the inside it looked a lot like Hell.

The people of Garth Court were thin and hungry. Only the cats were fat from all the rats they caught. Garth Court was no place for rats. The children who caught them were as deadly as the cats and ten times as hungry.

Just a year before our story started, an inspector had gone inside the court. He came out without his jacket, wallet, hat or overcoat.

After four long weeks in hospital he found the strength to write one last report and then he took a job as a shepherd under the free, fresh stars. He said he'd never go near a town again. His report was hidden by Mayor Twistle, ashamed of such a sight that stood to blight his Wildpool Town.

And so it went on.

Sir Oswald and Lady Twistle made sure no one else saw that shameful report.

*

When Liddle and Larch had marched through the town towards Garth Court it seemed a hundred people had followed them. The two old men were in step, truncheons raised high.

They marched past Master Crook's Crime Academy and the teachers and pupils slipped out to follow them. "Today's school trip is probably going to take us to Garth Court," Mr Dreep said.

"Yes, well don't walk too fast cos my legs ain't as young as they used to be … and neither is me head, me teeth or me stockings," Ruby Friday huffed.

The constables marched through the flock of geese that were being driven to the butcher's yard. The angry, clacking geese turned and followed them. There was nothing the goose-girl could do to stop them. The constables walked around a small herd of cattle on their way to the market.[24]

The cattle turned and followed. They marched down Low Street and past Smiff's house.

Smiff's mum came to the door. "Hello, Smiff! You and that handsome Mr Dreep coming in for a cup of tea? I made it fresh yesterday."

"We're busy at the moment, Mum – I'll have it after school tonight," the rough-haired boy said. "I'll bring you some sugar!"

Mrs Smith smiled at her neighbour. "I'm so proud of our Smiff. You should see his school report! Bottom marks for honesty, bottom marks for helping the police and no marks at all for being polite to posh folk!"

"Takes after his mum, then," the neighbour muttered.

The constables were being followed by every stray dog in Wildpool and children

24 They marched THROUGH the geese but AROUND the cows. You can't march through a cow. It 's like Ruby Friday said, "Only fight the battles you can win." So next time you see a cow in the road, walk around it. Next time you see a bull in the road just run. Unless you are a matador, of course.

were pouring out of the houses to join the stream down Low Street. "It's like a papered pie!" Mrs Smith chuckled.

"A what?"

"That story when we was kids. The children followed the Papered Pie and got lost in the mountains."

The neighbour frowned. "Don't you mean the Pied Piper?"

"That's what I said. Here! I'm getting my shawl. I'm not going to miss this!"

"But what's happening?" the neighbour asked.

"Haven't a clue," Mrs Smith shrugged, "but I don't want to miss out!"

It seemed as if half of Wildpool had gathered outside Garth Court. Mayor and Lady Twistle were already there, sitting silently in their carriage. The mayor stayed silent when the constables arrived. He simply raised a short arm and pointed a short finger at the entrance arch to the brown brick building.

Even the chattering children went quiet

when Liddle and Larch marched in. For a minute you could have heard a rat squeak.[25]

Smiff peered through the archway into the square courtyard. It was only a minute from his own home but it was very different. There was not a blade of grass in the square yard. He watched the policemen pick their way through piles of rubbish and broken furniture.

The windows were boarded but there were cracks in the boards and sly eyes seemed to follow the two men in navy uniforms. Someone had chalked words on a board beside a door-less entry:

WELCOME TO
THE EMPIRE OF HUNGER

25 Well you couldn't have heard a rat squeak because most of the rats had been eaten by the cats. The rats that were left stayed alive because they had the sense to stay quiet. Let 's say you could have heard a cat 's footfall. That 's foot-fall not foot-ball.

It seemed like only a minute had passed before the two constables came back out blinking into the light...

Thursday 15 March 1837

THE WILDPOOL STAR

COPS IN COURT CATCH COLD!

Today Wildpool's new police force, Constables Liddle and Larch, were caught cold when they tried to enter Garth Court by the riverside. The shocked constables gave our reporter an interview as they stood shivering outside the brown buildings.

"We entered the premises as ordered. The windows were boarded up so we used our lanterns," said the ageing Constable Liddle. "The door closed behind me. First I felt the lantern snatched from my hand and shone in my face. That blinded me. I then felt things swarm over my body. They could have been rats or they could have been human hands!"

His terrified partner, Larch, added, "The same thing happened to me. I reached for my police rattle to call for assistance but it was gone. I reached into my pocket for my police notebook, but it was gone too ... I mean the pocket as well as the notebook. After a minute the swarming hands stopped, the door opened and I was thrown out of the door."

"Me too," Liddle said. "In the archway I bumped into a man. I reached for my truncheon to defend myself, but it had gone, along with the belt I hang it from. I was about to strike this man when I realized it was Constable Larch.

I didn't recognize him because he was wearing only his underclothes – not even his boots. He looked embarrassed."

"And Liddle looked the same," Larch put in. "We were both stripped and thrown out within a minute. These people are expert thieves and it will take an army to get them out."

"The inspector said this was our chance to cover ourselves in glory," Liddle sniffled. "Now we're not covered in anything. Anything at all."

A little child giggled but no one joined in.

"Is that why we're here?" Alice whispered to Mr Dreep. "To learn from expert crooks on how to outwit the police?"

The teacher shook his head. "No, Alice, these are not clever crooks, just desperate people. We steal from the rich to help the poor. But we never make the constables look foolish. That would be a big mistake. Mayor Twistle will just be angry."

"So? What can he *do*?" Alice asked.

Samuel Dreep just nodded towards the mayor's fine carriage.

Mayor Twistle's face hadn't changed. He stepped out of his carriage. He pointed up to the railway line that ran above the docks. Locomotive No. 3 stood at the end of the line. It was on a platform that ended high above the river. The coal trucks could drop their coal into the waiting ships.

The engine driver waved back. He tugged on the whistle of the steam train giving three long blasts. There were twenty trucks but not one lump or chip of coal inside. From each truck six men stood up. Even from far below the crowd could see they were large men with arms of solid muscle and faces hard as iron. They each carried a tool – pick-axes and shovels, metal levers and bow saws.

They formed up in a loose line – as loose as a line of ants but just as determined – and began to walk down the path towards the quayside.

"Ah," Mr Dreep sighed. "Navigators."

"What?" Smiff said.

"We call them navvies," Ruby Friday said. "They're the men that are building the railways. I guess these are the workers building the Wildpool and Helton line that'll join up with the Great Northern line."

"A dangerous job," Samuel Dreep breathed. "Dangerous men."

The army of navvies didn't speak. When they reached Garth Court they split into two groups. Half formed a line like an iron wall outside the arch. The rest walked calmly through the archway into Garth Court. There was a splintering of wood.

There was no opening of doors that they could be locked behind, like the poor policemen. There were cries of frightened children, squeals of babies, quacks of ducks and screams of women.[26]

Soon after the last navvy had vanished into the last shattered doorway the brown-faced, frightened, shivering families began to stumble out.

The line of navvies in the roadway outside closed in so the Garth families were trapped. There was more splintering as the boards were hacked away from the windows to let in the light, let out the stench and uncover any dark hiding places.

When almost a hundred people were huddled into the ring of captors, one navvy, who seemed to be the leader, came to the door and nodded to the rest. They formed into a line two abreast with the families trapped between them and began to march up Low Street towards the High Street at the top.

26 I didn't mention the ducks before. It upsets me to think of the ducks. They are such comical and charming creatures. They lived in the room with one of the families. They were not pets. Their eggs were tasty. And when they stopped laying eggs ... what can I say? Duck soup is also very tasty. As I say, it upsets me.

They turned right on to the bridge and across it towards the workhouse at the far end.

The crowd who had come to see some sport had only seen half of it.[27]

Some of the navvies who had been inside came out and pushed the watchers back to safety.

Suddenly there was a crashing as the roof tiles exploded out. Pick-axes and crowbars appeared in the gaps and the rotting timbers started to tumble into the road below. When the roof had gone the navvies started to beat at the wooden walls. The worm-eaten timbers crumbled and showed the pitiful rooms that had once been home to a hundred humans. A few ragged blankets and clothes fluttered to the ground and the crowd covered their mouths to keep out the smell.

The mighty navvy arms worked as tirelessly as the pistons on Locomotive No. 3

27 When I say "sport " it was no more "sport " than throwing Christians to the lions in ancient Rome. Sport is when it 's a fair fight with rules. Sport is pelting your teacher with pellets dipped in ink and trying to get away with it ... not that someone as sweet as you would ever dream of doing such a thing, would you?

and in half an hour Garth Court was a tangled pile of timber.

The navvies left. The last one carried out two bundles of navy blue with silver buttons. He handed them to the two constables who scrambled into their uniforms.

At last Mayor Twistle allowed himself a smile. He reached into his pocket and pulled out a fat purse full of silver. He handed it to the head navvy. The man took it and tugged at the hair on the front of his forehead. He pointed to the pile. About five or six of his workers ran to the rubble with tinderboxes and set the filthy straw on fire. In minutes the timbers caught alight and the crowd had to step back and away from the furnace heat.

The mayor's horses snorted and reared in fear.

"Home James, and don't spare the horses!" Mayor Twistle cried and slid up the window.

The driver raised his whip. "He loves shouting that ... even if me name is Jack."

Chapter 7

PUDDINGS AND PLANNING

Thursday 15th March 1837

Alice White stood by the gates of the workhouse on the damp March day and watched the silent families troop in past Mr and Mrs Humble. The workhouse overseers rubbed their hands together and counted the pennies rolling through their doors.

It was noon and the previously fake but now real night soil men rumbled up to the gates. The taller night soil man grinned at Alice. "Thanks for speaking up for us in court," he said.

"It made all the difference," the smaller one

agreed. "Anything we can do for you, miss, any time? A free load of night soil ... it does wonders for your cabbages."

"I am *not* cooking cabbage in night soil!" the girl said with a shudder.

"Nah! You sprinkle it over your cabbage."

"I'd rather have salt and pepper," the girl said.

"I *mean* while the cabbage is still in the ground. The night soil helps them grow if you put it in the cabbage patch. When you pick your cabbage you'll be amazed!" the taller one said.

"I would," she nodded. "But I pick my cabbage from a shelf in the greengrocer shop."

"Oh, well, we can't do much for you then," the smaller man sighed.

"You're wrong!" Alice said quickly. "You *can* help me!"

And she told them how.

*

Millie Mixley climbed under the soil cart and clung to the axle. No one could see her unless they knelt down and peered *under* the cart. And *who* would do that?[28]

When the cart was through the gates of the workhouse Millie dropped down. "Ten minutes today," the smaller night soil man said. "The place was nearly empty. Tomorrow it'll take twice as long now that all these people have arrived. Tell your brother to be here in ten minutes. We can't hang around."

The soil men started their round of the workhouse while Millie ran off to find her twin brother. She was in luck.

Martin was sitting at a desk just inside the door with a quill pen and a pot of ink, making a note of the new arrivals. They stopped and waited as dull as donkeys while he spoke with his sister. He quickly explained the job he was doing and showed Millie the sheet he was filling in.

"You just fill in the name and the class—"

28 I will bet Queen Victoria's purse full of pound notes that YOU have never crawled under a cart full of poo. Have you? See! I told you. If you want to sneak someone into a guarded place use a muck cart. I always thought it would be a good way to rob a bank! I just never worked out why a muck cart would be driven through the bank doors. If you can think of something then do let me know.

Date	Name	Class	Age	No.
14 Mar 1837	Mixley, Martin	W	10	001
"	Beggar, Blind	S	55	002
15 Mar 1837	Jones, John	M	30	003
"	Jones, Jane	W	30	004
"	Jones, John junior	W	10	005
"	Jones, Jane junior	W	6	006

"Class?"

"M for men, W for women and children, and S for sick and old – see? I'm a child!

"Write their number on a piece of paper and give it to them. Once they have had a bath they'll get a uniform. They have to pin this number on that. Then you pass them on to the beggar and he sends them off to different parts of the workhouse. The women and children under six go to one part of the building, the men to another, the children age seven to fourteen to another and the old and sick go to the hospital. It's easy."

"But what about if a man comes in with his family?" Millie asked.

"They're split up," Martin said.

"That's cruel."

"It's the workhouse rules," her brother nodded.

Millie looked at the list. "There's a lot of John Joneses," she said.

Martin shrugged. "When they don't want to give a name they just say John Jones. It doesn't matter anyway. Once they're in here they're just a number." He passed across a piece of paper with 001 written on it and pinned it to a uniform. "Here. Put this on and you are number one."

Millie took his place at the table. "The muck cart won't be long," she said. "Hurry. It's the only way out."

He nodded and ran out into the yard. Millie smiled up at the family that were waiting. They didn't smile back.

"Name, please?"

"Jones," the man said.

Outside the night soil men rolled into view. Mr and Mrs Humble were watching the new families arriving and didn't see Martin duck under the wagon and cling to the axle. "Coming through!" the night soil men cried and the crowd shuffled aside to let the cart pass through the gate.

*

Constable Liddle and Constable Larch stood in front of Inspector Beadle's desk. They did not look happy.

"You entered Garth Court?"

"Yes, sir," lank Liddle muttered.

"And you let them strip you?"

"Yes, sir," large Larch sighed.

"How did Wildpool's wonderful police allow that to happen?"

Liddle and Larch looked at one another. "It was foggy, sir."

"Foggy!" Inspector Beadle roared.

"Yes, sir ... they'd lit fires in some of the rooms. That made the damp walls steam, sir. It was a fog!"[29]

29 This is a ridiculous excuse. People living in houses so damp they made a fog when they lit a fire. Ridiculous ... but true. I was once so poor I lived in a house like that. It broke my nose. I ran to the door through the fog and missed ... fog and mist? Get it? Oh, never mind.

"You have truncheons to deal with people who attack you. Did you use your truncheon, Liddle?"

"Yes, sir."

"And who did you hit?"

"Constable Larch, sir," the old man muttered into his moustache.

Larch nodded. "Made a right mess of my top hat, sir."

Inspector Beadle rubbed his eyes, eyes as small and dark as a pig's. "Get back on the streets. Our important visitor arrives at noon tomorrow. If anything goes wrong ... anything ... then I will use your truncheons to drive you over the edge of Wildpool bridge. Tomorrow is the most important day in Wildpool history. Nothing can go wrong. What can go wrong?"

"Nothing," the constables chimed together like the clock bell on Wildpool town hall.

*

The blind beggar showed a woman with her six children into a room like a cell. The walls were almost bare but there were straw

101

mattresses on the floor and a bucket for a toilet in the corner.

On one wall was a finely stitched piece of cloth in a frame.

"IF ANYONE WOULD NOT WORK, HE SHOULD NOT EAT"

ST.PAUL

The woman (who called herself Mrs Jones) looked up and said, "Saint Paul? Is he the bloke that built the cathedral in London?"

"What cathedral?" the beggar asked.

"St Paul's Cathedral."

"Oh, yes ... he's the same bloke. Very clever

he is. Goes around stitching little mottoes for the poor ... when he's not building cathedrals and things."

"If you don't work you don't eat, kids!" Mrs Jones said.

The six children nodded. "We *did* work, Ma," the oldest girl said. And it was true. Mrs Jones turned to the beggar.

"We worked ever so hard. We used to make matchboxes. If I made a hundred and forty-four then I got paid two pence. I picked up the cardboard and the sandpaper and made them ... but we had to buy our own glue. Of course as the kids get older they can help. In the end we was making a shilling and sixpence a day. Two days' work and we paid the rent for the week. After three days we could afford to eat!"

The blind beggar nodded. "So what went wrong?"

Mrs Jones sighed. "Little Jacob got too hungry. One day he ate the glue."

"Ah," the beggar nodded. "Made from the bones of old horses. Glue is very tasty they tell me."

"Very tasty," little Jacob nodded. "When do we eat?"

"After you've had a bath and got into your uniforms."

The oldest girl looked at him. "What's a bath?"

*

Back at the academy, Martin Mixley stood in the front of the class. He felt a little strange. Not only were the pupils Smiff Smith, Alice White and Nancy Turnip looking at him. So were the teachers Samuel Dreep and Ruby Friday.

Miss Friday had already told them that the secret of a good kidnap is planning. "If we are going to make life better for the people in the workhouse we need to kidnap Mrs Humble. Show her the power the poor have if she doesn't mend her ways. But we can never be caught or it will be worse than ever. There are three rules that you must never forget – planning, planning and planning."

"You forgot to mention planning," Alice said sourly.

"First we need our kidnappers to know the plan of the workhouse, then we need to know where Mrs Humble will be at a certain time, and then we need to work on our disguises," Ruby Friday said firmly. "Now, Martin. The drawing of the workhouse!"

Martin pulled the sketch from inside his workhouse jacket and handed it to Samuel Dreep who pinned it to the blackboard. It was a very neat plan and even had some labels.[30]

30 You may think Martin Mixley had a talent for drawing plans. You would be right. Many years later he became an architect and built some famous railway stations. He never did anything as great as St Paul's Cathedral ... but, then, neither did Saint Paul.

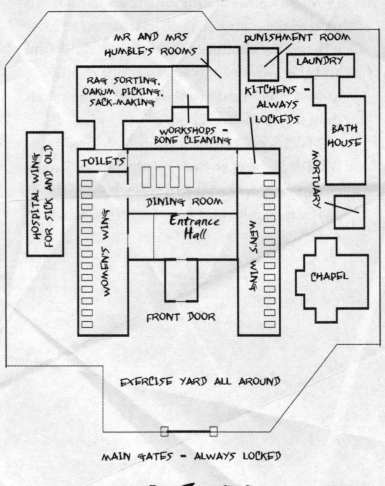

MAIN GATES - ALWAYS LOCKED

WILDPOOL
~~WONDERFUL~~ WOEFUL WORKHOUSE

"Mr and Mrs Humble also have a timetable," Martin said.

"Oh! Wonderful," Ruby Friday cried and threw her hands in the air.[31]

"Mrs Humble is asking to be kidnapped! Show us the plan."

FIVE A.M. Paupers rise and tidy their rooms, make the beds and wash the children while cooks prepare the gruel in the kitchen.

SIX A.M. Paupers gather in the dining room. They are served breakfast – one bowl of gruel each – and eat it in silence..

SEVEN A.M. Paupers go to workshops and begin work. Cooks prepare breakfast for Mr Humble. Bacon, eggs, sausage, lamb chops, kidneys, mushrooms, black pudding and fried bread with one pint of sweet tea and one pint of warm ale.

EIGHT A.M. Mr Humble arises, dresses, washes and has breakfast.

31 When they came down she tried to catch them but she couldn't because she'd thrown her hands in the air. Heh! Only joking. Let's face it ... "throwing your hands in the air" is one of the silly things writers say when they don't quite mean it.

NINE A.M. Cooks prepare a light breakfast for Mrs Humble – the same as Mr Humble but with toasted bread instead of fried bread plus buttered crumpets, kippers and coffee.

TEN A.M. Mrs Humble arises, dresses and has breakfast.

ELEVEN A.M. Mrs and Mrs Humble do the accounts.

TWELVE NOON Mr and Mrs Humble meet at the front door to start a tour of the workshops, inspect the work, punish the slackers with beatings.

ONE P.M. If the work is good enough the paupers may be allowed to eat a lunch of soup and bread.

TWO P.M. Paupers return to work until seven p.m. Mrs and Mrs Humble have lunch together – roast meat, potatoes and carrots followed by suet pudding.

SIX P.M. Mr and Mrs Humble have supper of tea, pie, sandwiches, cakes, biscuits, sweetmeats, custard and tarts.

SEVEN P.M. Paupers have supper of cheese and broth.

EIGHT P.M. Families have one hour to meet while children play. Mr and Mrs Humble entertain guests to a late supper of cold meats, chutneys, cheese, biscuits, fine wines and brandy.

NINE P.M. Pauper prayers and return to cells. Lights out at 9:15 p.m.

"So, class?" Ruby Friday asked with raised eyebrows. "When do we snatch Mrs Humble, eh?"

It was Alice White who slowly raised her hand and said, "There's only one time, isn't there?"

Ruby Friday nodded.

Smiff sighed. "All right, miss clever drawers. When is it?"

Alice gave a smirk like a well-fed cat. "Work it out, pudding-brain. Work it out."

Chapter 8

GRACE
AND GRUEL

Friday 16th March 1837

Mr and Mrs Humble were looking forward to the day ... well, they couldn't look back because it was early morning.

Mrs Humble made a huge effort to get out of bed before six a.m. She even had her breakfast sent to her in bed so she could save time later. It was a large meal so it took her a long time to finish it but by half-past six she was dressing in her best blue gown.

"What time do our visitors arrive, my duckling?" she asked her husband.

"At noon, my sweetness. It all depends on the tide, of course, but I think Mayor Twistle meets her at the south dock around now. He'll take her to his house in South Drive to rest from her journey. Then, at around half-past eleven, she'll ride here in the mayor's carriage in time to see the paupers working. By the time we've shown her around the building it will be time to watch the paupers eat."

"Then let's go down to the dining room and get them to practise," Mrs Humble said. "We don't want her to see them eating like termites at a timber-yard, do we?"

The couple linked arms and walked to the dining room where the paupers waited in silence for them to arrive. The cook had been told to serve no one till the Humbles arrived.

The families sat in rows on benches. Each had an empty bowl and a spoon. No one spoke. Even the babies were too weak to cry.

Mrs Humble smiled. "Today we will have a very important visitor. If you all behave well then you may get meat for supper tonight!"

"Then again, you may not," her husband muttered.

"There are ten rows of ten people. You are

seated there with number one at the front left and in order up to number one hundred at the back right. First numbers one to ten will line up and you will be given a bowl of gruel," she said, pointing at the front row. "You will return to your seats. But no one will eat till all hundred have been served. You all eat at exactly the same time. So much neater. Do you understand?"

Rows of dead eyes stared back at her.

"Excuse me, Mrs Humble!" the cook said. "I have spent an hour cooking this muck."

"So?"

"So . . . you can't expect me to *serve* it as well. That's not fair that's not. I am here as a cook, not a *server*. They told me a pauper would do the serving."[32]

Mrs Humble sighed. "Very well, number one can help."

32 There's always one, isn't there? Someone who does their job and nothing more? The teacher who says, "Oh, I am paid to beat children till they learn – you can't expect me to do yard duty." Or the cab driver who says, "I am paid to take you to the station – I'm not paid to carry your heavy bags to the train, you old goat." But I 'm here to tell you the story of the Wildpool kidnap, not ramble on about lazy teachers and cab drivers. So I 'll get on with it.

"Too small," the cook sniffed, looking down at Millie Mixley. "And dishonest too!"

"I'm not dishonest!" Millie cried angrily.

The cook waved a gooey ladle at her. "Yesterday you were wearing brown boots ... today they are black. Paupers can't afford *two* pairs of boots ... so you must have pinched them."

Millie's mouth moved like a goldfish. "Ah ... ah ... ah... I cleaned my brown boots with black polish by mistake!"

"I still don't trust you, boy. I don't want you helping me."

Mrs Humble ground her teeth. "Then number two can do it."

"I'm blind," the beggar said.

"So? That's no excuse." Her face began to turn red and angry. "Get yourself up on this platform and do as you are told otherwise you will be punished. You will spend a day in the solitary cell!" she raged. Then she lowered her voice. "There are no windows in the cell. Imagine that? Locked in darkness for a whole day."

"Ooooh! Sounds spooky!" the blind beggar gasped. "I'll serve the food."[33]

He stumbled on to the platform and picked up the ladle.

Mrs Humble clapped her chubby hands. "Numbers one to ten ... except for number two ... get ready ... wait for it ... and ... *go!*"

The paupers, led by Millie Mixley at number one, lined up at the table where an iron pot full of gruel stood. The grey mush was slopped into their dishes and they returned to their seats.

The gruel was served out; the gruel disappeared.

"Now, we say thanks to our Lord. Our visitor will expect it!" Mr Humble said. Suddenly the paupers spoke. They spoke with one voice ... but not the words Mr Humble expected. It was the pauper's grace.

"I thank the Lord for what I've had,
If I had more I should be glad,
But now the times they are so bad,
I must be glad for what I had."

---

33 A blind person would not be worried about being shut in a dark room. I KNOW that. So don't start jumping up and down and saying, "That 's silly! " or "My dog's got no nose" or something.

"That's enough of that!" Humble growled. "Get on with it, Mrs Humble, before I lose my temper with these ungrateful wretches."

*

In Master Crook's Crime Academy the pupils ate fresh white bread with butter. They drank tea with sugar and sat by a coal fire to plan their day. Sausages sizzled in the pan and flames flared when the fat landed on the coals.

"It's noon, isn't it?" Smiff said. "You said there was only *one* time we could kidnap her. It's noon."

Alice smiled cruelly. "It took you all night to work it out."

"Alice!" Ruby Friday said sharply. "Do not bully your classmates. Remember the school rule?"

Alice scowled. "Sorry, Smiff. You are correct. The only time we can kidnap Mrs Humble is at *noon*. That is the time when the night soil cart enters the workhouse. It takes twenty minutes to make its round and at twenty-past twelve we leave with her."

"And at noon we know where Mrs Humble

will be – in the entrance hall ready to start her rounds. We have Martin's timetable."

Ruby Friday nodded. "Two more things. We must be sure we know which one is Mrs Humble."

"Easy," Martin Mixley said. "She's the stout one in the white dress with purple sleeves and a purple apron."

"I'll know her when I see her," Nancy said. "If she's stout even I will have trouble carrying her!"

"She will struggle. We need to get a gag in her mouth and a sack over her head in an instant," the teacher reminded them.

"And after Nancy has done that, I tie the sack up with rope," Alice said.

"And someone needs to get Mr Humble out of the way for a few minutes – we can't have him coming to rescue his wife."

"My job," Smiff said.

"That's it then. This morning in class we will work on our disguises," Miss Friday said. "There's nothing that can go wrong. Nothing that I can see."

*

The soot-stained water of the Wildpool river stood still when it reached the end of the pier. It mixed with the green water of the sea and pushed at it like a wrestler. The river lost the struggle in the end . . . as it did twice every day.

The tide flowed in and the fresh sea pushed back the filthy river where it came from; the dark river with its coal-dust and sewage, its drowned rats, its ooze and oil, its bits of boats and ropes and sawdust from the shipyards, a basket, a bucket and broken branches from far upriver.

The tide flowed in and brought with it a fine, large yacht with shining white sails that lit up the dull air. Sailors hurried over her decks, hauling on ropes, lowering the sails and steering her towards a rowing boat. A bare-footed sailor threw a rope to the rowing boat and let the oarsman tow them towards the quayside.

A man stood at the front of the yacht – the "prow" if you want the proper word.

He was an old man but as upright as the yacht's mast and with a face as cold as the water beneath them. His dark coat was cut from the finest cloth and his shirt from the best silk. But people noticed none of this.

People noticed, first, his hawk nose between his hawk eyes. They noticed his gleaming boots, tall, black boots that came up to his knees.

The yacht bumped gently into the quay. The tall man walked to the door of the cabin and spoke quietly. "We are there, ma'am. We are at Wildpool."

The voice from inside snapped, "About time too. Even this bleak and black berth has to be better than another day at sea." Then the young woman's voice spat as if to a servant, "Dress me in my best purple dress. The one with the white collar, lace cuffs and hem. I suppose I will have to be polite to that awful little man. What's his name? Whistle?"

"Twistle, ma'am," the man on deck said. "Sir Oswald Twistle and Lady Arabella. He has a lot of power in this part of England."

"What do I care?" the voice called, muffled now as she wriggled into the too-tight dress.

"Not as much power as I will have soon. So long as he feeds me well."

"Yes, ma'am. I'm sure he will."

"But I will have breakfast first ... just to be on the safe side."

"Yes, ma'am."

*

At that moment the paupers in the workhouse put their spoons in their bowls and placed their bowls on their knees to show they had finished their pitiful meals.

Suddenly Millie Mixley rose from her seat and walked to the overseer, basin and spoon in hand. She said – shocked at her own courage – "Please, sir, I want less."

Humble turned very pale. He gazed in amazement at the small rebel for some seconds, and then clung to the table for support.

Mrs Humble was weak with shock; the paupers with fear. "What?" said the overseer, in a faint voice.

"Please, sir," replied Millie, "I want less."

The master aimed a blow at Millie's head with the ladle. "Did you hear that, Mrs

Humble? Pauper number one has asked for more!'[34]

"For more?" said Mrs Humble. "Calm down, husband. Are you saying pauper number one has eaten his gruel and is greedy enough to ask for *more* than the amount we decided is good for him?"

"He did, Mrs Humble," replied the overseer.

"That boy will be hung," said his wife. "I know that boy will be hung."

No one argued.

"Number two? Take him away to the punishment cell!" Humble ordered.

"If I can find it," the beggar said. "I'm blind, you know."

"Excuse me," Millie said in a piping voice growing stronger and angrier all the time. "But what is the charge?"

"Eh!" Humble exploded. "No *charge* ... it's free, you foolish boy!"

---

34 Yes, I know, that the famed author, Charles Dickens, wrote a famous scene that very year of 1837, in which a boy called Oliver asked for more gruel in the workhouse. It is clearly nonsense. NO ONE who has tasted workhouse gruel would EVER ask for more. Not even the twisting little Oliver. THIS is the true story.

"No, sir," Millie went on boldly. "I meant what crime are you *charging* me *with*? Remember Magna Carta?"

"Who's *she* when she's at home?" Humble sneered.

"An ancient law – no one can be arrested or locked away without being charged. It is my right as a freeborn girl. . ."

"Eh? You're a boy."

Millie looked down at her trousers. "Yes ... my right as a freeborn *boy* ... my right to British justice and a fair trial!" She raised a fist in the air.

Ninety-nine pauper mouths fell open. Then a bent old woman cried, "Well said, number one, lad!" and the room burst into applause.

(39)

No free man shall be seized or imprisoned, except by the lawful judgment of his equals or by the law of the land.

Humble bumbled and searched for words. He read them off the motto on the wall, "If anyone would not work, he should not eat – that's what Saint Paul said."

The old woman rose to her feet. "We mostly *did* work till we were thrown out of Garth Court. I did dress-making."

"I was a weaver," a man's voice called. "Even if the factories meant I didn't earn enough to feed a scarecrow."

"And I was a street-singer!" a young woman added. "I sang for pennies and I sang for my pride."

"I was an organ grinder ... till those navvies wrecked my machine when they pulled down our home!"

The voices rose to a roar and Mr and Mrs Humble were white with fear. "Silence!" Mrs Humble screeched and the noise fell away. "We have a very important visitor this afternoon. If they think we are doing a good job then they will give us money ... and the money will go to buy you better food, or finer clothes. You can work less hours and we'll even let you leave the workhouse to find better work. We promise that, don't we, Mr Humble?"

"We do. We promise!" he nodded.[35]

The paupers nodded. Humble turned to Millie. "As for you, I will spare you the punishment room this time. But no nonsense about asking for more at dinner time."

"More?" Millie frowned. "I asked for *less*! I couldn't *bear* to eat any more of that *slime*. I'd rather *starve*! But if you want me to ask for *less* when the visitor comes then I will, sir."

"No!" Mr Humble choked. "We want the visitor to think this is the best food a pauper has ever eaten!"

Millie nodded. "Right, so you want me to come and ask for *more*, do you?"

"Yes," the Humbles nodded.

"So the visitors think you starve us with too *little*."

Humble saw the trap too late. "No!" he moaned.

---

35 Of course YOU know that as soon as the important visitor has gone he would break his promise. People who want something desperately enough will promise anything. "Ooooh! Mum! Buy me an ice cream and I will tidy my room." Yeah. Right.

"So? What's it to be? 'Please, sir, I want some less' or 'Please, sir, I want some more'?"

The man's forehead was so creased his eyebrows touched his dark hair. His eyes looked as if they would explode. He had never had to think this hard in his life. "Say ... say ... 'Please, sir, I want some *more*'," he decided.

Millie grinned and looked at the paupers. "Great! Mr Humble said we could all have some more!"

In the rush to the front Mr Humble was trampled like a worm in a field of cows.

Chapter 9

PAPER AND PAINT

"The plan is in place," Ruby Friday said once the students of Master Crook's Crime Academy were back in the classroom. "Nancy Turnip, is the hiding place ready?"

Nancy smiled shyly. "The best place in the world, Miss Friday. The place where no one will ever look."

"Smiff, is the ransom note ready?"

"Yes, Miss Friday," he nodded and showed it to the class. It had a few blots and smudges but it was clear enough.

To Mayor Twistle,

We have Mrs Humble as a hostage.

She will live on gruel and water, just like the paupers, until you agree:

1. The paupers will be fed properly and that Police Inspector Beadle can check any time.

2. The paupers will be **PAID** for their work and the children will be **free to play**, not work

3. The paupers will be free to leave the workhouse to find their own work any time they like

4. The families will not be forced to live apart

5. The paupers will be given proper clothes and not forced to wear uniforms and be ashamed.

If you do not agree in one day then Mister Humble will be kidnapped too.

We can **kidnap anyone at any time**. Guess who will be next, Mayor Twistle?

Pin your answers to the town hall door where all Wildpool can read them.

"Very good, Smiff. Now all we need to do is make the disguises. I have here some paper bags that you can carry in your pockets then slip over your heads when you need them,"

126

Ruby Friday said and handed one each to Smiff, Alice, Martin and Nancy. "Martin, you'll be staying here so as not to blow Millie's cover, but you can still learn this for next time. Now first cut out the eye holes, of course."

Smiff put the bag over his head and the eye holes were neat as a knight's helmet.

Alice pulled her bag over her head to try it. Smiff looked at her and gasped. "Oh, Alice! I have said some unkind things about you before."

"Uh?" she said, muffled under the bag.

"But can I say," Smiff said with a sob in his voice, "I have never seen you look so beautiful!"

There was a silence and Nancy and Martin looked at one another, waiting for the fight to start. Alice spoke sweetly. "Smiff?"

"Yes, lovely Alice?"

"What did I do before I came to Master Crook's Crime Academy?" she asked.

"You were a match girl, Alice."

"I was a match girl. And I still have my matches," she said quietly.

"Good for you, Alice," Smiff said.

"What would happen if I struck a match

and set fire to your paper bag?" she asked.

Smiff slipped the bag off his head and placed it on the table. "Why not try it?" he asked with a grin.[36]

Alice pulled off her paper bag. "I hate you Smiff," she said.

Smiff gasped. "Oh, Alice! Put the bag back on your head, *please!*"

The girl's fists went tight and Ruby Friday spoke quickly. "I think it would be a great idea to decorate the fronts of the bags to really confuse the police . . . just in case someone sees you and reports you!"

She took a paint-box from the cupboard and gave the students brushes and water.

Smiff painted a pair of spectacles and a dark moustache on a dark-haired gentleman – it could have been Mr Samuel Dreep. Alice painted a rough-haired boy that looked a little like Smiff. Nancy painted a cat's face and Martin painted a pig.

---

36 At this point in the story I have to say, "Do not try this at home." If someone with a paper bag over their head annoys you it is WRONG to set fire to the bag. The whole house could burn down. And it 's a waste of good paper.

They had just finished and were washing their brushes when Mr Dreep swept into the room, his red-and-white striped scarf trailing like a sunset cloud and his top hat tilted back in the rush.

"Now, class, Mayor Twistle's guest has arrived and she is being driven up to his house right now," he announced.

"A woman?" Smiff said.

"Who is it?" Alice asked.

Dreep shrugged. "I didn't recognize her but she must be a really important lady because she has an armed guard on the yacht – a tall old man was their commander and he has a troop of ten men in British army uniforms."

"Can we see them march past?" Martin asked, excited.

"They stayed on the yacht. Maybe they think the lady is safe in Mayor Twistle's care," the teacher shrugged.

Ruby Friday was pleased. "The mayor will be so busy with his guest it will make the kidnap of Mrs Humble all the easier."

"The soldiers and their commander are a worry," Samuel Dreep said.

Ruby Friday laughed. "I helped the Duke of Wellington win the battle of Waterloo. I know how to deal with soldiers, don't you worry!"

*

Constable Liddle and Constable Larch stood in front of the inspector's desk in the basement of the police station on the High Street.

"You lost your trousers," the inspector said. "*The Wildpool Star* has told the whole town that the Wildpool police constables are clowns."

"We got our trousers back," Liddle muttered, "sir."

"No. Mayor Twistle's *navvies* got them back."

"We filled the workhouse," Larch pointed out.

"No, Mayor Twistle's *navvies* filled the workhouse. How many did *you* arrest?"

"Well," Liddle said eagerly, "there was that blind beggar!"

"And that chap on the corner of the High Street ... the blind beggar!" Larch added.

"Enough!" Inspector Beadle roared and he thumped the table with his massive fist. The police station shook. "Here is your chance to show the town ... and a VIP—"

"What's a *vipp*?" Liddle asked.

"V.I.P. a Very Important Person," the inspector explained. "Mayor Twistle will be taking her around the town this afternoon. I want you on the streets."

"Sweeping them?"

"Yes. Keeping the roughs and scruffs off the street, making sure there are no traffic hold-ups, no dogs fighting, no stray animals. Here," he said, pushing a sheet of paper in front of them.

WILDPOOL POLICE FORCE

ORDERS FOR VIP PATROL.

DATE: 16th March 1837

Polish your buttons and boots and brush your uniforms.

Proceed to the main streets of the town.

Patrol tirelessly. There must be NO farm animals being driven to market, NO stray cats or dogs. NO beggars or tramps.

ORDERS FOR VIP PATROL.

Make sure every shopkeeper sweeps the
pavement outside their shop.

Stop all vehicles if they are in the way
of Mayor Twistle's carriage and the VIP.
If you are asked to walk in front of the
carriage as a guard of honour then do it.
Then stand guard at the workhouse gates.
Wildpool needs you. Remember Mayor
Twistle's words: "Carry your truncheons
like flaming torches of justice. Bring
light to the darkness of our savage
streets."

POLICE INSPECTOR BEADLE

"Ooooh!" Constable Larch said. "It's a big
job."

"But someone has to do it, and it is our
proud duty," Liddle added with a sniffle.

"We are flaming torches!" Larch sobbed.

"No – you are flaming dribbling over my carpet," Beadle snapped. "Get out."

Mayor Twistle stood with his back to the fireplace. Lady Arabella sat on the sofa next to their VIP guest and looked up at her husband.

"I am proud to welcome you to Wildpool, ma'am," he said. "It's an honour."

"We know it is," the woman said sourly. She was short and stout with a pout to her snout that would have looked right on a pig. Talking of pigs, she was tucking into tea and scones with jam as her morning snack.

"When your dear uncle dies..."

"Won't be long now," the guest said and sucked thirstily on her tea.

"When he *does* die, then of course we will be proud to serve you ... and maybe you will do us the honour of making our humble town into a city?" the little man said, twisting his hands.

"Maybe," the young lady said through a

mouthful of scone. "Depends if we like the place. Doesn't look much."

"We are building warships for the navy – they will cruise the world, sail to every corner of the British Empire, and bring glory to the name of Wildpool City..."

"Town," she said.[37]

"Ah ... yes ... we built the best slave ships that crossed the oceans and made Britain rich."

The woman looked up sharply. "Slaving was banned three years ago," she said. "Go to America if you want to keep slaves these days."

"Ah ... yes ... but I meant—"

"And we do *not* mention the slave trade in London. It is not something we care to talk about," she said and rose to her feet. She was even shorter than the little mayor. "Now, we will rest," she said. "Then we'll get this over with."

*

37 It is sixty years on now. Wildpool never did become a city and I doubt it ever will. I think the old queen took a dislike to Wildpool. As for Mayor Twistle, he wanted to call himself LORD Mayor Twistle. A silly little thing I know ... and maybe I am becoming spiteful in my old age ... but I am very happy he never made it!

Ruby Friday's plans were finished. Now she had to wait till noon. There was time for a walk in the dank March morning air to clear her head. There could not be any mistakes.

She walked along the High Street to the end of the bridge. Across the bridge stood the workhouse, closed and barred and almost silent. Only the odd chink of a hammer breaking rocks into smaller stones could be heard.

In the mist-muffled air, horses' hooves clacked softly on the cobbles and gulls cried sadly as they soared and dived round the fishing boats.

Below the bridge was the fine, large yacht Mr Dreep had described. Ten soldiers had lined up on the quayside and were practising their drill. They wore red coats and navy trousers with white cross-belts.

They carried long muskets with wicked knives on the end to stab and tear the guts from enemies who came too close.

The sergeant on the end lined them up in two rows of five. The five at the front knelt down. They loaded their weapons faster than flying fish. They fired blanks towards the river and scared sixty seagulls into screeching flight. In moments the five in the back row had fired and by then the front row were ready to fire again.

They were good, Ruby knew. The very best the British army had. Ruby had mixed with soldiers all her life and had never seen better. Their faces were as hard as the concrete quay. What had the old Duke said in the Spanish wars about his own men? *"I don't know what effect these men will have on the enemy, but by God, they terrify me."* These were ten terrifying men.

Ruby Friday smiled. "They're the Duke of Wellington's own troop!" she laughed. She looked for their officer but he wasn't in sight.

There was an old gentleman stepping down from the yacht. He was not in uniform, yet he seemed to be in charge of the soldiers. His white hair and side whiskers curled out from under his hat. The troop stood to attention as he approached.

Ruby Friday strained her eyes. She rubbed them and looked again. But there was no mistake – even from the bridge high above the quay she could see his large nose and those long black boots. "Holy crumpets," she breathed. "The Duke of Wellington himself! What's *he* doing in Wildpool? Holy, holy, crying crumpets!"[38]

---

38 I am sorry if there are any younger readers or ladies reading this. I do not like repeating Ruby Friday's swearing. Polite writers, in the age of Victoria, would have written, "H—, H—, c— c—". But Victoria is dead ... as I may have mentioned.

Chapter 10

KIDNAP
AND CART

The new night soil men sat on their wagon at the end of the bridge. Alice gave them their last orders. They were about to set off for the workhouse at the far end of the bridge when they heard shouting.

"Move along there please! Get that wagon off the bridge!" Constable Liddle and Larch had turned from the High Street into Bridge Street and were using their truncheons to push people aside.

They sweated and panted up to the muck cart. "Get this to the side," Liddle cried. "Mayor Twistle's carriage is coming through. He doesn't want to be stuck behind a slow-moving vehicle."

Larch took the bridle of the horse in his hand and started to guide it towards the pavement then hurried on. No sooner was the cart at the kerb than the Twistle carriage clattered and rattled, rattered and clattled past.

The horses' hooves struck sparks off the cobbles and the mighty Wildpool bridge shook as they cantered across it.[39]

Dogs scattered and cats dodged. Liddle and Larch's boots sparked as much as the horses' hooves as they hurried to stand at the workhouse gateposts. They raised their truncheons in a salute.

The carriage skidded and bumped a little as it turned towards the Wildpool workhouse gates.

The sign usually said:

---

39 There should be a law against driving too fast in town. It 's even more dangerous now we have these smelly motor cars. The trouble is the really fast carriage and car drivers can't be caught by the police, can they? Well, not by police as old as Liddle and Larch. Maybe it 's not such a good idea after all.

Now Mr Humble had been up a ladder with a pot of whitewash and added to it:

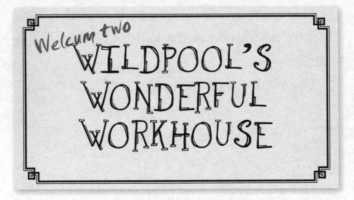

The gates swung open as the carriage arrived and swept in. The gates closed behind the carriage before Alice could see what happened next. And that's why the plan went wrong.

Mayor Twistle jumped down from the carriage and held the door open. He gave a nervous smile towards the Humbles. Mrs Humble was dressed in her best blue gown and matching bonnet and dropped into a low curtsey. Mr Humble pulled off his hat and bowed low.

The very important visitor in her purple dress stepped down, followed by Lady Twistle in pea-green silk.

"On behalf of a hundred happy paupers may we welcome you to Darlham Gaol," Mr Humble said.

"We're not there any more!" his wife hissed up at him.

"What?"

"We're not in jail."

"Ooooops!" the workhouse overseer said and smiled. "We are not in a jail. We are in a happy place full of happy people who love their work."

"Oh, please!" the little visitor said with a wave of her tiny hand. "No speeches. Let's get on with it." And the mayor led the way to the main door of the building.

It was exactly noon. The town hall clock chimed, *ding-dong* and all that. But there was another *ting-tong* of a smaller bell.

"Excuse me!" Humble said. "There's someone ringing the bell at the gate! Probably the muck men!" He shuffled across to the gate and lifted the bar.

*

Alice had run across to the workhouse gate but it had slammed in her face. "Holy crumpets," she snarled.[40]

She ran back to the cart. The girl lifted a canvas cover that had been thrown over the back. The cart had been scrubbed clean ... though it still smelled slightly worse than a coal-miner's armpit. Smiff and Nancy jumped

---

40 This is what Ruby Friday used to say. It just goes to show that adults can give young people disgusting habits like swearing. Do NOT do it, adults. And, young readers. Do NOT let me hear you repeat this disgraceful language either. Sadly I have a duty to report what was said. That does NOT mean you should copy.

down, climbed under the wagon and clung to the axle.

Alice pulled her paper bag over her head then nodded to the night soil men. They tapped the horse and guided it towards the gate.

"Halt! Who goes there?" the constables said.

Later, when the "Wanted" poster was put up around the town, they remembered that face...

Alice peered through the holes in her mask. "You can see who it is. It's the new night soil men – the ones you arrested. This is their punishment ... emptying the workhouse toilets for a week."

"So it is, little boy," Larch said and patted Alice on the head. He frowned. There was something not quite right.

Larch reached across and pulled the bell. The town hall clock was giving its twelfth *dong* when the gates swung open and Humble's flat face appeared.

"What do you want?" he demanded.

"Night soil men!" Larch cried. "It's all safe. We checked."

The overseer scowled till his thick eyebrows almost knitted themselves into a scarf over his nose. "We have a guest today. We have to be extra careful."

"We checked—" Liddle began.

"Checked? Did you check under the canvas cover? There could be a small army of assassins hiding there!" Humble cried.

"Well, they wouldn't be hiding in a pile of poo, would they?" Larch argued.

"And it's not our job to poke our noses into night soil," Liddle grumbled.

Humble stumped to the back of the cart and raised the canvas. "Hah! See?"

"See!" Liddle cried. "An army of assassins! Ooooh! I'll just run and get help."

"Stay there you cowardly cop. I mean, see, the wagon is clean and empty."

"So it is! That's all right then." Larch waved up to the drivers. "Carry on."

"Back in twenty minutes," the smaller night soil man said and whipped the horse into life.

The policemen took up their positions at

the gateposts again. "It would take a cunning assassin to get past us," Larch chuckled.

"Would it?" Liddle asked.

"Well . . . yes. Liddle and Larch are too clever to be caught out," Larch said. The constables shuffled their cold feet on the pavement. Their eyes were just a little uneasy behind the smiles.

"Oh, yes. Much too clever."

The wind off the river whipped at Liddle's flowing white moustache and they stood there for a silent minute. Finally Larch said, "That boy."

"Yes."

"When I patted him on the head. . ."

"Yes?"

"I thought I heard him . . . rustle."

"Me too."

"Very odd."

*

Alice stood at the south-west corner of the workhouse and watched the muck cart finish its round and roll towards her. She sped to the south-east corner, paper bag flapping in the wind, and waved at Smiff. The boy in the gentleman-faced mask ran in through the front door. The group of visitors stood in the entrance hall admiring the painting of Mayor Twistle that hung on the wall, grinning like the skull on a pirate flag.

"Fire!" Smiff cried. "Hurry, Mr Humble. There's a fire in the punishment room!"

The overseer dashed through the dining hall, past rows of astonished paupers waiting to start their meal, and into the dark cell.

"Fire? Where?" Humble grumbled.

"There!" Smiff pointed. "In that room!" As Humble leaned forward to look, Smiff pushed him inside and swung the door shut.

Mr Humble may have cried, "Help! Let me out!" But, if he did, no one heard a thing because the walls were as thick as a Wildpool policeman's head and the door as solid as their truncheons.

Smiff raced back through the dining hall, giving Millie a small wave as he ran past her. The Twistles, Mrs Humble and their guest were standing looking alarmed. "Mr Humble is dealing with it," he said quickly. "He says he wants you all to go into the dining hall. Dinner is served. Step this way!"

As the visitors moved towards the dining room door Smiff raised a hand and pointed. "That's her, Nancy ... the one in the purple dress."

Nancy, in her mask of a cat, paused a moment ... *"She's the stout one in the white dress with purple sleeves and a purple apron."* That's how Martin had described Mrs Humble. This woman was stout all right, but the dress was purple with white, not white with purple. Nancy gave a tiny sigh – boys had no interest in women's clothes. Martin had got it *wrong*.

Neither Smiff or Nancy noticed Mrs Humble in the blue dress, who had opened the door to the dining room to welcome the visitors.

"After you," Mayor Twistle said to their guest.

"No!" Smiff hissed to him. "The room is a mess! You and Lady Twistle go and sort it out."

The mayor gave a terrified grin. "Excuse us ... we ... the mayoress and I ... we just need to make sure everything is in order." Oswald Twistle pushed his wife ahead of him and closed the door.

The visitor blinked. Smiff smiled at her. "Here is a poem I wrote for you," he said. He stood with his back to the door as Nancy crept behind the guest. The boy chanted:

"Roses are red, pink, white and fancy.

Now it is time for the kidnap, dear Nancy!"

Nancy threw a sack from the sheep-head shop over the woman's head and clamped a hand over her mouth so she couldn't scream. The woman struggled and Nancy stumbled as she pulled her victim towards the door.

Using all of her strength, she lifted the chubby woman off the floor and carried her out of the door before the other visitors could come to find out what was happening.

Alice was waiting with a rope and tied it firmly round the sack so the woman's arms were tight against her sides and the sack held firm. The muck cart came around the corner at exactly the right moment and the victim was thrown on to the back.[41]

The canvas cover was placed over the top and Smiff ran to open the gate before climbing under the wagon with Nancy.

The policemen raised their truncheons in salute then realized it was the muck cart, not the mayor's carriage.

"Want to search the back again?" Alice asked through her mask.

Constable Larch's large nose twitched at the smell from the cart. "I don't think so," he said. "Not unless you are stealing night soil again!"

Alice laughed. "No, Constable. We have something much more disgusting on board!"

"Ho! Ho!" the policemen chuckled. "Off you go!"

Alice led the horse on to the bridge and turned into the High Street. Shoppers turned away and covered their noses as the cart creaked past. At Master Crook's Crime

---

41 Yes, clever reader, you remembered that NOW the cart was NOT empty but full of workhouse waste. This was sad but it couldn't be helped.

Academy, Smiff and Nancy dropped off the axle.

The boy ran into the school but Nancy climbed up alongside the night soil men. She whispered orders to the drivers.

"Where are you taking her?" Alice asked.

Nancy shook her head. "Secret, Alice. It's what Ruby Friday said. The less people know, the better."

Alice looked furious even through the paper bag. "You don't trust me!"

"Of course I do ... but, if you don't know where I'm going, you can't betray me. If the police tortured you then you might tell. You'd hate that, Alice."

The paper bag with the boy's face nodded and Alice turned to follow Smiff into the school.

The muck cart moved on.[42]

Alice and Smiff tore off their masks and ran into the classroom. Mr Dreep and Martin waited for them.

42 To where? I can't tell you. But it was just as Nancy promised. "The best place in the world, Miss Friday," she had said. "The place where no one will ever look."

"Well?" Dreep asked.

"Perfect," Alice cried. "Just perfect."

The constables stood at the gate and the wind off the sea blew it open.

"Hello!" Liddle said. "No one locked it behind the muck men. We don't want the paupers escaping. We'd better go in and bar it."

They stepped through into the courtyard.

From inside the workhouse came a roar like a train getting closer. It had started when Mayor Twistle had walked into the dining room. Now it was so loud it could be heard outside.

Millie had stood up to say to Mayor Twistle, "Please, sir, I want some more". The plan was that the rest of the paupers would join in and cause such a disturbance no one would notice Mrs Humble was missing ... or at least not until the muck cart was well away.

Millie had jumped to her feet and said, "Please, sir, I want some ... what's Mrs Humble doing here?"

"Eh?" Mayor Twistle said. He looked at the overseer's wife in her best blue dress and matching bonnet. "She works here, foolish boy."

"Yes, I know, but she was supposed to have been—" Millie started to speak but the blind beggar cut in.

"The lad was just about to ask for more!"

"Yes!" the paupers cheered. "We want more! We want more!"

Soon they were roaring their chant. The constables were hit by the wave of sound as they stepped into the dining hall.

"Is everything all right?" Larch asked the mayor.

"Just a stupid little riot about food."

"No," Liddle shouted so he could be heard. "We meant, is everything all right with the VIP?"

Mayor Twistle looked around. His eyes widened, his mouth worked but no words came out. He ran to the door and looked into the entrance hall. Only his own face on the portrait looked back.

He rushed into the courtyard where his driver dozed on the carriage seat.

"James! Have you seen our guest?"

"No, sir . . . and me name's Jack."

Sir Oswald Twistle dashed back into the room where the chanting had fallen silent. "Arabella," he asked, "where is our guest?"

"In the hall? Back in the carriage?"

"No, she's not," the mayor said in a voice like a frog with a sore throat.

But Lady Twistle's voice was strong. "Kidnapped!" she wailed.

Frantic, the mayor grabbed Constable Liddle by the front of his jacket. "Call the police!"

"We ARE the police."

"There has been a kidnapping!" he said, shaking him till his buttons rattled.

Millie was paler than the gruel. She looked at Mrs Humble – the woman they were meant to snatch – she looked at the trembling mayor. "But *who* has been kidnapped?" she muttered.

Chapter 11

SEARCHING AND SHOOTING

G o out on a moonless night and shine a lamp in a field of rabbits. Catch the eyes of a rabbit. The rabbit will be frozen with fear, unable to move. That makes it easy to shoot.[43]

That is how Mayor Oswald Twistle looked that day. His wife took command. "We must tell the Duke of Wellington at once," she said.

"He'll have me shot!" Sir Oswald sobbed.

"Probably," she agreed. "But if you *don't* tell him he'll find out sooner or later and he'll have you even *more* shot. It is *his* job to guard the lady. He thought she'd be safe in the hands

---

43 This trick, called "lamping", is used by poachers. This is one of the many useful tips you will pick up by reading my Master Crook chronicles. I ask for no further payment . . . just send me a tasty piece of rabbit pie.

of a mayor – he didn't realize how careless you could be, Oswald. But never mind. The Duke beat Napoleon – a gang of kidnappers will be no problem."

Mayor Twistle nodded and walked stiffly to his carriage. Constables Liddle and Larch wandered after him. "You two climb on the back," Lady Arabella ordered. Then she called to the coach driver, "Drive to the quayside, Jack, and drive as if your life depended on it!"

Jack cracked the whip and the horses trotted towards the workhouse gate. The paupers watched in wonder as the carriage skidded through the gates that the policemen had left open.

It bounced over cobbles and threatened to squash rats and cats flat. The constables were flung from side to side and their boots bounced up and down on the platform at the back. "I feel sick," Liddle moaned just as the carriage left the ground and crashed back down to send his stomach into his mouth.

The carriage reached the quayside and shot past boatyards and barns and barges and ballast and bollards with ropes wrapped round, past fish filleters, carpenters, captains and coal carters, riveters and riggers, boiler builders, smiths and sail stitchers, sailors and tailors, craftsmen and draughtsmen, mast-makers and mates, chandlers and horse handlers, clerks on barques, seamen on steamers, workers on wherries and fat men on ferries.

The soldiers were cleaning their weapons on the deck of the yacht. They jumped to their feet when they saw the careering carriage come to a halt. They lined up quickly as a guard of honour for their guest.

The Duke of Wellington came out from his cabin and pushed through them to see Sir Oswald Twistle tumble from the carriage. The Duke put on his hat and waited. "Oh, your Dukeship!" the little man wailed. "We have lost her!"

The Iron Duke's iron face hardly moved. "Lost?"

"We think she's been kidnapped," the mayor moaned.

"Tell me," the Duke ordered.

Sir Oswald's tale poured out. It was a jumble

of words about paupers and gruel but at last the Duke began to make sense of it. "I left her in your care, Mayor," he said.

"Are you going to shoot me?" Twistle whispered.

"God's teeth no, man! We need your help to find her! You are no use to me *dead*! No. We will find her first ... and *then* I'll think about shooting you."

"Thank you, sir," Oswald Twistle said with a weak smile.

The Duke of Wellington lined up the troops and the policemen on the quayside. He spoke quickly. "We came to Wildpool with an important visitor. We kept her name a secret because we feared she would be kidnapped. We left the soldiers on the yacht – we didn't give her a full army escort because we didn't want people to suspect she was *really* important. But she is. She is the most important woman in Britain and we have to find her. She is Princess Victoria. And, when the old king dies she will become Queen Victoria."

*

"Do you know who we are?" Princess Victoria said. She was bound to a chair and looked up at the cat-faced mask of Nancy.

"Yes," Nancy nodded. "You are Mrs Amelia Humble of Wildpool's Wonderful Workhouse."

The princess twisted her smooth, round face in scorn. "We are NOT."

Nancy sighed. "All right. You are Mrs Angela Harper of Darlham Gaol."

"We are most certainly *not* from a gaol. How dare you!"

Nancy shook her head. "It doesn't really matter what you call yourself today, the fact is you are our prisoner and you will sign this ransom note." Nancy thrust the note in front of the young woman's face.

My Dearest Hengist
They have imprisoned me in a secret hideout where no one will find me. Someone will deliver a note to you and Mayor Twistle soon. They will ask for the paupers to be well fed and clothed. Sign that note and I will be set free. Refuse and they say they will cook me in a large pot and feed me to the paupers. Please, my sweetness, do as they say.
Signed:

The princess glared at Nancy's cat face. "Do we *look* like a workhouse keeper?"

"Don't know. I never met Mrs Humble."

"Look at the ring on our finger ... it is a ring of state. We are going to tell you who we are. You are then going to set us free. If you *do* then you will go to prison for fifty years for treason. If you do *not* then the Duke of Wellington will find us. He will arrest you and shoot you. Do you understand?"

Nancy nodded. "I'll tell you what. I will go and talk to Miss ... our leader ... and see what she says." She turned to go.

"Wait!" Princess Victoria cried.

Nancy stopped.

"Get us a fresh set of clothes and a warm scented bath. We have been carried in some sort of muck cart! We! Princess Victoria. Future Queen of Britain! At least let us get rid of this disgusting stench."

Nancy nodded. "I will get the servants to set up a bath, towels and clean clothes through that door in the dressing room. When they have done it they will knock on the door. You will count to ten then enter and have your bath. The rooms will be locked on the outside. You can't get out. But you mustn't see the servants and they mustn't see you. Understand?"

The princess glowered. "We understand. Now untie us."

*

The Duke of Wellington leaned close to Mayor Twistle and breathed in his face. "I have heard stories about your work in Garth Court," he said, waving a hand towards the flat, bare patch of earth where the houses had stood. "You can command a hundred thuggish railway workers."

"Yes, Duke Wellington, sir," the mayor said, swallowing fear like it was a bumble bee.

"There are ... what ... two thousand houses in Wildpool?"

"Yes, Duke Wellington, sir."

"I want those hundred navvies to search every one. Every room, every attic, every cellar. It's only twenty houses each. They will kick down locked doors if they have to. They will be split into groups of ten – each group will be under the command of one of my soldiers. If anyone gets in the way my men have orders to shoot."

"Yes, Duke Wellington, sir."

The Duke pointed to Constable Liddle. "Run up the hill to the coal platform. There's a train unloading now. Take it to the end of the line and collect the navvies. Bring them back here. Well? What are you waiting for?"

"Do you know how old I am? I can't run," Liddle groaned and sucked on one end of his white moustache.[44]

The Duke drew a pistol. "I can shoot. If you are not at the end of the quay by the time I count to ten then I will shoot you."

Liddle found he could run after all.

The Iron Duke turned to Larch. "Run to the harbour-master's office. No vessel of any kind may leave the harbour until the princess is found."

Larch waddled away in a sort of run.

---

44 I sometimes do that when I get worried, do you? Let me give you one of my ever-useful tips. Do NOT suck your white moustache after you've been eating blackcurrants or beetroot – it turns your moustache pink and you look stupid.

"How many roads are there out of Wildpool?"

"Just the Great North Road – north and south, Duke Wellington," the mayor squeaked.

"Get your driver to drop you off at the southern end of town and stop all traffic ... he can then drop your wife at the northern end to stop our kidnappers escaping that way."

Mayor Twistle bounced down the gangplanks of the yacht to obey.

The Duke of Wellington turned to his troop. "Collect bullets and powder from the locker and be sure your muskets are loaded. We would like to capture these kidnappers alive ... but, if they die escaping, it's their bad luck." The rock-faced men moved quietly and quickly. The Iron Duke had fire in his iron eyes as if he were almost enjoying being back in action. "These kidnappers are good – but the world's best kidnapper is not as good as me. Hah! Not even Ruby Friday could beat me. I wonder what ever happened to old Ruby?"

*

Ruby Friday sat in the classroom of Master Crook's Crime Academy. The pupils looked at her and waited.

"So, Smiff, you never got to give the ransom note to Mayor Twistle?"

"Sorry, I waited at the corner of the High Street – the way we said. The carriage would slow down as it turned to the police station. That's what you said."

"So what went wrong?"

"It didn't go to the police station. It raced down to the quayside and along to the fine yacht that sailed in this morning," Smiff told her. "The mayor seemed to be talking to an old man on the deck then he raced off towards the Great North Road."

"Please, miss," Martin asked quietly. "What's going on? Millie's still trapped inside the workhouse. What will I tell our mum? If she doesn't come home?"

Samuel Dreep's fingers had been whirring like someone with invisible knitting. "Millie is safe enough in there for the moment. We need to work out why the kidnap of Mrs Humble caused such a panic. She's only the wife of a workhouse overseer."

"Because we didn't kidnap Mrs Humble," Nancy said, walking in the door. She had taken off her cat mask and her face was pale and frowning. "The woman I kidnapped is saying she is Princess Victoria. I think I grabbed the wrong person."

Ruby Friday frowned. "I should have guessed. *That's* why she has an armed guard led by the Duke of Wellington himself. Is she safely hidden?"

"Yes," Nancy nodded. "You told me to keep it secret."

"Better whisper it to me," Ruby Friday said.

As she spoke Ruby's round, rosy face split into a wide smile. "Oh, that is very good, Nancy . . . brilliant."

"But I'll have to let her go. We've failed, haven't we?"

Ruby shook her head. "Not yet, my girl. The best crooks can change their plans when things go a little wrong. Isn't that right, Mr Dreep?"

The teacher said, "It is."

"So, Smiff, get ready to write us a new kidnap note!"

Smiff lifted the lid of his desk and took out a fresh sheet of paper and a quill pen. He began writing.

Dear Mayor Twistle,

We have Princess Victoria as a hostage. Not even the Duke of Wellington will find where we have hidden her. Not unless we tell him. She will live on gruel and water, just like the paupers, until you agree:

1. The wicked Mr and Mrs Humble will be sacked.

2. A pleasant lady called Friday will come to you tomorrow. You will give her the job as overseer.

3. She will change the rules so the paupers are free to come and go as they wish and families will not be forced to live apart

4. The town council will build a new, clean Garth Court with proper windows, wide chimneys, good toilets and made of the

finest brick and plaster. When it is finished
the workhouse families will be able to rent
rooms for just one shilling a week.
If you do not agree in one day then we will
tell the Duke that YOU have kidnapped the
Princess Victoria. He will shoot you.
Sign below to show you agree to our demands
The Power to the Paupers Gang
Signed:

"What can I do?" Alice cried. "This is the most exciting thing we've ever done in class and I've just been a lookout and not much else."

Mr Dreep looked worried. "We could give you the job of delivering the note to Mayor Twistle but—"

"I'll do it!"

"But it could be very dangerous."

"Who says? You says?" Alice jeered. "Danger is my middle name."

"I thought that 'stupid' was your middle name," Smiff muttered.

"He headed off to the Great North Road, isn't that right, Smiff?" Alice asked.

"Probably to stop the kidnappers escaping," Samuel Dreep put in. "That's what I'd do."

"I'll find him," Alice said.

"You'll need your mask!" Dreep warned.

Ruby Friday scribbled a note in pencil and put it in an envelope. She dripped sealing wax on to the flap and shut it. "If Mayor Twistle refuses then give him this."

Alice snatched up both letters and ran off ... just in time. Mr Dreep locked the front door behind her. He returned to the classroom.

"What next, Miss Friday?" Martin asked.

But a hammering at the front door answered him. "Open up."

Mr Dreep left the classroom, walked down the corridor and unlocked the front door. A large man with skin as grimy as his work-clothes stood there. "I've come to search your house," he said.

"Have you a search warrant?"

The man let a slow smile spread across his face. "Yes."

"Can I see it?"

The navvy put three fingers in his mouth, turned and whistled. A soldier in a red jacket appeared in the gateway and raised his musket. It was aimed at a spot between Mr Dreep's eyes.

"Hmm," the teacher said. "That search warrant seems to be in order ... come in. Could I offer you a cup of tea?"

*

While the navvy started in the attic rooms of the Crime Academy, and barged through doors, Ruby Friday slipped out of the kitchen door. She climbed the fence into the police station garden next door and came out into the High Street from the police station gate.

The world's greatest kidnapper hurried along the High Street, past screaming children, sobbing women and cringing men. The people of Wildpool were gathering in the street as the army and the navvies stamped and stomped and stormed through their homes, shops, sheds and cellars.

Inspector Beadle stood at the door to the

police station. "What are they *looking* for?" a woman cried.

"It's a secret," the inspector said. "A secret you may never know."

But still they didn't find the princess.

Chapter 12

BACON
AND X

When Mrs Humble opened the door to the punishment room Mr Humble's face was white.

By the time he had marched to the dining room it was purple with rage. The paupers cheered him.

"What?" he roared.

"We want more!" they cried.

"More? More! You aren't getting *any*." He held up the key. "Some jester locked me in the punishment room. Our important guests went away in some sort of panic. You will *all* pay for that. The gates are locked. No one can escape. The kitchen is locked. No one can eat ... not so much as a spoonful of gruel. The men will break one ton of stone till their arms and backs ache. The women will pick ten sacks of oakum till their fingers bleed. The children will pick the seeds from ten sacks of cotton – and if there is one seed in the ten sacks they will be beaten by Mrs Humble's rods, won't they, Mrs Humble?"

"I'll enjoy it," the woman said.

"The sooner you start the sooner you will eat ... probably tomorrow afternoon," he said.

The starving paupers, defeated, trooped away to their tasks.

*

Mayor Twistle stood in the chill east wind and argued. A queue of carts and horses were getting angry. "No one may pass!" the little man cried.

"Why not?" a farmer in a filthy smock asked.

"Because the Duke of Wellington says so," the mayor argued.

"The Duke of *Wellington*? Old Welly himself in Wildpool? If Welly's in Wildpool I'll eat my wellington boots!" the filthy farmer jeered.

The horse began to plod forward. "Fine!" Oswald Twistle said. "So long as you let me look in the back of your carts I can let you go!"

"What you looking for?"

"It's a secret."

"I haven't any of those on board," the farmer laughed. "Just a few geese. Mind they don't bite you."

Mayor Twistle raised the canvas cover. A goose bit him on the nose.

After twenty carts had been searched Mayor Twistle was almost pleased to see a boy with scruffy hair and a black skirt on run up to him waving an envelope. "Message for you, Mayor Twistle," Alice said.

"Oh," he moaned, stamping his frozen feet. "I hope it's from the Duke telling me I can come back to town!"

He tore open Smiff's ransom note and read it. He began to choke as if someone was pulling his necktie tighter than a hangman's noose.

The mayor looked at Alice's painted mask. "This is nonsense. You can't expect me to give in to these ... threats!"

"You refuse to sign?" Alice sighed.

"Of course I refuse, you stupid little man!"

"Then you'll be shot ... you stupid little man!" Alice said and thrust Ruby Friday's letter into his hand.

The mayor tore open the seal and unfolded the letter. He wobbled. He swayed. He staggered a few paces. He dropped the letter. He sobbed.

Alice picked up the letter and peered at it through the eye holes in her mask.

Mayor,

Princess Victoria is a prisoner in YOUR house. See if you can explain THAT before the Duke shoots you. Sign our note or we will tell him WHERE to find the princess and that YOU are the kidnapper.

A Friend

"Ohhhh!" the mayor groaned. "I'm too young to die. What am I to do?"

Alice pulled a pencil from her pocket. "Sign the paper, of course," she said.

Mayor Twistle signed.

*

The grey-faced, grey-haired butler stood at the door to 13 South Drive – Mayor Twistle's home. He wore a black tail coat, grey trousers, white shirt and white cravat tie. "You rang?"

The navvy was broad as the door and carried the handle from a pick-axe in his hard hand. "I've come to search the house," the man said.

"Certainly, sir. Just show me your search warrant and I will be happy to show you round."

The man raised his pick-axe handle and pushed it under the butler's nose. "Here's my search warrant," he said, as he'd said at the other houses.

"Ah!" the butler smiled. "I can tell you have been sent by Mayor Twistle!"

"That's right."

"Then you will be delighted to know *this* is Mayor Twistle's house."

"So?"

"So-o-o, Sir Oswald would not send you to search his own house, would he?"

"No, but..."

"In fact he may be just a touch upset if you trampled your muddy boots over the carpet that the maid has just swept," the butler said quietly. "What is your name?"

"Me name? I don't have to give me name!" the navvy said in alarm.

"The mayor will be so pleased with your work. When it comes to rewards your name will be top of the list!"

"Well," the navvy said, "when I sign for my pay I usually mark it with a 'x'."

The butler passed him a scrap of paper and a pencil. "Just write it down here."

The man did as he was asked.

"Thank you!" the butler said. "I will see this is delivered to the mayor, in person, when he gets home. I will tell him what a fine man you are and the reward will be doubled."

"Thanks mate," the navvy said.

"Good night and good luck!" the butler said as he closed the door.

A girl stood behind the butler. She wore a paper mask with the face of a cat on it. "There you are, Nancy, you're safe," the butler said.

"Thank you," she said and squeezed the grey-faced, grey-haired man's grey hand.

"But the sooner you can get our ... guest out of the house the better. She has been given a meal of best bacon, had a bath and been dressed in one of Lady Twistle's dresses and bonnets."

Nancy nodded.

There was a sudden rapping at the door like the volley of shots from Wellington's troop of soldiers.

"That could be just what we're waiting for," the butler said and turned to the door. He opened it.

*

Princess Victoria wandered around the room. She searched in the drawers of the dressing table. There were some corsets, stiff with whalebones, meant to hold in the body of an even larger lady than her.[45]

There were bloomers and bustles, brooches and bracelets, powders and paints for her face. But no sign of the lady's name.

Then the princess found a small writing desk. Inside she found paper and a quill pen and a pot of black ink.

The room in which one was held prisoner has wallpaper with pale green and gold stripes. There is a dressing table in the French style: there is a writing table to match. The hip bath one used has flower patterns on the side And one was given camomile soap with which to wash.

45 Oh but it's a hard life being a whale. You are swimming around happily in the sea. Then, one day, someone stabs you with harpoons and drags you on to a ship. They skin you and gut you and what do they do with your bones? Wrap them round some large lady's body to squeeze her till she's thin. Me? I'd ban whale hunting, but I guess it will never happen.

In a white-painted cupboard there are clothes for a lady with a waist of fifty inches which are held in with a corset to make her forty inches. (One is far too small to fit them oneself.)
Her black shoes are made hand and are large enough to put on a lake and sail one's pet dogs. Enormous.
There are two brooches – cheap glass one should say, three rings, a diamond and ruby necklace, and a silver bracelet (too large for one's own wrist).

The lady uses a lavender and rose scent, white face powder and crushed red cheek powder.

With this description one is sure our police forces will find the room where one was held, put the villains on trial and hang them for treason.

Princess Victoria

She folded the note, placed it in a purse that hung from her waist and sat on the chair by the writing table. She waited for the kidnappers to make their next move.

*

Constables Liddle and Larch stood in front of Inspector Beadle's desk in the basement of the police station. They were damp from a shower of drizzle on the outside and damp with sweat on the inside.

The gigantic inspector looked at them. "Yet again you have disgraced the Wildpool police force."

"Sorry, sir," Larch muttered.

"You let the kidnappers escape with a princess. They passed through the gate of the workhouse. Who was guarding that gate?"

"We were, sir," Larch muttered.

"We were, sir," Beadle mimicked. "The only way they could have got out of the workhouse was on the muck cart. The one that you didn't search."

"Well, sir," Liddle argued, "one piece of

muck looks pretty much like the next piece of muck and we thought—"

"You *thought* ... well that *is* new. Constables Liddle and Larch *thinking!*" the inspector roared till Liddle's moustache trembled in the blast.

"Get out there and find the muck cart ... and arrest the drivers. Though I expect they will have escaped the town long before the Duke put up his road blocks."[46]

The two old constables tramped wearily up the stairs and on to the cobbled streets of Wildpool. People were gathering in huddles on street corners. "Who are they looking for?" the hat-seller asked.

"The Emperor of China, Mrs Potterwick has heard."

The hat-seller patted her dog on the head. "I bet my Alfie could sniff them out. He's trained, you know."

"What? To sniff out Emperors of China? How does he know what they smell like?"

46 They had. The two men went off to Darlham where they did a wonderful job of stealing night soil. In fact they did such a good job the Darlham Council paid them to work there. Two villains became two honest working men. It's a funny old world – smelly, but funny.

"I own a china teapot," the hat-seller said proudly.

*

At 13 South Drive the butler opened the door. It wasn't Wellington's troops. It was Alice. She stood there in her scruffy-haired boy mask. She saw Nancy and waved the ransom note under her nose. "He signed," she said. "Get the princess."

"I wish I'd snatched Mrs Humble instead. The princess has been nothing but trouble."

"Don't worry, we can still make it work for the paupers of Wildpool. The princess's yacht is in the harbour. Let's get her back there, set Millie free from the workhouse, and we've done it."

Alice and Nancy ran upstairs and snatched a sack from a table at the top of the stairs. They tugged their masks firmly into place and unlocked the door. "We are setting you free."

"Has the Duke paid a fortune for our release?" Victoria asked.

"We don't want your money," Alice said.

"Now we are going to take you back to the quayside."

"Is it far?" the princess asked carefully. "We are not used to walking far."

But Alice was too clever to walk into the trap. "You will never know how far it is. You'll be blindfolded so you can't trace the house."

"Our feet will know," Victoria cried. "Our poor little feet!"

"Then we'll take you in a wheelbarrow," Alice said. "Now, sit still while I place this sack over your head."

"Umm-mmm-mmmf mmmf?" came the royal voice.

Nancy raised the sack. "What?"

"We said . . . where did you get this stinking sack from?"

"From the sheep-head shop," Nancy said pulling it down.

"Umm-mmm-mmmf mmmf!!!"[47]

---

47 You may think it's bad having your head stuffed into a stinking sack from the sheep-head shop. Baa! Just remember this: it was much worse for the sheep.

Chapter 13

BARROW
AND BULLETS

"Please sir," Millie Mixley said to Mr Humble. "I have picked all the seeds from my cotton. Can I have *more* work?"

"We don't have any more cotton," Mr Humble snarled.

"No, sir, but perhaps I can help the women to pick oakum?" she said brightly.

"You *could* ... but it's hard work. Makes your fingers bleed."

"I don't mind, sir. It's just so nice to live here I'll do anything to help!"

"The boy's sick," Humble muttered. "Must be feeding him too much gruel." He unlocked the door into the women's work room. Thirty weary women took ropes and pulled them apart until they were left with a pile of loose strands. "There you go," he said. "You have half an hour then it's a quick spell in the exercise yard."

Mille nodded and said to herself, "Half an hour to take the pieces of rope and knot them into a rope ladder. A ladder long enough to reach the top of Wildpool Wonderful Workhouse's wall and down the other side."

*

The wheelbarrow rattled down the streets of Wildpool. The cargo under the sack wriggled and moaned, wobbled and whinged its way to the quayside. The troop of soldiers were gathering on the windswept deck of the yacht.

The wheelbarrow was tipped on to the cobbles and the two masked kidnappers ran up the hill towards the high street.

The Duke of Wellington paced up and down with a face as furious as a giraffe with neck-ache. "They can't have escaped the town by road or by sea. So where is she?"

"We are here," Princess Victoria snapped as she stamped up the gangplank and on to the deck.

"You are free, ma'am!" the Duke cried.

"No thanks to you," the pouting princess said sourly. "We have been kidnapped in a muck cart, held against our will, had a sheep-head sack wrapped over us and been transported in a wheelbarrow back here. Someone will have to be hanged. We cannot have these kidnapping criminals loose in our country!"

"And what did the kidnappers look like, ma'am?" the Duke asked.

"One looked rather like a cat ... and the other was a very small boy with scruffy hair."

*

The wind blew wild down the valley and pushed the creeping constables back to Wildpool.

"My feet hurt," Liddle sighed.

"I'm hungry," Larch moaned.

"But we can't rest till we've arrested someone."

They passed the house with the sign, "Master Crook's Crime Academy" and stopped. "We could slip into the police station. Inspector Beadle will be in his office. He'd never know if we had a quick cup of tea and a slice of bread and cheese," Liddle said.

Larch's mouth began to water and dribble like a baby's.[48]

At that moment they saw a rare sight. Inspector Beadle stepped out of the doorway to the police station. He placed a large top hat on his large head and stepped into the street.

"We're supposed to be searching!" Liddle squeaked and dragged Larch back behind the gatepost of Master Crook's Crime Academy to hide till the danger was past.

*

Nancy and Alice panted up the steep hill, past Smiff's house. Smiff's mother, Mrs Smith, stood on the doorstep. "Ooooh! Hello there, Smiff," she said to Alice." "You should be wearing a hat – that's a nasty cold wind. We don't want you catching a fever, do we?"

"Hello, um . . . Mum, must dash," Alice said, backing away up the street.

"You've lost a bit of height, son," the woman said, squinting at the retreating girl.

48 Babies have lots of disgusting habits. Some of them involve nappies. Know what I mean? So, if Constable Larch 's only baby habit was dribbling then the people of Wildpool were very lucky indeed.

"Had a hot bath ... I shrank in the wash," Alice said quickly.

"Ohhhh! I did that to one of your vests – shrank terrible it did. Tried to put it on you. Nearly strangled you!"

"Must dash!" Alice said.

"Been getting yourself a new cat?" the woman asked, pointing at Nancy.

"Yes ... must go."

"Does it want a saucer of milk?"

"No. It only drinks blood. Bye!" Alice cried.

"Miaow!" Nancy said ... and waved a paw.

The two girls sped up the street and turned into the High Street. The people on the corners were returning to their houses and work. "Looks like they found the Emperor of China then," the hat-seller said. "They're getting that yacht ready to sail." She stepped back into the hat shop, tugging her dog behind her on its squeaking wheels.

Alice slowed to a walk. "We've done it, Nancy!" she sighed as she stepped through the gates of the Crime Academy. "Safe at last!"

A long, white, bony hand rested on her

shoulder. "I arrest you in the name of the law!" Constable Liddle said. "You're the fella that was with the night soil men at the workhouse. Well, Wildpool's wonderful police force has triumphed again! I wouldn't be surprised if they don't hang you for this."

"What do we do with him?" Larch said, clamping handcuffs on Alice's thin wrists. "Inspector Beadle's just gone out."

"Let's take him to the Duke on the yacht. He'll know what to do."

"What about the cat?"

"Let it go," Liddle said.

"You mean let's not purr-sue it?" Larch joked.[49]

They dragged Alice into the High Street. Nancy raced into the school to report on the disaster that had struck.

*

In the workhouse Mr Humble was struggling to write his report.

---

49 It wasn't a very good joke but the policemen were so giddy with happiness they thought it the funniest thing in the world. Better than being slapped in the face with a wet kipper anyway.

WILDPOOL WORKHOUSE

DATE: FRIDAY 16TH MARCH 1837

REPORT: LOST PAUPER.

PAUPER NUMBER ONE IS MISSING. HE WAS WORKING IN THE OAKUM ROOM. AT THE EXERCISE BREAK HE DID NOT RETURN. MAYBE HE WAS SO SKINNY HE SLIPPED UNDER THE DOOR. THE WOMEN PAUPERS DID NOT TRY TO STOP HIM. THEY WILL BE PUNISHED.

Mrs Humble looked over his shoulder. "Don't be stupid. If we report a lost pauper they'll stop paying for him."

"What do we do?"

"Find a uniform. Stuff it with oakum and sit it in his cell. We'll pretend he never escaped."

*

The yacht was almost ready to leave when Constables Liddle and Larch marched up to it and said, "We have the kidnapper! We have the kidnapper!"

The Duke came on to the deck followed by Princess Victoria. "Is this the villain?"

"You appear to have one of them," the princess said. "We wish to see him hanged."

"No time if we're going to catch the tide," the Duke said. He shouted orders and the soldiers ran back on deck. Then he spoke to Liddle and Larch. "Unfasten the prisoner's handcuffs. Cuff his hands behind him, around that lamp post, so he can't get away.

"Yes, sir," the policemen said and hurried to obey.

The Duke lined up the soldiers facing Alice. "It is our duty to execute this traitor. Line up. Aim for the heart."

"We don't wish to watch!" Victoria said and scurried below decks again.

"I think I'm going to be sick ... again," Liddle groaned. He turned away.

"What have we done?" Larch gasped. "Let's get back and report to Inspector Beadle," he said and the old constables hurried off. At the bottom of Low Street they passed a group of people sprinting down the hill. The old men didn't even notice them. They just repeated, "What have we done?"

The soldiers stood in a row and raised their rifles. The Duke walked over to Alice. "Do you have a last request?"

"Yes," she said from behind her paper bag. "I'd like to die of old age if you don't mind."

"Request refused," the Duke said coldly. He stepped to the side. "Guards, take aim ... and—!"

A small shape as quick as a rat's tail flew along the quayside. Millie Mixley threw herself between the firing squad and her friend Alice. "Remember Magna Carta!" she cried. "No free man shall be seized or imprisoned, except by the lawful judgment of his equals or by the law of the land."

The soldiers' muskets wavered a little. "The lad is right, sir," the sergeant said to the Duke.

"This is *treason*," the Duke explained. "He is guilty – you all heard the princess say so. Now. Take aim..."

Millie had not changed the Duke's iron mind. But she had put off the shooting for one precious minute. That minute was enough for the students and teachers of Master Crook's Crime Academy, who had listened to Nancy's tale, to hurry down to the quayside.

"Wait!" Samuel Dreep cried. He reached across and ripped off Alice's paper mask. "It's a girl! What sort of cowards shoot down a girl in cold blood."

The soldiers' rifles lowered again. "It's one thing shooting French soldiers at Waterloo," the sergeant said quietly. "For you, sir, we'd even shoot a traitor without a trial ... but a little girl!"

The soldiers rested their rifles on the ground and turned away. The Duke's face glowed an angry pink in the cheeks. He drew a pistol from his belt. He aimed it at Alice's head. "I'm not scared of you," she snorted, looking him in the eye.

"Little girls don't plan kidnappings. Tell me who was behind this – we'll shoot them instead," the Duke said.

"Me!" Samuel Dreep said. "We planned to kidnap the workhouse keeper's wife – the princess was a mistake. But if you are going to shoot anyone shoot me!"

"Fine," the Duke said. "Sergeant, unfasten the girl. Put this man in her place."

The last person to arrive at the quay was the slowest. "And me!" Ruby Friday said. "You'll have to shoot me too. After all I am the real mastermind. The world's greatest kidnapper."

The colour ran from the Duke's face. "Ruby Friday? After all these years?"

"Perhaps we'd better have a little word, before you shoot me," she said with a smile. In the watery light the Duke read the paper she held in front of him.

The Iron Duke's face became harder than iron.

BRITISH ARMY HEADQUARTERS, WATERLOO

17 June 1815

My Dear Bonaparte,

Just a little note to say I am looking forward to a jolly fine battle tomorrow. But I do hope you will lose! You see, British secret agents have kidnapped your dear wife Josephine. She is now my prisoner. She is comfortable but hidden somewhere that you will never find her.

Her guards have orders. If it looks like your French chaps are going to win the battle they will stuff your dear lady into a cannon and shoot her back to you. It could make a bit of a mess of your uniform with all those shiny medals.

This is frightfully unsporting, old chap, I know. But all is fair in love and war, as they say. Just *make sure you _lose_ the Battle at Waterloo tomorrow or we blow Jo.*

Send a reply with this messenger and we will spare the empress.

Best wishes and see you tomorrow,

Arthur Wellesley

Duke of Wellington and Baron Douro, Duke of Ciudad Rodrigo, Marquis of Torres Vedras, Count of Vimeiro.

By the time the Wildpool clock struck four o'clock the teachers and pupils of Master Crook's Crime Academy were walking up the hill and back to the school.

The yacht was sailing out of the river on the cold westerly breeze and the strong tide.[50]

50 You will have forgotten what I said at the start. The mayor 's wife of 1901 was quite right when she said "Queen Victoria never came to Wildpool ". But the mayor 's wife was quite wrong as well. See? Victoria came to Wildpool as a princess. She never came when she became queen. She refused! And she never allowed Wildpool to become a city. Now you know why!

On the quayside there were still the boatyards and barns and barges and ballast and bollards ... but no bodies or bullets or blood.

The night began to close in on one of the strangest days in the strange history of Wildpool.

Chapter 14

RENT AND ROCKS

Saturday 17th March 1837

Lady Arabella Twistle sat in the dining room of 13 South Drive. The butler served soup silently.

"I promised to sack the Humbles and rebuild Garth Court," Mayor Oswald Twistle sighed.

"Nonsense," his wife snorted into her soup spoon. "They said they would tell the Duke that Princess Victoria was a prisoner in this house. So what? She is gone now. They can *never* prove that she was here. The Humbles stay. We save the money and *don't* build a new Garth Court with cheap rents to help the poor. Let the kidnappers go hang."

"If you say so, dear," Mayor Twistle sighed.

"I do."

The butler took the empty soup plates away.

He hurried to the kitchen and scribbled a note.

N

I THINK YOU OUGHT TO KNOW. MAYOR TWISTLE WILL GO BACK ON HIS WORD. HE SAYS YOU CAN'T PROVE THE PRINCESS WAS HERE. SORRY. LOOKS LIKE THE WHOLE PLAN HAS FAILED.

B

He wrote "Nancy Turnip" on the front of an envelope. A maid was sent to deliver it to Master Crook's Crime Academy.

Monday 19th March 1837

On Monday morning the pupils met in the classroom of Master Crook's Crime Academy.

"Well, Ruby? What did you say to the Duke?" Alice asked. "Mr Dreep would have been pushing up daisies by now if you hadn't done something."

Ruby smiled her apple-cheeked smile. "I told him he was a hero because he won the battle of Waterloo. But he wouldn't be a hero much longer if I told the world how he *cheated* ... how *I* was the real hero that kidnapped Napoleon's wife! And I still have the note he wrote. Holy crumpets! He *had* to let you go."

"Princess Victoria wouldn't be pleased," Alice laughed.

"She wasn't," Mille Mixley said. "I saw her raging at the Duke as they sailed out of the harbour."[51]

"So? What went wrong with our kidnap that almost got us shot?" Mr Dreep asked. "The best schools don't mind pupils making mistakes ... but they *learn* from their mistakes.

51 As I said, there were eight attempts to kill Victoria in her long life. Every one failed. Every time she demanded the assassin should be hanged. Every time she raged because they weren't! Vicious Victoria.

How did we end up with Alice and me in front of a firing squad?"

Smiff took a sheet of paper and wrote on it.

What went wrong?

Nancy snatched the wrong woman in purple and white

Alice kept her disguise on too long

"But what have we got *right*?" Ruby Friday cried. "Look on the bright side!"

WHAT WENT RIGHT?

MAYOR TWISTLE PROMISED TO SACK HUMBLE AND REBUILD GARTH COURT

WE KIDNAPPED THE MOST IMPORTANT WOMAN IN

THE LAND ... AND ALMOST GOT AWAY WITH IT!

"And we won't make the same mistake next time. Let's get on with planning the *next* kidnap," Samuel Dreep said with an excited wave of rippling fingers.

"Who's the victim?"

Nancy took an envelope from her pocket and passed it to the teacher. "Ah!" Dreep nodded. "I think I have the answer. I will have a word with Master Crook first."

Samuel Dreep took the letter and disappeared through a door that led into the basement at the Crime Academy. The basement room was almost dark, lit by a single candle. A door opened behind a curtain and a deep voice spoke. "Well, my friend Samuel. What do we have today?"

"A small problem, Master Crook."

*

In Wildpool police station, Constables Liddle and Larch stood in front of Inspector Beadle's desk.

He had two sheets of paper.

WILDPOOL POLICE FORCE

WHAT WENT WRONG?

Wildpool police allowed their VIP to be
kidnapped under their very noses. They
failed to find where she was held prisoner

"But what have we got *right*?" Liddle cried.
"Look on the bright side!"

WILDPOOL POLICE FORCE

WHAT WENT RIGHT?

The alert police spotted one kidnapper and
delivered him to the Duke. Wildpool police
managed to place one blind beggar in the
workhouse

Inspector Beadle nodded. "As usual, gentlemen, Wildpool police have succeeded in keeping the town safe from the villains who roam its gutters. And you get to keep your jobs..."

"Thank you, sir!"

"...for another month at least."

"Ah!"

Tuesday 20th March 1837

In the Crime Academy basement room the next day Lady Twistle sat and faced the curtain. A sheep-head shop sack was pulled off her head and left her with a red face and battered bonnet. "This is disgraceful. Someone will hang for this!"

She turned and looked at the kidnapper who had led her down the stairs. For this kidnap Alice had painted her paper mask with the face of Lady Twistle herself. "Urrrrggggh!" Arabella Twistle cried. "What an ugly old woman!"

She was right!

"If anyone is to hang it will be you, Lady

Twistle," the deep voice said from behind the curtain.

"Eh?"

"Princess Victoria was held prisoner in your house, your room. When the Duke of Wellington finds out you will be arrested."

Her ladyship's mean eyes looked suddenly as sly as a dog in a sausage shop. "Ah, but you can never prove that!" she cackled.

Alice unfolded a piece of paper and held it so Lady Twistle could read it. The note was written by Princess Victoria. It described the room where she had been held prisoner ... Lady Twistle's room. The woman tried to look defiant but she only looked defeated.

"I slipped this out of the princess's purse before we dumped her out of the wheelbarrow," Alice explained.

Friday 30th March 1837

The families from Garth Court were given a day off by the new workhouse keeper, Ruby Friday. The well-fed and happy groups crossed the bridge and wandered down to the riverside. A fine new building was rising in the place where Garth Court had stood.

A sour-faced Mayor Twistle and his wife stood behind a table in the weak sunlight. Spring was struggling to come to the skies over Wildpool. But summer seemed to have arrived for the paupers. One by one families signed up to take new rooms when they were finished.

"How much?" Mr Jones (the organ grinder) asked.

"One shilling a week," the mayor said through his teeth as though the words hurt him.

"That's cheap!" Miss Jones (the street-singer) said.

"We can easily make it double ... treble!" the little man said quickly.

Behind him a small figure stood. She had a face that looked very much like Lady Twistle's. She coughed. "The Princess Victoria note," she said.

Mayor Twistle took a deep breath. "One shilling ... no more," he sighed.

"I'll take it!" Miss Jones laughed.

"I thought you might," the mayor said.

*

The workhouse was almost empty. Only the blind beggar and two new inmates were there. The woman sweated over piles of ropes, unpicking them till her fingers bled to make oakum.

The man, in the men's yard, ached as he smashed large rocks into small stones and sweat ran down his forehead.

Ruby Friday brought the register up to date.

Date	Name	Class	Age	No.
22 Mar 1837	Harper, Hengist	M	33	101
	Harper, Angela	W	34	102

The blind beggar was not working. As Hengist Harper slaved over the broken rocks the blind beggar looked on. "I can't break rocks – I'm blind! I may hit someone over the head by mistake! Anyway, I have a visitor." The High Street hat-seller had taken an hour off to visit him with his dog.

"Are you happy here?" she asked.

"Happier since Miss Friday arrived," the beggar said. "And you?"

"Happier since I have your dog with the waggly tail for company!" she giggled.

"So," the beggar said. "Everybody's happy!"

Hengist Harper looked up. He looked as if he wanted to use that hammer on someone's head.

Which just goes to show ... not everyone can have a happy ending.

THE END

MASTER CROOK'S

CRIME ACADEMY

SAFECRACKING FOR STUDENTS

Before word

IF CRIMES WERE MOUNTAINS THEN BANK ROBBERY WOULD BE MOUNT EVEREST.

BANK ROBBERY IS TOP OF THE TREE, PICK OF THE PILE AND BEST OF THE BESTEST. IT IS THE GREATEST WORK OF ART SINCE WILLIAM SHAKESPEARE GAVE UP PAINTING.

SADLY, THERE IS A LITTLE COUNTRY ON THE OTHER SIDE OF THE ATLANTIC CALLED THE UNITED STATES OF AMERICA. IN THE US OF A THEY DO NOT TREAT BANK ROBBERY AS AN ART, THE WAY WE DO.

THERE ARE THESE TERRIBLY ROUGH CHAPS CALLED "COWBOYS" - MAYBE BECAUSE THEY ARE HALF COW AND HALF MAN - AND THEY CARRY GUNS. THEY WALK INTO A BANK, THEY SHOOT A FEW PEOPLE, THEY STEAL SOME MONEY AND THEY RIDE OFF ... PROBABLY ON A COW.

POLICE OFFICERS CALLED "SHERIFFS" RIDE AFTER THEM, CATCH THEM AND TAKE THEM BACK TO TOWN TO BE HANGED.

ONE OF THE MOST FAMOUS COWBOYS WAS BILLY THE KID. NOW, AS YOU KNOW, A KID IS A SMALL GOAT. SO BILLY THE KID MUST HAVE BEEN BILLY THE GOAT. MAYBE HE WAS HALF GOAT AND HALF MAN.

THEY SAY HE HAD "BUCK TEETH". A BUCK IS A RABBIT . . . SO PERHAPS I'M WRONG. PERHAPS HE WAS HALF RABBIT AND HALF GOAT.

HIS WANTED POSTER MUST HAVE BEEN A BEAUTY!

NOW, WHERE WAS I? OH, YES, US BANK ROBBERS. BORING.

BRITISH BANK ROBBERS? THAT'S A DIFFERENT STORY. BRITISH BANK ROBBERS WERE MEN OF SKILL. NO ONE WAS HURT . . . NOTHING WAS HURT, EXCEPT THE POCKETS OF THE RICH.

ONE OF THE MOST DARING BANK ROBBERIES TOOK PLACE IN THE LITTLE NORTHERN TOWN OF WILDPOOL. WILDPOOL HAS BEEN DESCRIBED AS A "POOR LITTLE, MUDDY LITTLE, COLD LITTLE, WIND-WRACKED, WAVE-WASHED, SMOKE-CHOKED, RAT-RIDDLED, SOUR-SMELLING LITTLE TOWN."

I SHOULD KNOW. I WAS THE ONE WHO DESCRIBED IT THAT WAY. PEOPLE OF WILDPOOL DO NOT LIKE READING THAT ABOUT THEIR TOWN. "IT'S A LOVELY PLACE," THEY SPLUTTER ANGRILY. "AHA," I REPLY. "I AM WRITING ABOUT THE WILDPOOL OF OVER SIXTY YEARS AGO. I WAS THERE – YOU WEREN'T. BELIEVE ME, IT WAS AS GRIM AND GRIMY AS A TRAMP'S SOCKS."

AS WELL AS THE TALE OF A WONDERFUL BANK ROBBERY WILDPOOL HAD ANOTHER STRANGE TALE TO TELL. THE TALE OF A SCHOOL THAT WAS SET UP JUST TO TEACH YOUNG PEOPLE HOW TO BREAK THE LAW … AND NOT GET CAUGHT. DON'T YOU WISH YOU WENT TO A SCHOOL LIKE THAT?

IN WILDPOOL YOU COULD. IT WAS CALLED MASTER CROOK'S CRIME ACADEMY AND THIS IS ONE OF ITS GREAT TALES. I WAS THERE AND GATHERED THE FACTS FROM THE ROBBERS.

IF YOU WANT TO WITNESS THE WONDER OF WILDPOOL THEN READ ON.

IF YOU WANT A TALE OF GUNS, HANGINGS AND KIDS THAT ARE BOY-COWS THEN GO TO THE US OF A.

MR X

23 APRIL 1901

Chapter 1

SIGN AND
SECRET

Wildpool Town – Monday 3rd April 1837

I t took three men to put up the sign. It was a large sign painted in red with gold lettering.

They dug two holes, placed a post in each hole and then heaved them upright.

The men didn't know they were being watched. Across the road was an old house. The house had a sign outside its door too.

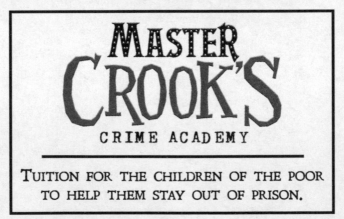

MASTER
CROOK'S
CRIME ACADEMY

TUITION FOR THE CHILDREN OF THE POOR
TO HELP THEM STAY OUT OF PRISON.

Five pupils stood at the window of an upstairs classroom and watched the men across the High Street. The pupils were in the top class of Master Crook's Crime Academy.

They were also in the bottom class.

Master Crook kept school records, of course. The records for the class of April 1837 looked like this:

NAME: Smiff Smith,
REGISTERED: January 1837,
TEACHER'S COMMENT: Shoplifter. Could turn out to be a top criminal. Keen to learn and good at talking his way out of trouble.

NAME: Alice White,
REGISTERED: January 1837,
TEACHER'S COMMENT: Match girl and beggar.
Bad-tempered and wild but has a lot of common sense
and a kind heart (under that fierce scowl).

NAME: Nancy Turnip,
REGISTERED: February 1837,
TEACHER'S COMMENT: Serving maid. A quiet and
nervous girl but very determined to rob the rich and
help the poor. Strong as a carthorse, gentle as a lamb.

NAME: Martin Mixly,

REGISTERED: February 1837,

TEACHER'S COMMENT: Schoolboy. Looks like a quiet, honest boy but that's an act. Determined to make the rich pay for their crimes. Bright as a button.

NAME: Millie Mixly,

REGISTERED: February 1837,

TEACHER'S COMMENT: Martin's twin. Quick-thinking and brave as a lion. Always ready to help someone in trouble.

"It's a prison! They're building a prison," Millie Mixly breathed, watching the men across the High Street. "They're going to lock us all away if we get caught."

"Who says? You says?" Alice White snorted. "There's a perfectly bad gaol in Darlham. There's not enough crime in Wildpool to have a prison. Anyway ... we're not going to get caught, Millie Mixly. Not unless you're really stupid ... like Smiff Smith!"

Smiff sniffed ... sort of smiffed. He wasn't going to let Alice upset him. "You can't tell what it'll be till it's finished. They've only built the ground floor so far. Why do you think it's a prison, Millie?" he asked.

"All the windows have thick bars across them," she explained. "To keep people in."

"Sometimes bars are used to keep people out," Nancy said quietly. "When I worked for Mayor Twistle he had iron bars on his wine cellar to keep the servants out."

"Did it work?" Martin Mixly asked.

"No. He gave the key to the butler every

time he wanted wine. The butler had a copy made. We could get in any time we liked."

The pupils nodded. Sometimes the rich and greedy could be very stupid. The classroom door opened. A man walked in. He wore a shabby top hat and a red-and-white striped scarf around his neck. His gooseberry-green eyes bulged like a bulldog's. His fingers were thin and they rippled when he talked.

"Good morning, class, and what a fine spring morning it is too." The class kept their eyes fixed on the workmen as they struggled to raise the sign that would be nailed to the boards. The man sighed. "And good morning to *you*, Mr Dreep. Yes, it is a fine day," he said to himself.

Alice White turned. "Oh, it's you, Mr Dreep."

"What a pleasant way to greet your teacher. You have the manners of a farmyard goat, Alice."

"Oh, sir!" Smiff cried. "That's a rotten thing to say about a goat."

Alice looked as if she wanted to butt the boy. Butt she didn't.

"Please, Mr Dreep," Nancy said quickly, "can you tell us what they are building across the road?"

The teacher nodded. "Master Crook tells me it is something we have always dreamed of!"

"I dream of pushing Smiff off a cliff," Alice said, suddenly sweet.

"I just dream of Alice losing her voice," the boy said.

"Look," the teacher said, "the sign is going up now."

The men pushed and struggled and wobbled and wibbled. But at last the sign was raised in front of the half-finished building.

"A bank!" Martin cried. "Oh that's perfect!"

"We don't have to burgle fifty rich houses . . . we just let them bring their stuff to the bank and we take it all at once," Millie agreed.

"We've never had lessons in bank robbery," Nancy said quietly. "Who will teach us?"

Samuel Dreep took off his hat and scarf and placed them on a hat-stand by the door.

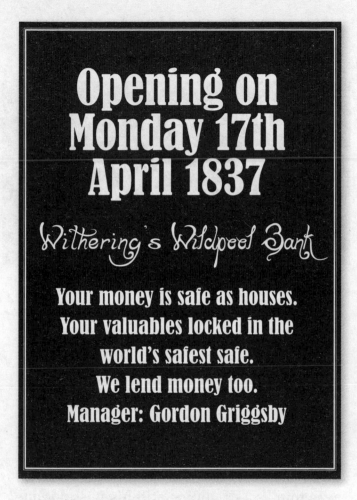

Opening on Monday 17th April 1837

Withering's Wildpool Bank

**Your money is safe as houses.
Your valuables locked in the
world's safest safe.
We lend money too.
Manager: Gordon Griggsby**

"There are two ways to rob a bank," the teacher told the class as they scrambled to sit at their desks.

He wrote on the blackboard with a stick of chalk:

How to rob a bank

1. rob the carts that bring in the money
2. wait till it's all locked away and crack open the safe

"Which will we do?" Smiff asked.

Mr Dreep's eyes glowed like Wildpool gas lamps. "Both," he said. "We'll try both."

Wildpool police station stood next to Master Crook's Crime Academy. Constable Septimus Liddle (PC 01) and Constable Archibald Larch (PC 02) sat in their room. Constable Liddle was thin as a drainpipe and his wispy, white moustache drooped sadly.

Constable Larch opened the newspaper to look at the horse-racing results. His round, red face was as gloomy as doom. "Oh, dear," he sighed. "Lost again. I've never seen one of my horses win."

"No ... funny that ... you never see one of your *horses* win. But you see invisible dogs!" Liddle sniggered.

Larch glared. "Don't mention invisible dogs. You promised not to mention them ever again."

"Sorry, Larch." Liddle was polishing his top hat. He looked over the top of the hat to the front page of the newspaper. "Oh, dear, oh dear, oh dear! A dead policeman!"

Constable Larch's piggy eyes peered, squinted and almost disappeared into the folds of fat in his cheeks. "Where? I can't smell no dead policeman!"

"On the front of your newspaper!" Liddle cried.

"There's a dead policeman on the front of my newspaper? How did he get there?"

"No, no, no ... there's a *report* about a dead policeman. Who is it, Larch?"

"How would I know? It's not you and it's not

me ... though I sometimes wonder about you, Septimus," the lardy lawman said. "Let's have a look," he muttered, turning the newspaper.

He read slowly. "We are sad to announce that John Constable has died in London at the age of sixty-one. Mr Constable was famous for his painting."

"Aw! That's nice. A policeman that paints. He could come round to my house!" Liddle said.

"Why's that?"

"Well, my house needs a lick of paint."

"I don't think he's that sort of painter," Larch said, frowning. "I think he paints pictures."

"Oh, a policeman that paints *pictures*. Nice. I could do that. What did he die from? Was he attacked while he was on duty?"

"It says here he had an attack of indigestion. I get that very bad myself. Especially after I've eaten one of Mrs Bunton's meat pies. Ah, it says Mr Constable is famous for painting Salisbury Cathedral!"

"I thought you said he didn't paint houses? If he painted a cathedral he could paint a house. Big things is cathedrals. He must have had very long ladders!"[1]

"And he's famous for painting a cornfield," Larch gasped.

"A cornfield! He must have used a hell of a big brush," Liddle said.

"Language, Liddle."

"Sorry, Larch. But he was a busy man. Where did he find the time? I mean we have a full-time job being constables. We couldn't fit in painting a cathedral."

"We wouldn't have to," his portly partner said. "There aren't any cathedrals in Wildpool."

Constable Liddle blew out his thin cheeks. "I'm pleased about that. I mean. I'm nearly sixty-one myself. If I had to run up and down ladders painting cathedrals I'd probably drop dead too. This job's hard enough."

1 John Constable WAS famous for painting pictures, as you probably know. But Liddle makes a good point. What did Mr Constable do when Mrs Constable said, "The house needs painting, John"? Did he pay a house painter to do it? Did he give the man a free painting. Or did he get out a bucket of paint and do it himself? It is one of the great mysteries of life. Someone should ask him. I suppose him being dead is a problem though.

"What job?" came a deep voice from the doorway.

Liddle and Larch jumped to their feet, jammed their top hats on their heads, and saluted. "Mornin' all!" they said.

"What job is hard enough?" said the man in a black suit. He was so enormous he made large Larch look like a puppy.

"Oh, Inspector Beadle," Larch said, "we were just reading about this constable that died in London. He was attacked by indigestion. We were just saying what a hard job it is being a constable."

The inspector walked into the office and the floorboards creaked. "John Constable was a famous painter. He wasn't a policeman," he explained.

Liddle gave a slim smile. "That's how he had time to paint cathedrals then," he nodded.

"And you have time to paint cathedrals too. You could do it while you're sitting here in the police station," Beadle growled.

"No, sir," Larch said, shaking his head till

his chins wobbled. "There's no cathedral in Wildpool."

"And we haven't any ladders long enough," Liddle added.

Inspector Beadle closed his eyes and counted slowly to ten. His fists were so tight the knuckles turned white. At last he said, "I have a special job for you two. A job so secret you must tell no one. No one at all."

"I can't even tell Liddle?" Larch asked.

"Liddle will know," the inspector sighed.

"So it's not a secret!" Larch said.

"Liddle will know because I will tell you both," the inspector said. He rolled his eyes. "Sometimes I worry about crime in Wildpool," he muttered.

"It's all right, Inspector, sir," Liddle said. "Like Mayor Twistle said, we'll carry our truncheons like flaming torches of justice. We will bring light to the darkness of our savage streets."

"Sometimes you have to stay in the dark," Inspector Beadle said and tapped his nose in a wise way. "And I am sending you somewhere very, very dark. I will explain when you get back from your morning patrol."

Liddle and Larch left the police station and blinked in the early spring sunshine. "I hope we don't get attacked by any of those nasty indigestions like that London constable," Liddle said and his wispy moustache, thin as parsnip soup, trembled at the thought.

Chapter 2

ROBBERY AND
RAT-POISON

The manager of Withering's bank stood and watched the men heave the sign into place. Gordon Griggsby was a round sort of man. He had a round, shining head on a round body that was bursting the buttons on his black suit. Even his legs looked like two balls balanced on top of one another and the round toe-caps of his black boots made his feet look round too.[2]

Once he was satisfied the sign was in place, Gordon Griggsby turned and walked the short distance across the High Street to Master Crook's Crime Academy.

2 Except the soles and heels of the boots. They were flat. Flat as the Earth ... otherwise he'd have had trouble walking, wouldn't he?

"Who's that man? What does he want? Do you think he knows we plan to rob the bank?" Millie Mixly cried as she watched him turn into the driveway of the school and waddle up to the front door.

"He'll tell the police! They'll come to arrest us all," Martin moaned. "We'll all be hanged. We'll swing in the breeze like apples on a tree."

"Like *what*?" Alice White sneered.

"Apples! It's a figure of speech."

"Core," she said with a wicked smile.

"You won't be laughing when you're on the gallows."

"No, I won't be laughing. I'll be too busy swinging like an apple," she agreed.

Gordon Griggsby's fist was as round as a ball and it bounced against the red front door.

"I'll get it," Nancy Turnip said. She'd been a maid-servant for years and she was used to answering doors. The girl hurried downstairs and tugged the door open.

Gordon Griggsby smiled at her as she bobbed down in a curtsey. "Good afternoon, sir," she said. "Whom do you wish to see?"

"Well, this is Master Crook's academy so I hoped I would catch Master Crook himself."

"Sorry, sir, Master Crook never sees anyone ... and no one sees him," the girl said.

"Are you a pupil here?"

"Please, sir, yes sir," Nancy said carefully.

"Then you have a teacher?"

"Oh!" she smiled and her pale moon face turned bright.[3]

"We have Mr Samuel Dreep to teach us."

"A man with curly side whiskers, a top hat and a red-and-white scarf? I just saw him come in here. Perhaps I could have a word with Mr Dreep."

"Who should I say is calling, sir?" Nancy asked politely.

"Gordon Griggsby, the manager of Withering's bank."

"I'll fetch him, sir. We're just in the middle of a lesson."

---

3 When I say "moon" face I mean a full moon ... round and white. I don't mean a new moon or a half moon. If she had a half-moon face she'd have had half a face, wouldn't she? One eye, one ear, half a nose and half a chin. She would also have half a brain ... just like anyone who thought I meant half-moon.

"No, I'll come to the classroom. I want to see you all," Gordon Griggsby said and stepped inside the house, closing the door behind him. Nancy felt suddenly trapped as the man's round body blocked the way out and the door shut out the light.

"Upstairs, sir," she said and led the way.

The stairs creaked and wheezed, and so did Gordon Griggsby, as he climbed. "So what lesson is it today?" he asked.

"Errrr ... banks and locks!"

"River banks and Scottish lochs, eh? Geography, then?"

"If you say so, sir."

They entered the classroom. Three pupils sat at their desks, their faces frozen and the itch of the hangman's rope felt around each neck. Smiff was standing at the blackboard with a cloth ready to wipe it but stopped with the cloth in his hand. He used it to wipe his nose instead.[4]

4 Please don't try this in school. It makes a snotty smudge on the board and when the teacher comes to write over it the chalk makes a horrible screech. It also leaves chalk on your nose. If you HAVE to wipe your nose then use your sleeve like everybody else.

"This is Mr Griggsby, the bank manager," Nancy announced to the class.

Samuel Dreep stepped forward to meet the man. He stretched out his fine fingers, as thin as October ice, to shake the round hand of the bank manager.

"Welcome, Mr Griggsby. I am so pleased to see you. The class are all great admirers of banks and money, and of course of Wildpool's wonderful police force. There could hardly be better men to guard the riches of the town. What can we do for you?"

Gordon Griggsby turned and let his twinkling dark eyes look over the five frightened faces.

"I understand you are a Crime Academy?"

"So what?" Alice said.

"So, you are learning how to fight crime, are you not?"

Alice felt the air rush out of her as if she'd been holding her breath for five minutes ... which she probably had. "Yeah, that's right."

"One day you will take the place of the

great constables Liddle and Larch?" Gordon Griggsby asked.

"Right," Smiff Smith nodded.

"So, today, I am here to give you the chance to take part in a little experiment," the bank manager went on. He smiled at Martin Mixly. "You will have seen they are building a bank across the road."

"Are they?" Martin gasped. "I never knew that. Did you know that, Millie?"

"No, Martin. I never guessed. Fancy that. Goodness me. How amazing. I never knew."

"That's two never knew," Martin said. "Did you knew, Smiff?"

"I never knew."

"Did you knew, Nancy?"

"I never knew."

"Did you knew, Alice?"

"Oh shut up, Martin. The bank manager isn't stupid. He knows we know and I know he knows we know and I'll bet he knows I know he knows we know. Isn't that right, sir?"

"I think so," the bank manager said. "But

my point is, the bank is always a magnet for criminals."

"Only if the criminals are made of scrap iron," Alice argued. "Don't tell me, it's a figure of speech?"

"I mean ... criminals from all over the north will come to see if they can rob the riches inside. Now there are two ways to rob a bank," the bank manager went on.

"You can rob the carts that bring in the money ... or you wait till it's all locked away and crack open the safe." Alice nodded. "We know that," she said glancing at the blackboard.

"Good!" the bank manager chuckled while his round head bobbed back and forth. "That means you can help the Wildpool police force. We need people we can trust for a very special job."

"What do you want us to do?" Millie Mixly asked.

Gordon Griggsby spread his round hands. "Why, I want you to rob a cart that is bringing in the money!"

235

The class were stunned. They were speechless. They could not find the words to even say how shocked they were. So they said, "...!"

A house near Darlham – Monday 3rd April 1837

The man was not tall but he seemed to fill the fine room. His dark brown hair was swept back from his forehead and hung, too long, over his bone-white, starched-hard, sharp-edged collar. His eyebrows hung like curtains over his eyes and his beard was cut as square and heavy as a church door.

His back was to the fire which crackled and warmed the rich room, with chairs of violet velvet and carpets of white wool, that was lit with the greeny glow of gas lights. They sparkled on the wine-and-white woven wallpaper, the crystal clock on the marble mantelshelf, the cheerful china figures in clear cases and on the portraits that peered at you from glittering gold frames.

A girl watched him from the table where she played with a large dolls' house. "I don't want this dolls' house any longer," she said.

"Too old for dolls, my cherub?" the man asked.

"No. I mean I want a *palace* not a house. I want it covered with gold and lit by lanterns with windows made of rubies and diamonds, emeralds and sapphires."

The woman in the corner of the room kept her head down over her embroidery and her fingers fluttered like butterfly wings. "Oh, Charlotte!" she breathed. "We mustn't be greedy. Your father is a rich man but he isn't a prince. And I'm not sure you deserve a new toy after what went on at your school."

The girl gave her mother a glare hot enough to peel paint from a lamp post. "You can buy me a golden palace, can't you, Daddy?"

The man's moustache moved as if he were smiling behind the beard. "There are people out there who want to take our money from us, Lottie. Today I could buy us *all* a palace covered in gold. Tomorrow we could be robbed of every penny."

Charlotte scowled. "I like my money, Daddy. I don't want to lose it," she said fiercely. Her pink satin dress rustled like a snake's dead skin and her ringlets trembled with rage.

"Your money?" her mother said and gave a soft laugh. "It's your *father's* money, my dear."

"When he dies it will be mine," Charlotte said with a shrug. "The Sharkle fortune will be all mine ... when you and Daddy are dead and in the Sharkle tomb. And *no one* is going to steal it from *me*."

The man chuckled. "That is why we are putting money towards building Withering's bank in Wildpool. It will have the safest safe in the strongest strong-room. The inspector of police is a man called Beadle. He has told me his wonderful Wildpool police force will make sure no thieving thugs get within a mile of our hordes of treasure. Never fear, Lottie my lovely. The bank manager, Mr Griggsby, has even arranged a test to show the world how safe our fortune is."

"Show the world?" the girl said sharply. "What does that mean?"

"It means, little Lottie, that any Wildpool

villains are welcome to watch and see how we deal with robbers."

Charlotte Sharkle lifted a wooden doll from the house. It was dressed like a serving man in a perfect little black suit and white shirt and tiny leather shoes. "Ooooh, dear, Mr Wildpool villain," she said to the doll. "I think you stole my missing watch. How do you plead?"

The girl held the doll up to her face. "Guilty," she answered in a squeaky voice. She didn't move her lips.

"Then I sentence you to die," she said.

"Fair enough," the doll replied.[5]

"I hereby execute you!" she said suddenly and pulled off the doll's head.

"Ouch! That hurt!" the doll cried.

She pulled off the arms and then the legs. "Ouchy, ouchy-ouch!" the doll cried. "That'll teach everyone that you don't steal from a Sharkle, I suppose."

She threw the bits of doll on to the fire. Her

5 The girl does not seem to be a great actress, you may think. If a judge says, "You will die for your crimes," then you will say a lot of things. You may say, "Help!" or "Stone the crows." You would NOT say, "Fair enough."

father laughed. Her mother shook her head and tutted.

"Yes, that's the sort of thing we need to do in Wildpool. Make an example of the thieves," Silas Sharkle sighed. "But they won't let us tear off the heads of all the villains in Wildpool."

"Why not?" the girl asked.

"I don't know, my dear," the man said and spread his hands.

"We should leave everything to the police," Mrs Sharkle said.

"But what if the police are useless?" Charlotte asked.

"Our police are wonderful!" her mother cried.

Charlotte pulled a letter from the pouch that hung from her pink belt. She handed it to her father. "I just had this from Piggy Trotter at our school. See what she has to say."

Darlham Ladies College

2nd April 1837

Dearest Charlotte,

I hope you are well. The girls are so-o-o-o missing you. It was jolly rotten of Miss Peach to suspend you from school. I mean, all you did was put rat-poison in the teachers' salt cellar at dinner. The food is so rotten here the old dears didn't even taste the stuff. Miss Kilbey will be out of hospital soon so where's the harm? Miss Meldrum probably won't be back – ever. But she was old anyway. It's tennis season soon and they'll have to take you back. You're our star player, Lottie. I mean to say, it was April Fool's Day. What did they expect?

Anyway, our Papas pay their miserable teacher

wages. (Except Bunty McGurgle, of course. They say her Pa has gone completely broke in some business deal. He can't afford to keep her here. Last we'll see of her, poor sop.)

Silas Sharkle shook the letter. "Lottie, why am I reading this drivel?"

"Oh, Daddy, turn it over. See what Piggy says about Wildpool," the girl said.

The man turned over the paper and read.

On Saturday we went over to Wildpool to see our new yacht in the harbour. The coachman had left a rope trailing at the back of our carriage, careless clot. Anyway there were two policeman in the High Street. One stopped the carriage and said there was a rope hanging loose. Daddy said it was all right ... it was our guard dog following behind. The fat policeman said there was nothing on the end of the rope. Daddy said it was an invisible dog. Then he took one of my marzipan sweets and asked the policeman to feed it to the dog! Would you believe it? The fat clown tried! He was crouched down saying, "Good boy, sweetie!" while the whole street watched. Then Daddy said, "April fool!" and we drove off. Oh, we laughed.

Anyway. Hope to see you back in school soon. Next week we start the school summer play and you definitely should have got the lead because you are the best actress ever.

Lots of love

Piggy

Silas Sharkle nodded slowly. "So, Lottie my dear ... useless policemen ... we need to do something, don't we?"

Chapter 3

MCGURGLE AND GUNS

Wednesday 5th April 1837

Gordon Griggsby, manager of the new bank, explained how money would be carried from the station to the bank on a cart with a locked strongbox. He left the students to work out how a gang of villains might rob it.

Nancy Turnip stood in front of the blackboard while Mr Dreep sat at the back of the classroom. "You are our expert at highway robbery, Nancy. Remind the class how we do it."

The girl blushed a little and pointed to a sketch of Wildpool High Street she had drawn. It showed the police station, the crime academy and the new bank. On the sketch she had drawn an "X" on the pavement and two Xs at the police station.

"First you have to stop the coach," Nancy said. "Any ideas how we'd do that?"

Smiff Smith raised a hand. "Please, miss, we could throw Alice White in front of the horses! When they trample her, the driver will have to stop. Great idea or what?"

Nancy didn't laugh. Her serious face frowned. "Yes. A great idea."

"Oh, thanks, Nance!" Alice cried.

"Yes," Millie Mixly said, excited. "But we don't want Alice to get hurt."

"That's right," Martin agreed. "We just get Alice to lie down in the middle of the road ... pretend she's been hit by a runaway horse. The driver will get down to help her!"

"Then two of us open the back of the cart and steal the loot?" Millie said.

"Hah!" Alice laughed a sharp and scornful laugh. "See that cross on the corner. That's the blind beggar that always sits there. He'll see what's happening and call the other two Xs ... the constables at the front of the station. You'll be arrested before you get the doors open. Call yourselves crime academy students? You know nothing."

"The blind beggar won't see anything ... he's blind!" Nancy argued.

"Yes ... and I'm the Duchess of Wildpool," Alice snorted. "Anyway, the street will be full of people – farmers driving animals to the docks to sell, shoppers and street sellers, road-sweepers and sailors and singers and butchers and bakers. They are just going to stand there and watch, are they? This is not like your highwaymen on the heath, you know. This is a crowded street, you dummies. Master Crook would be ashamed of you."

Nancy's mouth fell open. Her lips moved.

No words came out. The rest of the class looked at their desks.

"So what should they do, Alice?" Mr Dreep asked.

Alice marched to the front of the classroom and jabbed a thin finger at the map. "Millie stands on the corner here. She gives a signal when she sees the bank coach coming. I lie down in the road."

"Hope there's a farmer driving cattle to the docks!" Smiff chuckled.

"I – lie – down – at – the last – moment!" Alice said angrily. "The driver gets down. I tell him I want him to carry me to the corner of Bridge Street. Then I say I need him to carry me all the way to the hospital on the north side of the bridge. The driver is right out of the way, see?"

"No," Smiff said. "How does that help?"

"Because *then* Nancy can climb up to the driving seat and take the whole cart away. We take it to a quiet spot. Smiff and Martin unload the loot. We open it in secret. No one sees us. Job done."

The class nodded. Mr Dreep's fingers

rippled. "Gordon Griggsby said the police know about this test robbery. Even though we can use this to our advantage, this is to help them after all. Do you think they haven't thought of this?"

Alice rolled her eyes up to the ceiling. "They're cops. It's their cop brains against the brain of Alice White. Who do you think has the better brain?"

"A sheep has a better brain," Smiff said quietly.

"Or a beetle brain is better," Martin agreed.

"Even a Beadle brain," Smiff agreed. The boys' eyes twinkled as they waited for Alice to explode.

"OK class, now we have our plan. It's time for lunch." Mr Dreep led the class down to the kitchen where he served up big bowls of hot tomato soup with bread and butter.

Tap! Tap! Tap!

There was a soft knock at the front door. Smiff went to answer it, as Nancy was helping to serve.

He opened the door to find a girl stood

there. Her dress was plain, dark blue. Her face was just like a little china doll's. Her hair was dark and in ringlets and her hands were clutched nervously in front of her.

"Is this Master Crook's?" she asked in a voice as soft as tissue paper. "I desperately need your help."

Smiff couldn't help but smile at the girl and quickly ushered her through to the kitchen.

Mr Dreep jumped to his feet as Smiff brought in the nervous girl. "Come in, my dear. What's the matter?"

"Master Crook?" she asked.

"Master Crook is the owner of the school. I am one of his teachers," Samuel Dreep explained.

"May I join your school?" she asked shyly. Her voice was the voice of a lady and Alice's face twisted in disgust.

"Errrrgh! *May I join your school?*" she

mimicked like a purple parrot.[6]

"Alice!" Samuel Dreep said sharply. "Remember the school rules!" He pointed to the list on the noticeboard. Alice didn't need to look to know what rule he meant. Rule ten.

---

10 PUPILS MUST NOT PICK ON OTHER PUPILS. NO MATTER HOW WEEDY AND WORTHLESS A CLASSMATE LOOKS THEY ALL HAVE A PLACE AT MASTER CROOK'S. BE WARNED. BULLY NOT OR YE SHALL BE BULLIED.

"Puh!" Alice said.

"Sit down," Mr Dreep said. "What's your name?"

"Bunty, sir. Bunty McGurgle."

"BUN-TEE!" Alice cried. "Mc-*GURGLE*! What sort of name is that?"

---

6 Purple parrots are best. Forget your green-and-red parrots, your white cockatrices and your pink parakeets. You cannot beat a purple parrot. They taste really delicious with orange gravy and red onion sauce.

"It's *my* name," the girl breathed.

"Second and final warning, Alice," Mr Dreep said. The class had never seen him angry. He'd never had to punish anyone. Now it was like watching two people about to draw their guns in a western boy-cow gunfight.

"Mr Dreep, *sir*," Alice hissed. "Master Crook has a school for *poor* kids. Not for posh snobs like *Bunty* McGurgle."

"The school is for everyone who wants to see a world where money is shared around. A world where no one is poor."

Before Alice could reply Bunty put in, "We are poor, sir. My father was a rich man once, but then he fell in with a villain. That villain – his name was Silas Sharkle – took all our money and spent it on a trading ship. He filled it with muskets and cannons, powder and bullets. Then he sent it over the seas to the China seas where there was a war. He said we would sell the weapons to the war lords and get ten times our money back."

Samuel Dreep shook his head sadly. "Don't tell me. The ship sank?"

Bunty gasped. Even the class took a sharp breath. "How did you know?"

"An old, old trick," Samuel Dreep sighed. "He sent out an old, worm-eaten ship full of crates of scrap metal – not precious guns. The villain paid the crew to sail it out of sight and sink it. He kept the money that your father gave him."

"That's what I thought happened," Bunty whispered. "I came here hoping ... hoping Master Crook could find a way to get our money back."

"What?" Alice jeered. "You want us to swim out and un-sink the ship?"

"No," Bunty said. "Mr Sharkle is putting all his money – *my Daddy's* money – in a new bank ... Withering's Wildpool bank. I thought..."

"You *thought* we could get your rich Daddy's money *back* for him?" Alice shouted. "Well think again, brainless Bunty. We don't rob the rich to *pay* the rich, you posh-faced prawn. We're not here to risk the rope just so you can warm your white little hands and wear your blue little dresses and your bows and button-boots and crimp your curls with serving girls..."

"*Enough*, Alice," Mr Dreep said. "You were warned. There's the door ... get out."

"What?" Alice blinked.

"You are suspended from the school for breaking rule ten. You can get back on the street corner where we found you – try selling matches for a day. It will give you time to cool off."

Alice snatched her shawl from the back of the chair and raced from the room. She slammed the door behind her as hard as she could.

In the silence of the kitchen it was lucky no one dropped a pin. It would have deafened the pupils.

At last Mr Dreep said, "Lunch is over, time to get back to lessons."

"What about the cart robbery, Mr Dreep?" Nancy asked.

"Bunty can take Alice's place there too. Can you lie down in the road and pretend to be hurt, Bunty?"

"Yes, sir," she said eagerly.

"Good! Then let's carry on with the plan, Nancy."

*

"Push off," Alice said.

The blind beggar, sitting on the corner of the High Street, looked up at her. "You what?"

"Are you deaf as well as blind?" the girl asked.

"No, but. . ."

"Then push off. I'm begging here for the next couple of days," the girl said.

"I *always* sit here!" the man argued. "I need the money to feed me poor little cat."

"It's a stuffed cat," Alice said. "What does it eat?"

"Stuffing," the man said.

"So get back to Wildpool workhouse and feed it. Or else."

"Or else what?"

"Or else I will report you to those two policemen," she said.

Liddle and Larch had just stepped out of the police station on their afternoon patrol and were sniffing the fresh April air. They could smell the fug from the gasworks and the fog from the coal-fires, the horse droppings, rats' nests and open toilet pits, the slime and grime from the shipyards on the riverside and the rotten stink of the river. But in the weak sun a few blades of grass were poking their brave heads through the cracks in the cobbles.

"Spring in the air," Larch said.

"Eh?" his thin-boned friend said.

"Spring in the air."

Liddle scratched his head. "Why should I?"

"Why should you what?"

"Why should I spring in the air? I mean, at my age, my bones aren't as young as they used to be. I might hurt myself, springing in the air like that. I'm not a rabbit you know."

"Officers!" Alice cried. "I wish to report a beggar."

"What do you want us to do about it?" Liddle asked.

"Arrest him."

"Oh, but we have to fill in so many forms!"

Larch moaned. "Tell you what ... we will get him to move along."

"Yes. Move along," Liddle said.

"Where to?" the beggar asked.

"Somewhere else. We've had a complaint. Move along."

The beggar picked up his cat and his cap full of money. "I was just off for a cup of tea anyway," he grumbled and stepped off the pavement. A greengrocer's cart full of carrots almost knocked him over. "Watch where you're going!" the greengrocer cried.

"Can't you see I'm blind?" the beggar shouted back.

"You need a guide dog then," the carrot cart driver called over his shoulder as he rattled off down the High Street.

"I've only got a guide cat."

"Not my problem," the carrot cart driver called as he vanished round a corner.

"Sometimes it's no fun being a blind beggar," the man moaned. But no one was listening. Constables Liddle and Larch were on the march. Alice and the beggar watched as they turned off the High Street and into a shop next door to the apothecary.

GEORGE GREEN
GUNSMITH

OPEN FOR ALL YOUR PISTOLS, MUSKETS AND HUNTING GUNS NEEDS

"Oh, dear," Alice whispered. "Oh, no! I wonder if Mr Dreep knows where they've gone? I have to warn him!" She ran towards Master Crook's Crime Academy. Then her boots skidded to a halt on the greasy cobbles. "No I *don't*," she said. "No I don't have to warn the miserable trout and little Miss McGurgle about anything. Let them find out the hard way. That'll teach them. Oh, yes. That'll *teach* them."

*

Liddle and Larch entered the shop. The shopkeeper, George Green, was small and bald and wore round glasses. "Good morning, gentlemen. I know what you've come for."

"The guns," Liddle said. "The special new guns you've made for us."

"They are ready. Come into the backyard and I will show you how they work."

*

Darkness fell over the grimy, gloomy streets of Wildpool. But in Master Crook's Crime Academy the gas lights gave off a cheering glow and the coal fires were warmer than toast.

The Mixlys and Smiff went home to their families. In one of the bedrooms of the Academy Bunty McGurgle looked around and sniffed.

"That's your bed over there," Nancy said.

"There are no bedclothes on it!" Bunty gasped.

"No, the bedclothes are in the cupboard by the fireplace keeping warm," Nancy explained.

"But . . . but I can't make my *own* bed," Bunty gurgled. "At home I always had a servant to do it for me. *You* used to be a servant, Nancy, so *you* could do it for me, couldn't you, sweetie?"

"I suppose so," Nancy said and quietly took out the sheets and blankets. "I think Smiff likes you," she said with a shy smile.

"Lots of boys like me," Bunty sighed. "It's a nuisance. It's a curse, in fact. *Beauty* is *such* a *curse*. You should be pleased you have such a plain face, Nancy."

"Yes, miss."

"Oh! And I'd like a cup of tea in bed at nine o'clock tomorrow morning."

Nancy nodded.

"Two sugars."

*

Darkness fell over the grimy, gloomy streets of Wildpool. And the last of the winter chill returned with it. Alice wrapped her shawl around her thin body and huddled in the doorway to the hat-seller's shop.

The hat-seller opened her door and looked down. "Here, a young girl like you shouldn't be trying to sleep there."

"No?" Alice said, hopeful. "You want to take me in and give me a cup of hot chocolate?"

"No, I want you to shove off and find another shop doorway to sleep in. You're making my place look untidy."

Alice moved down the road to the greengrocer shop and settled down again, this time with the smell of cabbage and carrot.

Constables Liddle and Larch wandered past. "Evenin' all!" they said. "Here, a young girl like you shouldn't be trying to sleep there."

"No? You want to take me to the station and give me some supper?"

"No. We want you in the workhouse. That's where homeless kids belong."

Alice let them lead her down Bridge Street and across to Wildpool's Wonderful Workhouse.

The old rosy-cheeked keeper, Miss Ruby Friday, opened the gate. "Oh, Alice! Lovely to see you!"

"I don't suppose you're going to give me hot chocolate or some supper?" she asked.

"No ... I'm going to give you both! Come on in."

In the darkness the town hall clock chimed the end of the day. *Ding-dong, ding-dong, ding-dong...*

Chapter 4

BRICKS AND
BULLETS

Friday 7th April 1837

Locomotive No. 3 pulled into Wildpool station with a hiss of steam and a screech of cast-iron wheels on cast-iron rails. The choking smoke from the chimney floated up to the grimy glass roof of the station and the soot drifted down like black snow.

Two horses munched their oats in nose-bags as their wagon stood beside the railway carriage, waiting to be loaded.

The wagon driver sat quietly reading the morning newspaper. His dark eyebrows hung like curtains and his beard was cut as square and heavy as a church door.

On the back of the four-wheeled cart was a box like a large model of the bank. It was painted bright red with letters of gold.

Two railway porters heaved a heavy chest from the railway carriage. The chest was painted red and looked like an even smaller model of the bank – small enough to fit inside the bank on the back of the wagon.

Martin Mixly stroked the ears of the horses, turned to his sister and said. "It's as if they *want* someone to steal it."

"They *do* ... this time. Us! But it's full of bricks, isn't it?" she said.

Martin nodded. "That's what Gordon Griggsby told us." He looked towards the groups of people who stood around the station buildings.

There were ragged men and women in shivering huddles in the shadows. There were rich men with gold watches on chains, tucked into fine silk waistcoats, and with thick whiskers bristling under finer silk top hats. The women with the rich men carried parasols as bright as parrots and wore bonnets trimmed with the best lace. They warmed their white hands in fur gloves.[7]

"*We* know it's full of bricks," Martin nodded, "but those thieves don't. They may try to rob it before we do!"

"No," the driver of the carriage said suddenly. His white teeth glinted through the dark beard. "They will watch and see what happens. They will not try to rob it this time."

"But if they see *us* get away with it they will try next time," Martin argued.

"Hah!" the driver laughed. "But you won't get away with it. They will see you caught and they will never try to rob a Withering's bank wagon ever again."

Millie scowled at him. "We have a great plan," she said.

"So do the police," the driver said with a shrug. He jumped down and slipped the nose-bags off the horses. The cart springs groaned

7 Yes, the ladies warmed their hands in dead animals. They wore dead animals around their necks and trimmed their dresses with dead animals. They still do! Some women wear so much fur they are scared to go into the forest in case a hunter shoots them. Why do they do it? I ask. What's it all fur?

as the heavy chest was slid inside the back door of the van. The porters groaned and wiped sweat from their brows.

"It's done, driver!" one of them called. The driver tipped his hat in thanks. (The porters wanted him to tip them with some money. No chance. The driver's wallet was closed as tight as an oyster.)

That is how he became so rich.

*

"Buy my matches!" Alice cried in a pitiful voice. "Buy a poor girl's matches."

The sign by her side was scrawled on the back of an old advert for shoe polish.

"I'll buy a box of your matches," the blind beggar said.

"I haven't got any."

"Not got any matches?"

"No."

MATCHES

BUY THESE MATCHES FROM THE POOR LITTLE MATCH GIRL WHO IS TRYING TO FEED HER MOTHER, FATHER AND TEN BROTHERS AND SISTERS.

1P A BOX.

SPECIAL OFFER

BUY ONE GET 2 FOR 2P

"So you can't sell me any?"

"That's right," Alice nodded.

"So ... so, why are you shouting, 'Buy my matches'? Eh?" the beggar asked.

Alice gave a long sigh. "I am a spy. I am here to see what's going on in the street. The match selling is just a cover story. No one will think I'm spying. They'll think I am selling matches."

The blind beggar nodded. He watched the spring lambs being driven towards the quayside and the shoppers with their baskets prodding potatoes, squeezing sausages and sniffing scented soaps.

"Wouldn't it be a good idea to have a few matches to sell?" the beggar said after a while.

"Nah! I might get arrested by the police for begging," she explained.

"Right," the blind beggar nodded. He stroked his stuffed cat and leaned against the wall of the hat shop. "So what are you spying on?"

Alice looked towards the corner of the street where Smiff Smith stood. A red wagon was trundling along from the station. Smiff waved a hand to someone across the road from Alice . . . a girl in a blue dress. "I'm spying on a robbery," Alice said.

The slow wagon was being followed by fifty eyes as the gangs of thieves from the station followed it. "Those ragged people going to rob it?" the beggar asked.

"No-o-o! They're hopeless thieves! That's why they're ragged! It's the ones in fine clothes that will try."

"They look rich!"

"Of course they do!" Alice groaned. "That's what I'm saying! They are *rich* because they are *good* robbers. They're the ones the bank will have to watch. You are as brainless as your cat."[8]

"Suppose so," the blind beggar nodded.

"Now, let's see what a mess Master Crook's clowns can make of the robbery," she smirked.

The girl in the blue dress waved back at

8 Oh dear. What a cruel thing to say! I hope you're never that cruel. And it wasn't even a clever thing for Alice to say! The blind beggar's cat had a big brain. Yes, it was a brain made of cotton wool, but that's not the point. What is the point? I don't know.

Smiff and stepped off the pavement. She pushed her way through a flock of lazy lambs, threw the back of her hand to her forehead and gave a cry. "Woe!"

"Whoa!" Alice gasped. "Whoa? Is she trying to stop a horse?"

"Woe is me!" Bunty McGurgle cried even louder and staggered into the road. The shoppers and the gangs of thieves stopped to watch. Shopkeepers came to their doors and even the lambs gazed as hard as they usually grazed.

"I think I am going to faint!" Bunty croaked.

"I think I am going to be sick," Alice spat. "That is the worst acting I have seen since the dancing cow in the Christmas show at the Apollo Music Hall."

"I thought it was a good dancing cow," the beggar said.

"It fell off the stage into the orchestra!" Alice cried. "It climbed out with a French horn stuck on its head."

"All cows have horns on their heads," the beggar said.

"Shut up," Alice said.

Bunty fell slowly, and carefully, into the road – she found a patch where there were no sheep or horse droppings and lay down.

The wagon driver said, "Whoa!"

"*He's* at it now," Alice muttered. The driver climbed down and raised Bunty's head.

"Thank you, sir," she whispered.

"Poor child," Silas Sharkle said. "Can I help?"[9]

"You can carry me home, sir," she said. "Take me to the Wonderful Wildpool Workhouse across the river."

"Climb on to the wagon and I'll drive you there!" he offered.

"No!" the girl squawked ... then remembered she was supposed to be faint. "No ... I suffer wagon-sickness. Carry me there, good sir ... Miss Friday, the kindly workhouse keeper will care for me!"

Silas Sharkle picked Bunty McGurgle up

9 You should have already guessed Silas Sharkle was driving the wagon. You had enough clues. They were staring you in the face and if you didn't see them then you should get a job as a blind beggar.

and marched to the corner of High Street where he turned into Bridge Street. As soon as he was out of sight Smiff Smith darted out from a shop doorway and jumped up on to the driving seat. He released the brake and cracked the whip.

The carriage rolled forward and the horses seemed to sense he was in a hurry. They broke into a canter and clattered through leaping lambs.[10]

The cobbles clattered as the wheels whirred and the steel rims struck sparks. The gangs of thieves were too surprised to move but Alice knew what to expect and she was scurrying towards the east end of the High Street. She was just in time to see the wagon skid round into the back lane behind Low Street.

Women had hung out their washing in the spring breeze and it flapped in Smiff's face. He tore bloomers from his brows, trousers from his teeth, and knickers from his nostrils. He tugged on the reins as he reached a back gate

10 YOU would leap if a pair of charging horses were heading towards you.

where a woman waited. Her hair was like a bird's nest – only not so tidy and not so clean.

"Hello, Ma," Smiff grinned. "Is Nancy there?"

Smiff's schoolmate was in the yard with a rope ready to drag the treasure chest out. "Open the door, Smiff, we'll hide the chest under a heap of coal here. Then you can drive on to the docks and dump the wagon."

Smiff walked to the back of the wagon. "We'll break up the chest for firewood and even if they search the whole of Wildpool they'll never find out where their treasure went."

Nancy sighed. "Shame it's only a box full of bricks. The plan is perfect!"

Smiff shrugged and threw open the back door of the wagon. Inside was gloomy. Not a lot of sunlight fell between the high walls of the black-bricked back lane. Even less fell inside a covered wagon in that lane.

The chest sat there, glowing a dull red.

And behind it were two white circles. Smiff squinted hard. The circles were two pale faces.

Beneath them four pale hands held silver tubes.

The faces smiled. "Mornin' all!" Constable Liddle said.

"Put your hands up or we will shoot," Constable Larch added.

"Run, Nancy, run!" Smiff cried.

Mrs Smith darted back into her yard and bolted the door. Smiff grabbed Nancy by the arm and tugged her up the lane towards the safety of Master Crook's Crime Academy.

"Stop or we will shoot," Constable Larch called after them. The constables stood in the doorway and raised their rifles.

"They'll shoot us!" Nancy cried as she struggled.

"No they won't!" Smiff argued. "They're too soft. They wouldn't harm a fly."

Constables Liddle and Larch fired their weapons. *Crack! Crack!*

Which just goes to show...

Chapter 5

SPLOTTS
AND SHIPS

Saturday 8th April 1837

... something.

The newspaper told the amazing tale.

8 April 1837

THE WILDPOOL STAR

BANK ROBBERS 'BUNGLED'

Wildpool's wonderful policemen, Constables Liddle and Larch showed the world just how hard it's going to be to rob Withering's bank. With the help of some fake thieves, the bank set up a fake robbery to test the security of the bank and the skill of Wildpool's police force.

Little did the fake thieves know that the cunning constables were concealed under the cover at the back of the wagon.

Constable Liddle told our reporter, "Little did they know we were concealed under the cover at the back of the wagon."

Constable Larch joked, "You could say, Liddle did they know! Hah! Hah!"

The driver of the wagon was the rich businessman Silas Sharkle. "Stopping the thieves is easy – you just need an armed guard. But catching them alive is the tricky part. And that's where my amazing invention is so brilliant," he said. "The net gun can catch them alive so we can hang them in front of Darlham Gaol. That will show every villain for fifty miles you can't steal from a Sharkle."

Mr Sharkle's invention was made by Wildpool gunsmith, George Green. He told our reporter, "The net gun doesn't fire bullets – it fires a short dart like a harpoon. Fastened to the end of the dart is a rope and a net. The officers aim over the head of the fleeing thieves. The nets drops on them and they are caught."

Mayor Oswald Twistle said he planned to give the courageous constables another medal to add to their collection. "There will be no crime in Wildpool as long as I am mayor!" he said. "Vote for me next month."

Wildpool Star has a sketch of the wonderful new crime-cracking weapon, free to all readers. Collect it from the offices and pay just two shillings for delivery.

Little match girl Alice White said, "I saw it all. What a bunch of bungling buffoons. They couldn't steal milk from a cat. Heh! Heh! Serves them right." Our reporter was unable to find out just what served the thieves right.

The pupils of Master Crook's Crime Academy looked at the sketch that Samuel Dreep stuck to the blackboard. It had come free with the newspaper.

"It's clever," he said and tugged at his side-whiskers.

"It's cheating," Smiff snarled. "How's an honest bank-robber supposed to make a living when they come up with weapons like that?"

Nancy studied the plan. She shook her head. "No. I can't see any way round it. They have us beat."

When the train pulled out of Wildpool station that day it was filled with thieves. The ragged failed thieves and the rich successful thieves left the town. They left behind crumpled copies of the newspaper. They left behind broken dreams.

They went off to simpler crimes like stealing sheep from sheds or whipping washing from lines, pinching pennies from poor-boxes in church or snaffling sausages from butchers' stalls.

"No one can rob Withering's Wildpool

bank," a man in a golden waistcoat moaned.

"You could walk in with a gun and threaten to shoot the manager, Gordon Griggsby," the woman in the emerald dress told him.

The man gave her a sour look. "I am an honest thief ... not some American boy-cow," he said.

Monday 10th April 1837

But in Master Crook's Crime Academy the students did not give in so easily.

Dreep faced his students. "Now, class, we used this test as an opportunity to discover the bank's strengths and weaknesses. Is there any way to escape the net gun?"

"We could carry a pair of sheep shears," Smiff said, "and snip our way out of the net!"

Millie Mixly nodded. "Yes ... you could *get away* doing that ... but you still wouldn't have the chest of treasure, would you?"

"It looks like there's no way round it. The treasure is safe in the bank wagon," Nancy said.

Martin Mixly sighed, "I wish Alice was here. She'd think of a way. She has the brain of a great criminal."

"Yes, and the great criminal wants it back," Smiff snorted. "We can do this without awful Alice," he said.

Bunty McGurgle raised the back of her hand to her brow. "Poor little Alice. Where is the dear little child? Still on the street selling matches? Oh, what a waste of a sweet young life! I feel it was all my fault."

"She was rotten to you," Nancy said.

"I forgive her," Bunty said and fluttered her eyelashes like an angel.[11]

"You're very kind," Nancy said.

"Thank you," Bunty said and brushed away a tear.

"You're the nicest person I know," Smiff sighed. "Twice as clever as Alice and ten times as pretty."

"Thank you," Bunty said and pushed a handkerchief to her lips to choke back a sob.

Martin Mixly looked at his sister and put two fingers down his throat as if to throw up.

11 As you know angels flutter their eyelashes a lot. It helps them to fly. Those wings are not enough. They also grow their toenails long and flutter them too. At least that's what I was told by the last angel I met.

Millie nodded. "Smiff's brain is turning to water," she murmured.

"Alice can return when she says sorry," Mr Dreep said. "Now, let's get back to the problem we have to solve. The bank is almost finished. It will be filled with gold and silver, jewels and priceless works of art before the week is out. Master Crook needs us to set the treasure free so we can care for the poor and needy in Wildpool."

"Please, sir," Bunty said. "If Master Crook is such a *master*, then why can't *he* come up with a plan?"

"How would you learn if Master Crook always gave you the answer?" Samuel Dreep asked. "But he does like to help along the way so at ten o'clock we will have a guest who can help us with our problem." Dreep pulled a cheap watch from his waistcoat pocket and looked at it. The clock on the town hall chimed the hour. *Ding-dong, ding-dong, ding-dong. . .*

There was a knock at the door. Nancy trotted off to answer it. She led a man into the classroom. He wore a brown corduroy suit that was stretched over a body that seemed to be made of granite. His weathered face was as rough as a rock too and his cap sat on his thick hair like a saucer on a lion's mane.

"Welcome, Mr Craggs!" Samuel Dreep cried and reached out a thin, twiggy-fingered hand to their guest.

Craggs shook hands with the teacher. There was a crackling of bones and a whimper of pain from Samuel Dreep. "Ooooh!" He pulled his hand free and shook away the pain. "Welcome to Master Crook's Crime Academy ... Class, this is Mr Norman Craggs from Wildpool shipyard."

Craggs looked at the class a little shyly. "I've never taught in a school before," he said. "In fact I've never been inside a school."

"No, but you are a master of the new art of building iron ships, Mr Craggs," Samuel Dreep said.

"It's my job," the man said with a shrug.

"So ... we're going to get an iron ship, sail it up the High Street straight into Withering's Wildpool bank are we?" Smiff jeered.

The teacher ignored him and turned to the ship builder.

"You are so good at building watertight, iron ships the bank has given you a special task, haven't they?"

"They have. They asked me to build their thief-proof safe," Craggs said.

"Now my class are very interested in safes ... and crime ... and Master Crook invited you here to show the students how you build a thief-proof safe. What are its strengths ..."

"And its weaknesses," Smiff said.

Norman Craggs pulled a piece of paper from his pocket and unfolded it. The teacher copied it on to the blackboard.

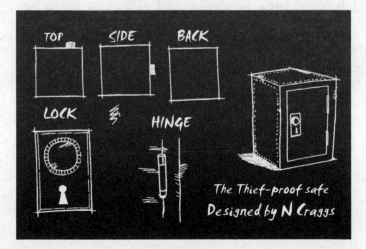

The Thief-proof safe
Designed by N Craggs

And for half an hour the class tried to find a way into the safe. There were two locks. One key was held by Gordon Griggs, the bank manager. The other key would be held by his chief clerk.

"We could kidnap the manager and the clerk. . ." Smiff began.

"What do you mean?" Norman Craggs said, alarmed.

Samuel Dreep stepped forward and said quickly, "It's a game! We sometimes *pretend* to be criminals so we can see how their minds work. What Smiff *meant* to say was a *criminal gang* could kidnap the key-holders and force them to open the safe."

Craggs nodded. "That's why Mayor Twistle has said the manager and the clerk must be armed with a pistol at all times. If anyone tries to take the key they will be shot."

"Oh! Oh! Oh!" Bunty McGurgle cried. "I am fainting at the very thought. Shot on the spot with my blood going splott."

"Don't worry, Bunty," Smiff said softly. "I would stand between you and the gun if I had to."

Bunty's mouth turned down. "Thank you Smiff, dear, but then it would be *your* blood that went splott on my clean blue dress. It's bad enough to have one's own blood, but to have someone else's blood is just too, too hideous! If you have to bleed please do it well away from me!"

"Sorry, Bunty," Smiff said.

Mr Dreep spread his hands. "Thank you *so* much, Mr Craggs. The class are happy knowing the thief-proof safe will keep the riches of Wildpool safe."

Craggs smiled and stretched out a hand to say goodbye. Mr Dreep said, "Nancy, please show our guest to the door."

"It's impossible," Bunty McGurgle said.

"Ah, but Master Crook's Crime Academy students enjoy the impossible, don't we?" the teacher asked.

Millie and Martin nodded excitedly. Smiff just looked at Bunty while saliva dribbled down his chin.

"What can we do now, Mr Dreep?" Millie asked.

"Go to the theatre, Millie," the teacher said. "Tonight we will all go to the theatre."

"Buy my matches!" Alice sang on the street corner. She sat under the canopy of the hat-seller's shop window. "Buy a poor girl's matches."

MATCHES FOR SALE

BUY MY MATCHES OR SEE ME STARVE.
DO YOU WANT THAT?
NO? THEN PUT MONEY IN MY MATCH TRAY.
LOVE FROM ALICE
P.S. JUST DON'T ASK FOR ANY MATCHES.

"Mornin' all!" Constables Liddle and Larch said. They wore Mayor Oswald Twistle's shiny brass medals with pride.

"Morning, constables," Alice said.

"You're not *begging*, are you?" Constable Liddle asked and his thin moustache dripped a little from the April shower that had just blown over.

"Begging?" Alice cried. "How *dare* you."

"Sorry, but I only asked because—"

"Yes, yes," she said, jumping to her feet. "Now shut up and get out of my way. I want to see what's going on over the road."

The policemen stepped back and followed Alice's stare. Wagons were rolling up from the riverside and the sweating horses stopped outside the bank. Each cart held a part of the safe. Alice counted the three walls, a side with a cut-out for the door, the square roof to the safe and the heavy door itself.

"It's the thief-proof safe," Constable Larch said.

Alice smiled. "Thief-proof? Who says? You says? I think not. Oh, no. Not thief-proof at all. But I wonder if those dummies in Master Crook's Crime Academy have worked out how to rob it?"[12]

---

12 And I wonder if you have? Maybe you don't have the mighty criminal brain of Alice White. In that case you will have to read on to find out how to crack Withering's thief-proof safe.

Chapter 6

MAGIC AND MONKEYS

Monday 10th April 1837

In the evening the Apollo Music Hall glittered under the gas lamps and looked like a magical palace.

In the grey daylight it looked like a shop that sells shoddy and was as shabby as a sixty-year-old slipper. But in the evening it shone – warm and welcoming.

The board outside promised the most marvellous and mellifluous melange of mind-boggling masterpieces ever to be seen on a star-spangled stage for superior supporters of sparklingly supreme sophistication and evenings of endless elegant and erudite entertainment.[13]

The poster that week would tempt any tightwads to cough up their coins.

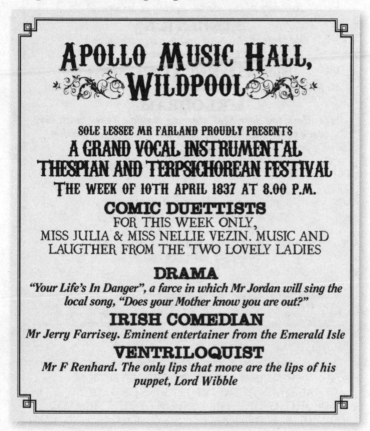

APOLLO MUSIC HALL, WILDPOOL

SOLE LESSEE MR FARLAND PROUDLY PRESENTS

A GRAND VOCAL INSTRUMENTAL THESPIAN AND TERPSICHOREAN FESTIVAL

THE WEEK OF 10TH APRIL 1837 AT 8.00 P.M.

COMIC DUETTISTS
FOR THIS WEEK ONLY,
MISS JULIA & MISS NELLIE VEZIN. MUSIC AND
LAUGTHER FROM THE TWO LOVELY LADIES

DRAMA
"Your Life's In Danger", a farce in which Mr Jordan will sing the
local song, *"Does your Mother know you are out?"*

IRISH COMEDIAN
Mr Jerry Farrisey. Eminent entertainer from the Emerald Isle

VENTRILOQUIST
Mr F Renhard. The only lips that move are the lips of his
puppet, Lord Wibble

13 Don't worry if you don't understand what that means. No one ever does. It just sounds GREAT and that's all that matters. Get the public to pay their pennies to put their pants on the seats.

MAGIC
*The Fakir of Ava will do tricks that are the eighth
wonders of the world. Seeing is believing!*

SENSATION
*Old Mother Hubbard and her wonderful dog!
Clever canine capers*

SENTIMENTAL SINGER
Mr F W Montague. If you have tears prepare to shed them

MELODRAMA
*"The Alarming Sacrifice" starring Matilda Heron, with her
stock company from the "Adelphi Theatre" in London*

DANCE
"La Zingarella," with Mr Smith and Miss Annie Walters

PRESIDER : MR EDWIN VILLIERS.
STAGE MANAGER : MR A MAYNARD
CHAIRMAN : MR T NORRIS
ORCHESTRA LEADER : MR WILSON
PIANIST : MR SOLOMON

Admission: Boxes 1 shilling; Balcony 9 pence; Stalls 6 pence; Back seats 4 pence.
Entertainment will start at 8:00p.m. doors will open half an hour earlier.
No dogs, no drinking your own drink, no spitting and ladies are not allowed
to smoke. Food and drink are served at the intervals, before and after the show.

A REWARD OF 20 SHILLINGS WILL BE PAID BY
THE MANAGEMENT ON THE DETECTION
AND CONVICTION OF PERSONS DESTROYING
OR MUTILATING THE POSTERS OF THIS THEATRE.

The pupils from Master Crook's Crime Academy walked through the stage door behind Mr Dreep. "Where are we going?" Smiff demanded. "I want to see the show."

"And so you shall, Smiff. But first I want you to meet a friend of mine."

"Is he in the show?" Millie Mixly asked, excited. "Is he famous? I always wanted to meet someone famous."

"Ooooh!" Bunty McGurgle cooed. "If I met someone famous I'd faint."

"Don't worry, I'd catch you before you fell to the floor," Smiff promised.

This time Millie joined her brother in sticking fingers down her throat. Nancy caught sight of them and smiled.

Mr Dreep tapped on a dressing-room door.

"What's a *fakir*?" Smiff asked. "Someone that goes around *faking* things?"

"A *fakir* is an Eastern Holy Man who has magical powers ... Ava is in Burma," Samuel Dreep explained.

"Come in!" a voice called from inside the room.

The teacher opened the door and the students of Master Crook's Crime Academy crowded into the small room. A cheerful young man sat in front of a mirror and was rubbing brown boot polish into his face. "Hello there, Samuel," he said. "Excuse me if I don't shake hands." He waved a brown-stained hand at the teacher.

"You're excused, Isaiah," Dreep laughed. He introduced the students.

"So where's the fakir?" Smiff asked.

The young man went on rubbing in the brown boot polish. "I am Isaiah Hughes in the daytime ... but when I go on stage I become the Fakir of Ava."

"Oh, so Smiff was right," Martin Mixly said. "You *are* a *faker* after all?"

"A magician, if you don't mind. One of the best. You can see me cut off a boy's head, stick it back on, and see him walk off the stage."

"It's a trick, right?" Bunty McGurgle said.

Isaiah tugged at a cloth that was covering a hump on the dressing table. A head gazed up at them. Glassy blue eyes stared at the ceiling and a freshly chopped neck glistened wet and red.

Bunty threw a hand to her brow, "Oh, too, too horrible for words. I think I'm going to faint."

Millie Mixly muttered, "It's all right, Smiff will catch you."

"It's a wax model of a head," Martin said.

"But it's a good one," Smiff nodded. "I bet it looks just like the real head of the boy you use in the act."

"Of course," the magician laughed. "There's no tricking a trickster, young Smiff. The boy ducks his head below his collar and it's the fake head I cut off."

"Then you put it back on, the boy hides the wax head and his real head pops up?" Martin said.

"Exactly. But go out and watch the show. Then tell me how I make a young woman disappear completely!"

"We'll do that," Samuel Dreep said and waved his twig-fingers towards the door. "Come along, class ... it's show time."

They slipped through a door that led from the dressing rooms into the theatre and they settled in red velvet seats. The place smelled of pipe-smoke and cheap perfume, stale beer and sweating bodies.

A stagehand switched on a powerful arc lamp and a brilliant beam dazzled on the red curtains. The orchestra, just in front of the stage, played a jolly tune and the burbling audience settled down. They didn't just come to watch – they came to join in.

The class's favourite was Irish comedian, Mr Jerry Farrisey. He started his comic song and a sheet rolled down from above the stage so they could all join in with his song about a trip to Wildpool beach.

> Martha swallowed a jellyfish,
> Janie got the cramp,
> My ma-in-law began to roar
> because the sea was damp!
> While I was floundering through the waves,
> A crab got 'old of me!
> And when we looked for the bathing-machine,
> It had drifted out to sea.

The evening romped along like a playful pony – except there weren't any ponies in the show. Just dancing dogs and a monkey that walked a tightrope.

Then the crowd's cheers died down to silence.

A back-cloth dropped down to fill the stage. It was painted with a scene from an eastern market. There were stalls painted with weird fruits, mud-walled houses and a domed temple.

Then the stage manager covered the spotlight with blue glass and the whole scene looked like a moonlit night. The orchestra played eastern music.

The chairman, Mr Norris, spoke in a hushed, hoarse voice from his platform at the side of the stage. "At this point in the entertainment we ask that nervous ladies leave the theatre – you will see the dreadful death of a simple serving lad, live on this very stage and before your very eyes. See his head severed with a slice from the sharpest scimitar this side of Suez."

"Ooooh!" the audience cooed. No one left. Not even the nervous ladies.

"If you stay you will see the weirdest, most wondrous events ever seen in Wildpool's Apollo theatre. Put your hands together in awe and amazement for Burma's most brilliant beheading beast ... the Fakir of Ava, Chief of Staff of Conjurors to His Sublime Greatness the Nanka of Aristaphae."

"Ooooh!"

"I give you ... the Fakir of Ava!"

Applause shook the walls of the hall and feet stamped on the floors, raising clouds of sawdust in the smoky air.[14]

Isaiah Hughes glided on to the stage and began his magic act. The dim blue light helped to hide his hands as he produced a boy from a bowl of water. Then the boy's head was sliced off as ladies screamed in terror.

Isaiah the Fakir held up the head so the

14 Sawdust? you cry! Yes, I know you go to the theatre today, in 1901, and expect to see carpets. Sawdust is for the filthy taverns that fester in awful alleys. Sawdust soaks up the spit and spilled ale. Yes, dear reader, the sawdust in the Apollo was there for just the same reason ... in 1837 the spitters and spillers spat and spilled in the theatres.

blue eyes gleamed in the blue spotlight. Then he covered it with a hood and placed it back on the boy's shoulders. He covered it all with a cloth and when the cloth was removed the boy jumped up, screamed when he saw the sword and ran off the stage.

Now the audience laughed.

Martin said, "It's not so much fun when you know how he did it," and the others agreed.

But they fell silent as the Fakir of Ava spoke for the first time. "Iggle, glumpa wompo lickety duck!"

The chairman said, "Ladies and gentlemen, the Fakir has asked for a young lady to help with his next trick..."

"Nuppa-luppa, choppa uppa!"

"But he says the lady will NOT have her head chopped off!"

A woman in the front row called out, "Here! I'll have a go," and she was cheered as the chairman helped her up the steps to the stage. "What is your name, young lady?"

"Peggy Maginty," the girl said.

Fakir Isaiah led her to one of the striped

market stalls that was more like a sentry box for a soldier on guard. He waved a hand to show he wanted young Peggy to look around it. She walked around and rapped on it.

"Solid as my boyfriend's head!" she said.

The Fakir opened the door and waved her inside. She trembled and giggled as she stepped into the box. The magician closed the door and rapped on the box. Peggy Maginty knocked back.

The drummer in the orchestra gave a long rattle on the drum as the Fakir waved his hands and cried, "Abracadabra!"

He threw open the door to the box ... and Peggy's face looked out, "Coo-ee!"

The audience groaned.

The Fakir looked annoyed and tried again. He closed the window then picked up a chain. He wrapped it around the box twice and fastened it with a padlock so no one could get out.

Then he threw a large sheet over the box.

This time he shouted "Abracadabra-cadabra-cadabra!"

He took his slicing scimitar sword and pushed it through a joint in the box. The tip of the sword came through the other side. The audience gasped.

"Ooooh!"[15]

"Here!" the chairman wailed. "You said the lady would not be hurt!"

The Fakir seemed to go into a rage. He picked up three more swords and jabbed them into the box. Even the gentlemen in the audience were screaming now.

Isaiah the Fakir raised his arms high above his head and the audience fell silent. Then he unwrapped the chain, took hold of the door and peered inside. He turned to the audience and gave a blue-toothed smile. He flung the door wide. Four swords criss-crossed the inside of the box.

But Peggy Maginty was gone.

The chairman strode down from his

15 Let's face it, YOU would gasp if you saw a sword being stuck through a young lady. Of course you would gasp a lot MORE if the sword was stuck through you. There is nothing so gasp-making as a blood-soaked sword sticking through your chest. It makes me gasp just to think of it. Gasp!

platform on to the stage. He pulled out the swords, stepped into the box and rattled all the sides. "Amazing! I thought there must be a hidden compartment ... but there isn't. Would any gentleman from the audience care to examine the box?" Several men came forward, rattled the box, rapped it, tapped it, tipped it, poked, prodded and picked at it. They left, shaking their heads.

The chairman spread his hands in wonder. "Peggy Maginty has vanished into thin air!"

Smiff leaned across to Bunty. "The chairman is part of the act."

"Really?" the girl breathed.

"Oh, yes. And so is that Peggy Maginty."

"Oh, Smiff, you are so very clever," Bunty squealed.

"I know," Smiff said.

"So?"

"So what?"

"So how did he do the trick? I mean, where did she really go?"

"Ah ... ummm ... ahhhh..." Smiff stammered.

"We'll go back stage after the show and ask him, shall we?" Samuel Dreep said.

"What has this to do with robbing a bank?" Nancy asked him.

"Maybe nothing ... maybe everything. If Isaiah knows how to make a girl disappear from inside a locked box then maybe he can help us make money disappear from inside a locked safe."

The act ended with the chairman opening the door to the box. Peggy staggered out and cried, "Ooooh! I had the strangest dream – I dreamed I was in Burma."

"Uppa-cuppa boogle woo!" the Fakir said.

The chairman explained, "The Fakir says that's because you WERE in a village in Burma – the Fakir magicked you there!"

"Ooooh!" Peggy sighed. "Fancy *that*!"

The audience cheered, long and loud, the Fakir took his bow and the show carried on.

*

At the back of the theatre, Alice White stood and watched with a faint smile. "Very clever, Master Crook – you've given your class all they need to rob Withering's Wildpool bank. There's only one thing going to stop you pulling it off. One little thing..." she said.

Chapter 7

SACKS AND SHOCKS

Isaiah Hughes was scrubbing off the face-colour when the class crowded into the dressing room after the show.

"Splendid show, Isaiah," Samuel Dreep said.

"Not bad," the Fakir of Ava chuckled. "So, did you spot how I did the disappearing girl?"

"That Peggy was part of the act," Smiff said. "And so was the chairman."

"And the gentlemen from the audience?"

"No-o-o," Smiff admitted. "They gave it a good looking-at and they didn't see a back door. Peggy didn't slip out the back."

The magician soaped his face and washed it then dried himself with a towel. "Come on stage and have a look yourself," he said, slipping a jacket on and leading the way.

The theatre was empty now but the smell of the audience remained. Isaiah Hughes asked a stagehand to help him move the disappearing cabinet into place. Master Crook's Crime Academy class crowded round the box and rattled it, rapped it, tapped it, tipped it, poked, prodded and picked at it.

Bunty McGurgle cried, "I know how he did it!"

The class turned to her in surprise.

"How?"

"It was magic! He magicked her away to Burma," Bunty whispered.

The Fakir shook his head. "If I was that clever I'd magic myself into your bank, load up with money and magic myself back out. I wouldn't be sweating on stinking stages like Wildpool Apollo for five shillings a night! No, I cheated." He stepped inside the box but left the door open. He waved to the stagehand at the side of the stage. The man turned a handle.

The class groaned as they saw the floor of the box open and allow Isaiah to lower himself through a trapdoor in the stage. He waved goodbye.

The stagehand turned the handle the other way and the trapdoor and the floor of the box closed again. Isaiah had stepped off beneath the stage. The box was empty.

A minute later the Fakir appeared from the side of the stage. "There's a lot of room under that stage. Peggy can go out the side door, the way I just did, and disappear forever! Or she can step back on the lift and pop back into the box."

"So, it's not magic after all?" Bunty said, a little disappointed.

"Not real magic," Isaiah said.

"But it helps us rob that bank. Doesn't it?"

"It does," Nancy said.

"It does," Millie and Martin Mixly said.

"Does it?" Bunty McGurgle asked.

"Remember the plan of the safe that Norman Craggs showed us?" Smiff asked. "It had three walls, a door and a roof – all too solid to cut through."

"But it doesn't have a metal floor!" Nancy

said. "We get into the bank and dig under the safe ... we come up inside. Perfect!"

Tuesday 11th April 1837

Millie Mixly was given the job of writing the shopping list.

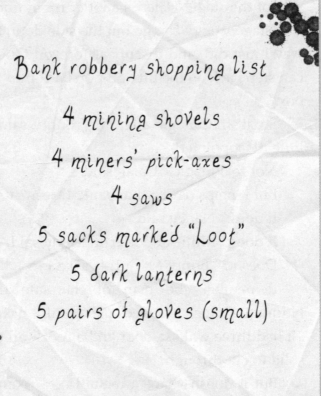

Bank robbery shopping list

4 mining shovels

4 miners' pick-axes

4 saws

5 sacks marked "Loot"

5 dark lanterns

5 pairs of gloves (small)

Smiff and Nancy were given the money to go to the ironmongers at the end of Low Street.

Outside hung tin pots and clothes-pegs, china cups and pewter mugs. They stepped inside and made their way through the piles of ropes and riddle, candles and cart-grease, buckets and brooms, knives and forks, hammers and handsaws.

The thin old owner, as grey as February, peered at the boy. "You again," he said. "You're not after cheating me out of another mop bucket, are you? You're out of luck cos I'm out of mop buckets. Some woman keeps coming in and buying them."

"That'll be my Ma," Smiff sighed. "She reckons you can never have too many mop buckets."

"Woman with hair like a bird's nest? Seems she's come into a bit of money," the old man said.

"I make a good living now," Smiff nodded.

"So what can I do for you?"

Smiff passed the list across the counter. The old man disappeared into the back of the shop and came back with the items on the list. "Now, son. I haven't any bags with 'Loot' on them but I have these," he said. He showed Smiff the bags.

"They'll have to do," Smiff said.[16]

"Sorry we don't have 'loot'. The 'loot' bags are very popular with the criminals in the county. You see, if the police stop them, and ask them what they're carrying, they say they have *tools* in the bag. When the police ask why it has 'loot' written on, the villains say they spelled 'tools' backwards so no one would pinch their tools. See?"

"Not really," Smiff sighed. "How much do we owe you?"

"Two guineas ... but since you're such a good customer I'll let you have the lot for two pounds."

Smiff nodded and handed the money over. He and Nancy loaded everything into a wheelbarrow at the front door to the shop

16 You can see the bag in Wildpool Museum. But which careless criminal from Master Crook's class left this clue behind? Or were they all caught? Wait and see.

and trundled it back along to Master Crook's Crime Academy.

"He charged us too much," Nancy said.

"I know," Smiff laughed.

"So what's so funny?" she asked.

"The old thief was so pleased with himself, he didn't notice we went off with one of his wheelbarrows! Heh! Heh!"

Wednesday 12th April 1837

The class were shocked, stunned, dazed, flabbergasted – their flabbers had never been so gasted – dumbfounded more than their founds had ever been dumbed. They were astonished.

A man stood in front of the class who looked like Samuel Dreep with his red-and-white scarf and shabby top hat. He even had Mr Dreep's gooseberry-green eyes and those fingers that were as fine as twigs on a vine, and that rippled when he talked.

But the face was brown as the Fakir of Ava, the side-whiskers were shaved and the hair as short as a worn yard-brush.

"Good morning, class," the figure said – and he even had Mr Dreep's voice.

No one answered. The man grinned. "So? Do you like my disguise?"

"Mr Dreep?" Nancy asked. "It's wonderful – except you've spread a bit of brown boot polish on your collar. It gives you away a bit."

"It's a fine day today. I want you to go into the back garden of the academy and practise your digging. You can even plant a few vegetables while you are there. The seeds are in the kitchen dresser."

"Where will you be, Mr Dreep – while we do all the hard work?"

"Finding you an easy way to get inside the bank," the man said and tapped his nose. He left a white spot where the polish rubbed off.

The class gathered the pick-axes and spades and went into the garden. "Ohhhh!" Bunty McGurgle sighed. "My poor hands are too soft and feeble to hold a spade. Nancy can do my share of the digging, can't you Nancy?"

"Yes, Bunty."

"I'll do some too," Smiff offered.

"Good idea!" the girl in the blue dress cried. "Smiff can start while Nancy makes me a cup of tea."

"Yes, Bunty."

"Two sugars."

Gordon Griggsby stood in front of the new bank building and looked at it proudly. The last tiles were being placed on the roof. A brass sign was being screwed on to the deep-red front doors...

Withering's Wildpool Bank

MANAGER: GORDON GRIGGSBY

BBC, BARF, MONICA

Gordon Griggsby rubbed the brass plate with the sleeve of his suit and looked at his own (round) face beaming back at him.

Workmen hurried past him carrying counters and carpets and cabinets, taking tills and tiles inside, dragging desks and drawers and deed-boxes, and pots of paint and pictures for the walls of the halls, glass lamps and gas lamps, sliding-in signs and stools and banking tools (like pencils and pens and pots of ink for quires that the quills would quickly fill) and lifting the ledgers and carefully carrying those little sponge-things-the-clerks-use-to-wet-their-fingers. It was more like a beehive than a bank it was so bustlingly busy.

Cough!

Gordon Griggsby tightened his tie in the mirror of the brass plate and smiled at the round face that looked back. "Good morning, sir, and welcome to Withering's Wildpool bank. How may I help?" he asked himself.

Cough! Cough!

"Yes I will happily lend you money ... and if you fail to pay me back I'll snatch your house and throw you out! Ha! Ha! Won't that be funny?"

Cough! Cough! Cough!

Gordon Griggsby suddenly realized a man was coughing. "Mr Griggsby ... BBC, BARF, MONICA?" the man asked.

Griggsby kept the smile fixed on his round face and turned around. He saw a tall, thin man with shining brown skin and glowing green eyes looking at him. "Yes, sir? How may I help?"

The man reached inside his pocket and pulled out a business card.

Mr Samuel Preed
BBC, BARF, MONICA

Inspector

"Ah!" Gordon Griggsby cried. "A fellow member of the BBC?"

"The British Banking Corporation," Dreep nodded.

"And BARF."

"Bankers Association Royal Fellowship."

"And MONICA too."

"Member Of the National Institute of Chartered Accountants," Dreep agreed.

""How can I help a fellow banker?"

"As you see, I am an inspector. I have been sent by the BBC to make sure the building meets our standards."

"Oh, but it does!" the manager said smugly.

"The new standards – passed last week in London by BARF."

"Ah ... oh ... I didn't know about them," Griggsby said and the smile slid from his face like jelly off a wet plate.

"I will just have a quick look around, if you don't mind."

"Please, Mr Preed, let me show you this fine building," Griggsby cried and led the way inside.

Dreep pretended to be interested in the cash tills and the little barred windows, the desks where the clerks would sit and the tiny toilets they could use – but no more than twice a day.

At last they reached the monstrous safe that stood in the back room like a silvery dinosaur with its door a gaping mouth. Workmen were bolting on the door. Dreep stepped inside. He tapped his foot on the wooden floor. It sounded as hollow as a wood floor should. He gave a thin smile.

Then he stepped outside the safe and walked around the room. The brick walls were bare. "Night safe," he said.

"Night safe?" Griggsby frowned.

"The shops of Wildpool close at around six o'clock in the evening. The bank closes at five. The shopkeepers can't pay in their money. They have to keep it in their shops overnight. That is dangerous."

"Dangerous?"

"There are so many criminals around," Dreep said in a low voice.

"So I've heard."

"Most banks have a 'night safe' ... a hole in

the wall where the shopkeepers can drop their money through … with a note to say who it's from, of course."

"Of course!"

"Now BARF says *every* new bank must have a night safe. Here is the design."

Dreep pulled out a plan.

"It will be done by tomorrow," Gordon Griggsby said with a smile.

"I'll be back on Friday to test it and to collect a copy of the key. BARF keep copies of every night-safe key in the country, just in case some careless manager loses his key. Hah! But you wouldn't do that, Mr Griggsby, would you?"

Griggsby laughed – roundly. "There is more chance of me losing every penny from my thief-proof safe!"

"Exactly!" Dreep cried. "You have a truly wonderful bank here, Mr Griggsby, and Wildpool is lucky to have a truly wonderful manager."

Dreep's fine white fingers rippled in a wave of goodbye.

Griggsby glowed, then a little crease of worry formed in the corner of his eyes. That wave. Those fine white fingers. There was something ... something ... not quite *right*.

He just couldn't work out what it was.

Chapter 8

PRETTINESS
AND PLOTS

S amuel Dreep crossed the High Street to where Alice White sat with her match tray and her sign. He knew that despite his disguise, her clever criminal mind would recognize him.

NO MATCHES.

DON'T EVEN ASK.

JUST LEAVE YOUR MONEY.

I AM NOT BEGGING.

JUST ASKING POLITELY.

"Come back to Master Crook's Crime Academy, Alice," the teacher said. "Master Crook has your money put away safely. You don't need to beg."

The girl glared at him. "I am not begging."

"Then what are you doing?"

"Keeping an eye out."

"For what?"

"That's my business."

"Then at least come and sleep in the warm bedroom at the academy," Dreep sighed.

Alice jumped to her feet. "I am not sharing a room with Miss hoity-toity, namby-pamby, simpery-whimpery, high and mighty, pretty-witty, lardey-dardey, wishy-washy, snooty-snotty, goody-goody, burgling McGurgling Bunty!"

Samuel Dreep nodded slowly. "OK, there's plenty of room, but you still need to say sorry."

"I am *not* saying sorry! Alice White does not say sorry. Alice White does not know the meaning of the word. Alice White can't even spell the word and she certainly doesn't say the word."

"What word?"

"Sorry!"

"What word?"

"Sorry!!!"

"Apology accepted. Now come back to class," the teacher said. "We all miss you. Nancy has been miserable since you walked out."

"Since I was *thrown* out."

"The Mixlys miss you ... even Smiff misses you."

Alice took a deep breath. "I think I may be more use here," she said quietly. "You'd be surprised what you see, sitting on the corner."

Samuel Dreep leaned towards her. "What have you seen, Alice?"

There was a gleam in her eyes as she said, "Sparrows."

"What?"

"Good day, Mr Dreep. Tell dear Nancy I'll be back as soon as Miss McGurgle is gone."

Friday 14th April 1837

Inspector Beadle's chair creaked.[17]

He looked at his constables standing in front of his desk, their buttons shining silver, medals shining brass and faces shining with the rain of an April shower.

"The bank opens in three days' time," he said.

"Yes, sir, I can't wait to get some money out," Constable Larch said with a smile.

"Do you have money in Withering's bank?"

"No, sir."

"Then you can't get it out," the inspector explained.

"Can't I? I didn't know that," Larch said, disappointed.

"Not unless you go to Mr Griggsby and borrow money – but of course he will make you pay back a lot more than you borrow."

"That's not fair!" Larch complained.

"It's how banks work," the inspector said.

"I know how you can get money out of Withering's and not pay," thin Liddle said.

---

17 You would creak if you had his great bulk sitting on you.

"How?"

"Rob it! Heh! Heh!"

"I'm glad you mentioned that, Liddle, because of course *now* is the time when thieves will be gathering to spy on the bank," the inspector said. "Here are your orders for tonight."

WILDPOOL POLICE FORCE

ORDERS FOR
NIGHT PATROL

DATE: I4th April I837

Proceed Withering's bank, High Street, Wildpool.

Patrol the outside of the premises.

Seek out and arrest anyone acting suspiciously.

POLICE INSPECTOR BEADLE

"Over the next few nights villains will be hanging around to look for weaknesses. Trying to find a way to rob the bank."

"We have our net guns!" Liddle said.

"They are for guarding the money wagons. We can't have officers on the streets with weapons like that. You can be clumsy. You'll probably net Mayor Twistle!"

"It wouldn't be hard to catch him," Liddle moaned. "He's only the size of a gnome."

"Just go on patrol and keep a record of what you see. Dismissed."

"Yes, sir. Evenin' all!" the constables said. They saluted. They gathered their truncheons, handcuffs, dark lanterns and rattles and set off into the sunset.

WILDPOOL POLICE FORCE

DATE: I4th April I837

At eight p.m. Constables Larch and Liddle proceeded through the town to

Withering's bank. A blind beggar sat
in the doorway to the butcher shop
chatting to a match girl. The beggar
was told to proceed to Wildpool's
wonderful workhouse. Constable Larch
proceeded with him.

The girl said she was waiting for
a tree to grow so she could chop it
down and make some new matches. She
then told Constable Liddle to shut
his tatty moustached-mouth as there
was something she wanted to see.
Constable Liddle saw a man proceed
from the direction of Wildpool
station and stop outside the house
known as Master Crook's Crime
Academy. He was a very respectable
gentleman. He was the respectable
gentleman who drove the money
wagon, with a big beard, last Friday.
(The man had the beard, not the
wagon.)

The gentleman blew a whistle. A pupil

from the school came to the gate and
had a talk with him for about five
minutes. "Aha!" the match girl said.
"Just as I thought." But she wouldn't
say what thought she thought that
was just as she thought.
Several people proceeded past the
bank when the taverns closed for
the night. No one looked like a bank
robber. But Constables Liddle and
Larch agreed they do not know what
a bank robber looks like as they
have never seen one before. I mean a
bank OR a bank robber.
Constables Liddle and Larch
returned to the police station at
eight a.m. daybreak for a cup of tea
and a bowl of porridge (each).[20]

20 However, someone as bright as you will see there is more to
this than meets the eye. YOU are as smart as Sherlock... Liddle and
Larch were as smart as sherbet.

Alice heard the last three words that Silas Sharkle spoke to Bunty McGurgle as he walked back to the train station. "Same time tomorrow, Lottie."

Saturday 15th April 1837

Smiff marched into the police station. "Mr Dreep has lost his dog."

Constable Liddle took out a pencil and report sheet and asked, "What does he look like?"

"He's about six foot tall and always wears a top hat and a red-and-white striped scarf."

"A dog like that should be easy to spot!" Liddle cried.

"I think the young gent was describing Mr Dreep, Liddle," Larch said.

"Ah . . . so what's the dog like?" Liddle asked.

"Bones. He likes bones," Smiff told him. "And chasing cats."

"I meant what does he *look* like?"

"Four legs, a tail."

"He'd be easier to find if he had *five* legs," Larch sighed.

"Or a top hat and scarf," Liddle nodded. "What's his name?"

"Samuel . . . Samuel Dreep."

"Clever dog! Here! It's not that dog that's been on at the Apollo Music Hall this week, is it? Old Mother Hubbard's dog?"

"No," Smiff said.

"I want to go and see that show on my night off."

"When's that?"

"Sunday."

"It's a good show – the Fakir of Ava is wonderful," Smiff smiled. "If you are out on patrol you might spot him."

"The Fakir of Ava?"

"The dog. You may spot him."

"Aha!" Liddle cried and wrote on the form. "It's a spotted dog then."

"So," Smiff asked, "when will you be out on patrol? I mean, when can we expect a result?"

Constable Larch took a sheet from under the desk. Here you are," he said, showing the sheet to Smiff.

WILDPOOL POLICE FORCE

DUTY ROTA

Sunday 16th	Day off
Monday 17th	Liddle: Guard bank. Larch: patrol docks
Tuesday 18th	Liddle: Patrol taverns. Larch: guard bank
Wednesday 19th	Liddle: guard bank. Larch: patrol streets
Thursday 20th	Liddle: patrol posh houses. Larch: guard bank.
Friday 21st	Liddle: guard bank. Larch: patrol shops
Saturday 22nd	Liddle: check for beggars. Larch: guard bank

"See?" Larch said. "The villains never know where we'll be next. Our patrols are a closely guarded secret."

"Ah, but there is always someone guarding the bank," Smiff said.

"Yes. The mayor said that is the most important thing. It would be a terrible disgrace if we ever let the bank get robbed. In fact he would even take our medals off us."

"You wouldn't want that," Smiff said.

"We couldn't stop him."

"You could keep them in the bank!" Smiff said.

"Good idea!" Liddle and Larch cried. "Evenin' all," they called as the boy walked out.

Samuel Dreep shook his head. "So the bank is always guarded."

"Yes," Smiff said. "Except Sunday."

"Ah, but the money doesn't arrive till Monday."

"No point robbing an empty bank," Martin Mixly said.

"If Alice was here she would think of a way to get the constable away from the bank," Nancy said quietly.

"But Alice *isn't* here, sweetie," Bunty McGurgle said. "Still, the good news is you have me instead. I am twice as bright as her!"

"And twice as pretty," Smiff added.

"True," Bunty agreed.

"I remember the theft of the Twistle treasure," Smiff said. "Alice reported a crime at the *north* side of town and the constables went off to investigate – we did a robbery at the *south* side," Smiff said.

Samuel Dreep shook his head. "They won't fall for that trick again."

Bunty clapped her hands. "What about if Inspector Beadle told the constables to leave the bank? They would *have* to go then."

Millie Mixly said, "Why would Inspector Beadle do that?"

"Because one of the rich men with money in Withering's bank would *tell* him to," Bunty said.

"We don't know any rich men with money in Withering's bank," Nancy said.

Bunty sat back in her chair and played with a curl. She looked as smug as a slug on a lettuce leaf. "I do," she said. "Remember Silas Sharkle?"

"Wasn't he the man that ruined your father and left you penniless?" Nancy asked.

"He was ... but, to be honest it was Mr McGurgle's own greed that ruined him."

"Mr McGurgle?" Smiff asked. "You mean your dad?"

"Yes, sweetie, my Papa. Anyway, Silas Sharkle has another ship ready to sail. This one really is full of muskets and cannons, powder and bullets this time. What if I tell him someone is planning to set fire to the ship – some rebel Chinese plotters who don't want the weapons to go to China?"

Nancy tried to say, "How do you know about the ship, Bunty?"

But her soft voice was drowned by the crow call of Smiff Smith. "Brilliant, Bunty! The police will go down to the docks and leave us free to get into the bank. Cor, Bunty, you really are twice as clever as Alice!"

"And twice as pretty," she agreed.

*

The blind beggar sat in the butcher's shop doorway, stroking his cat. He wondered where Alice the match girl was this evening.

Happy crowds strolled past on their way to the music hall or the taverns and happy people gave him happy coins. So everyone was happy.

High above Wildpool's gaslit glitter the town hall clock chimed the end of the day. *Ding-dong, ding-dong, ding-dong...*

A man walked from the railway station. The man was not tall but he seemed to fill the pavement. Crowds flowed round him like a stream round a rock. His eyebrows hung like curtains over his eyes and his beard was cut as square and heavy as a church door.

When he reached Master Crook's Crime Academy, he blew a whistle.

The door opened and a girl in a blue dress hurried to the shadow of the gate to meet him.

"Sign this," she said and passed him a letter.

Dear Constable Larch

As you know I deal in weapons. Weapons that
defend our great British Empire. But our Empire
has enemies! On Monday night of 17th April they
plan to attack my ship in Wildpool harbour and
burn it. There is enough gunpowder on board that
ship to blow Wildpool into the North Sea.

These attackers are cowards. If they see two
policemen on guard by the gangplank, they will not
attack. The ship sails on Tuesday. I humbly ask
that you send your brave constables to the docks on
Monday night at midnight.

God save King William and the Empire.

Your humble servant,

"Why would I want to sign this, child?" the
man asked.

"It will allow me to rob Withering's bank," she said.

"Remember all my valuables will be in there," he said quietly. "A hundred thousand pounds in bank notes and jewels. Do not take those."

"I know," she said. "But I will steal them and give them to you. Then Gordon Griggsby will be forced to pay you a hundred thousand pounds – or no one will ever use Withering's bank again."

"So I will have *two* hundred thousand pounds," the man nodded and a smile lit his eyes. "Clever child."

"Ah! But we can't allow the bank robbers to get away with a robbery," she said. "I will be first to leave the bank and I'll take with me all the Sharkle fortune. When you see me enter the bank send a second note to bring the constables up from the docks with their net guns. They will catch the whole gang."

The man shook his head. "They will catch *you*, child."

Bunty McGurgle sighed. "Of course you *tell*

them you have a spy on the inside who must go free."

"How will they know you?"

"Just tell them to look out for the girl in the blue dress," she said.

"Clever. It's an evil plot."

"I'm an evil girl."

"Yes. Very clever. I double my money – and you? What is in it for you?"

"I am doing it to help my dear father, of course."

He nodded. "Pass me the paper to sign – there you are – Silas Sharkle!" he said.

*

When the man had walked back to the train station and the girl had slipped back into Master Crook's Crime Academy, a shadow moved in the shadow of the bushes. Alice White gave a grim grin. "All arrested? Serves them right I suppose. Should I warn them?" She stepped into the High Street and crossed between carriages to the butcher's shop. "Nah! Better let beautiful Bunty's plan go ahead."

"Hello there," the blind beggar said. "Where have you been?"

"Spying," Alice said.

The man rose and stretched and picked up his cat and his cap full of coins. "Time to make my way to the workhouse," he said.

"The workhouse? Yes! That's just the place I need to be. I'll come with you."

"You can guide a poor, blind beggar," the man sighed.

"Hah!" Alice snorted. "That's what you have a guide-cat for. Now hurry up or we'll miss the plum pudding supper."

Chapter 9

OPENING
AND ORDERS

Sunday 16th April 1837

Nancy Turnip walked back to Master Crook's Crime Academy from Wildpool church. She smiled because the vicar's message had been a happy one that Sunday morning. "The poor are blessed," he said.

Mayor Twistle had turned red and looked furious. "The poor are a nuisance," he'd muttered to his wife, Lady Arabella. But he muttered so loud half the church could hear him.

As Nancy walked through the gate and into the crime academy she heard her name called. "Oi! Nancy!"

The girl stopped and peered into the bushes. Alice White's thin face looked out and her thinner finger beckoned. "Come here, Nancy! Come here, quick!"

"What are you doing there, Alice?" she asked. "Come inside."

"Nah! I'm not going back in that place while snooty-tooty, runty Bunty is there."

"I need to change into my boots and catch the coach to Darlham," Nancy said. "I'm going to visit Uncle Rick in Darlham Gaol."

"I know that," Alice sighed. "You *always* go there on a Sunday. *That's* why I need to talk to you. Before you go."

Nancy frowned. "Why?"

"Listen and I'll tell you," she said. Nancy hopped from foot to foot, knowing she hadn't time to stop and talk if she was going to catch the coach.

"There are a lot of villains in Darlham Gaol," Alice said.

For once Nancy's calm face creased crossly. "I know that, Alice. That's why they're in the gaol!"

Alice went on, "And villains know more about the rich than the rich know themselves. I want you to ask your Uncle Rick what he knows about Silas Sharkle."

"Silas Sharkle? Why?"

"It's a name I heard when I was spying. I want to know about his family..."

"But—" Nancy asked.

"Just do it," Alice snapped. "I am trying to save your miserable heads from the noose. Even Smiff who doesn't have a brain in that head of his. You have to trust me, Nancy." Her pale eyes stared hard at the crime academy pupil. "You do trust me, don't you?"

"Yes, Alice," Nancy said slowly.

"And find out if the prisoners know anything about the McGurgle family – and especially about their daughter Bunty."

"Are you doing this to get revenge on poor Bunty?" Nancy cried.

"I thought you trusted me," Alice hissed.

"I do, but—"

"Then don't ask questions," she said.

"You want me to go to Darlham Gaol."

"Yes."

"And ask questions."

"Yes."

"But you don't want me to ask questions."

"Right."

Nancy shook her head. Then the chimes of the town hall clock began to chime ten ... *Ding-dong, ding-dong, ding-dong...*

"I'll have to run!" Nancy moaned. "I'll be walking the streets of Darlham in my Sunday shoes. They'll be ruined."

"I'll buy you a new pair when this bank robbery's done."

Nancy hurried back into the High Street and Alice followed. "We have a brilliant plan to rob the bank," Nancy said.

"I can guess what it is," Alice said.

Nancy skidded to a halt. "You can?"

"Yes. And if I can work it out then so can the police."

"Constable Liddle and Constable Larch aren't that clever," Nancy said.

"No, but Inspector Beadle is. He's the one you have to watch. Him and Silas Sharkle."

Nancy hurried on. "Silas Sharkle ... Silas Sharkle ... I'll find out what I can," she promised.

The coachman was blowing a long horn to signal that the coach was about to leave. Nancy climbed up to an outside seat and turned up her collar against the cool breeze off the sea.

The rutted road threw up splashes of mud that marked Nancy's shining shoes. "I hope this is important, Alice," she said to herself. "I hope it's important."

*

Alice watched the coach roll along the road to the south then turned and walked down Bridge Street to the bridge high over the Wildpool river. Even the shipyards below were steeped in a deep Sunday silence and only the wheeling seagulls' harsh cries disturbed her.

"Right, Alice White," she said as she looked down into the wind-whipped waves on the river. "You don't know why this Bunty McGurgle would want to help Silas Sharkle, do you? No you don't."[18]

18 If you can't find anyone sensible to talk to then talk to yourself. Sometimes I can't even find an idiot to talk to and so I talk to myself. I do. Do you? Yes, I do. You should try it some time. Who me? Yes, you.

The tall walls of the Wildpool's Wonderful Workhouse loomed above her. The gates stood open, ready to welcome anyone unhappy enough to fall on hard times. They would be sure of a warm fire, a good meal and a bed here.

Families of children played happily in the courtyard. Alice marched through them with no time to stop and kick at the rag ball when it rolled in front of her.

Ruby Friday waited at the door and smiled at the girl. "Nice to see you, Alice. Come for a bed for the night? There's always one here for you. Better than a cold shop doorway."

"Not this time. I've come to ask a favour, Miss Friday."

"Always ready to help Alice White. Most of the people in here will be gone in a month when their new houses are built. But we won't forget who helped that to happen," the overseer said. "You and your friends at Master Crook's Crime Academy."

"I'm not at the academy at the moment,"

Alice admitted.

"You still haven't made up your little argument then?"

"No. They still haven't said sorry to me," Alice sniffed. "But you and the workhouse people can help."

"Name it," Ruby Friday said.

"I want you to take the blue uniform material..."

"Plenty of that stuff," Ruby said. "We don't force our guests to wear workhouse uniforms any more."

Alice nodded. "It was a sign that you were a pauper – something to be ashamed of."

"So what do you want with it?" the overseer asked.

"I want your best dressmakers to take that material and make some clothes for me."

"Clothes? How many sets do you need?"

"Five should do it," Alice said. "I need five."

Monday 17th April 1837

The pupils of Master Crook's Crime Academy stood at the window and watched as a piece of paper was pasted over the sign.

They watched as Gordon Griggsby stood at the door. His smile shone as brightly as his bald head in the April sunshine. He threw open the doors. He welcomed in the new

Opening on
M~~~~~~~
Open TODAY!
~~~~ 1837

Withering's Wildpool Bank

**Your money is safe as houses.
Your valuables locked in the
world's safest safe.
We lend money too.
Manager: Gordon Griggsby**

customers. He chatted brightly and shook hands.[19]

The people of Wildpool stood in an eager queue. Some clutched purses and piggybanks, some carried bags and others just clung tight to their pockets.

"We'll leave a lot of people miserable," Nancy moaned. "Some of those poor people are putting everything they have in the bank!"

"You are right," Samuel Dreep said. "But inside the safe there are boxes that the really rich put their valuables in. We'll rob those."

"I think we should steal from just *one* box. The Silas Sharkle box," Nancy said. "Uncle Rick in Darlham Gaol told me he is the richest."

"Sharkle is the man who robbed my father! Steal back the money and give it to me!" Bunty McGurgle said eagerly.

"I suppose we should give you the money

19 From their window in the academy the pupils could see he often wiped his hand on the side of his long black coat – there were some hands that were dirty from more than money. Let that be a lesson to us all. I will not explain. You may be eating as you read this and I don't want you to throw up into your porridge.

Sharkle cheated your father out of," Dreep nodded at Bunty. "The rest is profit for Master Crook's Crime Academy ... we share it out to the poor at the end of the year."

"If Master Crook's Crime Academy is still open at the end of the year," Bunty said softly to herself. "And if there are any pupils left to share it out."

Smiff didn't hear what she said. He just looked at her with a sickly smile – the sort of smile a rabbit has when it sees a bowl of carrots.[20]

Silas Sharkle took a large key from his pocket and opened the heavy lid of the heavy chest that stood in his office at Darlham. Beside the chest stood a red box with gold lettering.

He began to lift bags of gold and silver, bundles of bank notes and boxes of coins out of the chest and put them in the red box.

"Ohhhh!" Mrs Sharkle muttered and fluttered. "I hate to see our money leave the house."

Silas Sharkle gave a grunt. "Foolish woman. It's not safe here. How would you like to wake

20 Poor boy. Poor, poor boy.

up one night and find a gang of thugs breaking down our doors?"

"Gracious me, I wouldn't!" the woman whimpered.

"They *will* if they know I have McGurgle's hundred thousand pounds in the box."

"But you have the key, my love!" the woman said with a soft smile.

Silas Sharkle threw up his eyes till they disappeared into the hanging hedge of eyebrows. "They will simply carry off the whole box and smash it open when they get it back to their den."

"I never thought of that," his wife sighed. "I thought it would be safe. After all, no one knows it's here!" she said, feeling rather clever.

Her husband glared at her. "Ernest McGurgle knows it's here," he said quietly. "And if I were Ernest McGurgle – penniless and desperate – I would gather a gang of the vilest villains in the country. I would send them to smash down our doors and rob us of our riches."

"Would he do that?" she gasped.

"That's what I would do if I were him," Sharkle snarled. "It's just a matter of time before

McGurgle thinks of it – maybe he already has! So we don't just have to move our money to Withering's thief-proof safe, we have to let the whole world watch us as we do it. See?"

"Ooooh, you are so clever, Silas, ooooh," Mrs Sharkle said, cooing like a dove.

The man slammed down the lid on the chest and marched to the door. "There you are, constables! All ready to go! Take it to the waiting wagon."

Constables Liddle and Larch shuffled into the room. Liddle looked at Larch. "We can't lift a big chest like that!" Liddle cried. "Our orders say nothing about that!"

"Nothing!" Larch agreed and pulled out his orders.

WILDPOOL POLICE FORCE

ORDERS FOR DAY PATROL

DATE: 17th April 1837
     Collect Net guns from Wildpool police
     station store cupboard.

Proceed to Sharkle Hall near Darlham.
Enter the premises. Escort the
treasure chest on to the Withering's
bank wagon.

Accompany the wagon to Helton
station, sitting inside the vehicle.
Beware highway robbers while
crossing the moors. Warn the driver
to stop for no one.

Escort the chest on to the Helton to
Wildpool train, sitting inside the
carriage. Beware train robbers while
travelling to Wildpool. Warn Driver
Rump to stop for no one.

Escort the chest on to the bank wagon
from Wildpool station to the High Street.
Beware gangs of wagon thieves and order
the wagon driver to stop for no one —
even girls lying down in the road.
Escort the chest into the safe and
see it safely locked away.

POLICE INSPECTOR BEADLE

Sharkle snatched the paper. "No need to warn the wagon driver – it will be me."

"Sorry, sir, but it doesn't say nothing about lifting heavy chests," Liddle said.

"It says lots about hundreds of robbers trying to murder us!" Larch moaned.

"Ah, yes," Liddle nodded. "It's all right to get murdered ... but it's not all right to hurt our old backs!"

"You're right," Larch agreed.

Silas Sharkle snapped, "I'll get the servants to carry it from here and the porters at the station."

As Sharkle left the room Liddle and Larch smiled at one another. "The public has to be told!" Liddle declared.

"Told what?" Larch asked.

"They can murder us as much as they like but they can't strain our backs," the proud policeman said.

Chapter 10

PIES
AND EYES

S amuel Dreep stood at the blackboard and
ran through the plan one more time.

Master Crook's Crime Academy :
Secret Bank Robbery Plan
READ AND LEARN TELL NO ONE

MONDAY AND TUESDAY 17/18TH APRIL

11:30 p.m.   Streets empty after taverns and
music hall close. Bunty approaches
Constable Liddle on duty at Wildpool
High Street. Gives him letter
ordering him to join Larch at docks.

11:45 p.m. Smiff, the Mixlys, Nancy and Bunty use Mr Dreep's key to open the night safe and climb into the bank. Mr Dreep (who is too big to fit) will pass through the tools and wait in the alley with the wheelbarrow. He will keep watch at the docks to make sure the constables stay there.

Midnight: Students remove the floorboards outside the safe. They dig into the earth and scoop out a tunnel under the safe. They saw through the floorboards inside the safe and climb in.

1:00 a.m. Millie and Martin empty the Sharkle box and pass the loot to Smiff and Nancy who place it in "Swag" sacks. Bunty loads the wheelbarrow with the sacks.

2:00 a.m. All return to Master Crook's Crime Academy.

"Any questions?" Mr Dreep asked.

"How will we know if the constables come back up to the High Street?" Smiff asked.

"I'll make sure I'm ahead of them. I'll whistle down the night-safe door and warn you to be quiet," Mr Dreep explained.

"But we'll be trapped inside," Nancy said.

"Not for long. Even if they stand guard all night the police night shift ends at eight in the morning. The bank doesn't open till nine. You have an hour to get clear."

"But the High Street will be busy by then," Martin Mixly argued.

"And all they will see is a couple of you wheeling a barrow with sacks across the road," the teacher explained. "But I'll do my best to get the constables away from the street – even if they do return. I'll think of something."

"The people in the High Street will see the tools – they'll know who did the robbery," Millie said.

"Leave the tools behind," Mr Dreep said.

"Then the police will check who bought

those tools. The shopkeeper will remember me," Smiff said.

"If that happens we'll have to get you out of Wildpool to a safe town where no one knows you," the teacher promised.

"What!" Smiff wailed. "Away from Master Crook's Crime Academy, away from my Ma? Away from everyone?"

Bunty McGurgle patted Smiff on the arm. "It's all right, Smiff, I'll visit you."

Smiff gave his stupid rabbit smile and said, "That's all right then."

"Millie and Martin, have you told your parents you'll be out for the night?" the teacher checked.

"Yes, sir . . . we said it's a school trip," Martin told him.

"And it is!" Millie chuckled.

"It'll be dark soon. Try to get some sleep," Samuel Dreep said. "And don't worry. Nothing can go wrong."[21]

---

21 People have horrible accidents – they are run over by herds of mad pigs, crushed by falling pianos and drowned in tubs of treacle. And what are the last words most of these unfortunate people hear before they go to their dreadful deaths? You guessed it: "Nothing can go wrong."

Withering's bank wagon rolled down Wildpool High Street. Dozens of ruthless rogues watched and sighed. Hundreds of itching fingers wriggled.

Alice White sat on the corner of the High Street with a soft smile on her lips. Bank porters hurried out and lifted the red chest from the wagon. Two old constables climbed out, stiff as bank-window bars, and raised their fearsome net guns towards the waiting crowds.

The driver with a beard cut as square and as heavy as a church door climbed down and handed the reins to a servant who carried a rifle. "Take it away, Herbert."

"Yes, Mr Sharkle," the man replied and touched the front of his hat.

"I'm going in to see my money safely stowed away."

The chest vanished safely into the bank, Silas Sharkle followed and the doors slammed behind him.

Dozens of waiting faces fell in disappointment. "Gone, gone, gone," a woman in a fine satin dress sighed. "I suppose we'll have to find something easier to rob."

The crowd of villains nodded and trudged slowly back to Wildpool station.

One of them stopped on the corner and smiled at the thin girl who sat there with eyes as fiery as the setting April sun. "I'll have a box of matches for my pipe, my dear," the man said.

Alice White glared up at him. "Do I *look* like a match seller?"

"Well ... yes. . ." and he glanced at her sign.

MATCHES

HIGH QUALITY, LOW PRICE

SOLD OUT

JUST LEAVE YOUR MONEY
AND SHOVE OFF.

I'M BUSY.

"Pipe smoking is bad for you," Alice said. "You are better off without matches."

"I suppose so."

"I am doing you a favour by not selling you matches," she said.

"Thank you."

"Don't thank me – just pay me."

The man left sixpence and hurried off to the train station.

The constables hobbled over the road to Wildpool police station for a cup of tea and to have a rest before their night patrol started.

Inspector Beadle was there to meet them. "The plan worked, then. Everyone knew our brave constables were guarding the cash. No one tried to rob it. It's a job well done ... a job *half* done. Now we just need to make sure it stays in the bank."

Constable Larch's round face broke into a happy, but weary, smile. "That's the easy bit, sir. Now it's in Withering's thief-proof safe."

"That's right," Liddle agreed and tugged on

his wispy moustache to pull it out of the way of his tea. "Nothing can go wrong."

Mr Dreep checked his notes for the last time.

> **11:30 p.m.** Streets empty after taverns and music hall close. Bunty approaches Constable Liddle on duty at Wildpool High Street. Gives him letter ordering him to join Larch at docks.

The streets of Wildpool were never empty. The streets were lit by glowing gas lamps but the back alleyways were as dim as coal mines on the dark side of the moon.

And in those shadows the cats stalked the rats in a never-ending game of hide-and-seek.[22]

The town hall clock struck eleven-thirty. *Ding-dong, ding-dong, ding-dong...*

---

22 Sometimes the cats caught the rats. Then it became a game of hide-and-squeak. Hah! Get it? Hide-and-squeak? Oh, dear, sometimes I'm so funny I could make a snake snigger.

Eleven-thirty didn't strike back.

This was the hour when burglars lurked.

This was the hour when children buried themselves under blankets to keep out the cold and to keep out spiky monsters that hid under beds to chew their toes.

This was the hour when the fine folk of Wildpool dined and wined. The hour when Mayor Oswald Twistle twirled his glass of port and passed a box of fat cigars to his rich guest.

"It's good of you to offer me a bed for the night, Sir Oswald," Silas Sharkle said.

Mayor Twistle was a small man, but no smaller than a gnome. His chest puffed out like a frog and his starched white shirt showed blotches of dropped dinner.[23]

"It is a pleasure," Mayor Twistle began. "No – it is an *honour* to welcome such a rich guest to my house. Nay, to the town of Wildpool. The town is richer for your visit. We have Withering's bank, of course, but what is a

23 Steak pie in mushroom gravy, if you want to know.

bank without a fortune in its thief-proof safe, eh?" he chuckled.

Sharkle stroked his beard and gave a sly smile. "I always take a walk after dinner, Sir Oswald," he said.

"I don't!" the little mayor squawked. "My feet hurt. It's these shoes, you know."

"No! No! No! Don't worry," Sharkle said swiftly. "I like to walk alone. It helps me sleep. I thought I'd take a stroll by the bank tonight."

"Ahhhh! You'll see one of our brave constables on guard there. Our constables have medals for their gallant acts you know?"

"I know. You're lucky to have such fine fellows," Sharkle said. He let the butler help him put on a dark cloak and he walked out into the quiet road that led towards Wildpool town centre.

When he reached the High Street he stood in the shadow of a shop doorway. He watched a girl in a blue dress pass a note to a thin policeman. In the breeze he heard the policeman read it slowly.

"Deal in weapons ... our Empire has enemies ... plan to attack my ship in Wildpool harbour ... blow Wildpool into the North Sea ... two policemen on guard by the gangplank they will not attack ... send your brave constables to the docks on Monday night at midnight ... God save King William and the Empire. Ooooh!" The constable groaned. "Inspector Beadle says I have to guard the bank."

"Guard what?" Bunty McGurgle laughed. "Who on earth is going to break into a bank when everything is locked away in a thief-proof safe."

"That's true. And if we don't stop the Chinese plotters Wildpool will be blown into the North Sea," the policeman groaned. "I have to stay and I have to go. What do I do?"

"It's a fine medal you have there, Constable," the girl said.

"The best I've ever seen," Constable Liddle said and spat on it before rubbing it with his sleeve.

"Imagine the size of the medal you'll get

when you save the whole of Wildpool! It will be the size of a dinner plate. It will be amazing. You will be Wildpool's greatest hero!"

"I will!" Liddle cried and he hurried off to Low Street and down to the quayside.

The girl in the blue dress smiled and rubbed her hands. The man in the dark cloak smiled and rubbed his hands. "Nothing can go wrong," he said.

*

From an even deeper and darker doorway, Alice White clutched at a soft bundle in her arms. She watched and waited.

She saw Bunty McGurgle wave a hand. Samuel Dreep stepped out from the gateway of Master Crook's Crime Academy. He trotted to the top of Low Street to make sure the constable was on his way. He waved back to the gateway. Four pupils from the academy stepped out with a wheelbarrow. The teacher checked his notes.

11:45 p.m. Smiff, the Mixlys, Nancy and Bunty use Mr Dreep's key to open the night safe and climb into the bank. Mr Dreep (who is too big to fit) will pass through the tools and wait in the alley with the wheelbarrow. He will keep watch at the docks to make sure the constables stay there.

Alice saw the pupils run across the road and disappear into the alley that ran by the side of the bank. She heard a key clink in the door to the night safe. *Clink.* "Careless," she muttered.

She heard muffled groans as one by one the pupils slid into the gap. She saw Mr Dreep run back and heard clanging of spades and pick-axes ratting on the iron door frame. *Clang.* "Ooooh!" she said to a passing rat. "If I'd been there I'd have wrapped those tools in sacking to muffle the sound."

"Squeak," the rat agreed.[24]

The great Wildpool bank robbery was under way. The robbery so secret no one should have been watching. But, in truth, eight eyes were watching the robbers' raid.

Oh, dear.

24 At least I think the rat agreed. My rat-speak isn't too good. The rat could have said, "Excuse me but could I buy a box of matches?" Luckily for the rat Alice's rat-squeak-speak wasn't very good either or it would have been (a) rat, then (b) splat.

Chapter 11

MIDNIGHT AND
MESSAGE

Alice White waited. She knew it would take at least forty to fifty minutes for them to break through the floorboards and reach the money. Even with Nancy-the-strong working her hardest.

Silas Sharkle waited. He knew it was no use calling the policemen back to catch the thieves until the girl in the blue dress had escaped with his fortune.

Samuel Dreep waited. He knew the class could do the job. He only wished Alice White was in there to drive them on. He watched the hands on the town hall clock creep round to midnight. His wavering fingers twitched at his notes.

Midnight: Students remove the floorboards outside the safe. They dig into the earth and scoop out a tunnel under the safe. They saw through the floorboards inside the safe and climb in.

Another pair of eyes watched and waited.[25]

Midnight chimed.

Mr Dreep was sure the constables were on the quayside. He took time to walk back up the High Street to check the alley at the side of the bank.

He could hear the sound of the class working but it was too early for them to be passing out the treasures. The teacher walked close to the doorway where Silas Sharkle was standing in shadow.

Sharkle stepped back so the teacher

25 Who could that be? you cry. I'm not telling you, I cry back. Wait and see or work it out from the clues I've given you. Clues? you cry. Now stop all this crying or you'll make the pages damp.

wouldn't see him. He stepped on to something soft but crunchy. "Hey! Watch where you're putting your shiny boots!" a voice groaned ... the voice of that fourth pair of eyes. The voice of Wildpool's blind beggar.

"Who are you?" Sharkle hissed.

"I'm a very disturbed beggar," the man said. "Who are you?"

Sharkle's smile glittered in the little light there was. "I am your best friend," he said. "And you are going to help me. You're just what I need."

"I am?"

"You are." He pushed a hand into a pocket of his jacket and pulled out an envelope. "I have a message here I need delivered."

"At this time of night?" the beggar asked.

"Yes. I want you to go down to the docks and give it to the captain of a ship called the *Guns of Doom*."

"You what?" the beggar cried. "I'm not going down to the docks in the dark. There's all sorts of rogues hiding in lots of back alleys just waiting to jump out and rob you. I'm scared of the dark."

"You're blind!" Sharkle argued. "It's always dark to you."

"So I'm always scared. You wouldn't get me going to those docks ... not for ten shillings, you wouldn't."

"What about for a guinea?" Sharkle asked and jingled some coins.

"I'm your man!" the beggar said and he was on his feet faster than a cat after a rat.

"Here's the money and here's the note." The clock chimed quarter-past midnight. "Time to go," Silas Sharkle said.

The beggar set off towards Low Street. Sharkle shrugged himself inside his cloak and set off back to his comfortable bed in Mayor Twistle's house. He knew the plan would be safe in the hands of the girl in a blue dress.

Mr Dreep hurried back to the end of the High Street. He looked down Low Street to watch for police. He saw the back of the blind beggar hurrying down the steep, cobbled street.

Now there was just one pair of eyes peering at the alley by the side of the bank – Alice White's.

She decided it was time for her to make her move.

Inside Withering's bank, the class worked steadily – but noisily. Floorboards splintered and were thrown against the wall, shovels crunched into the stony soil and earth was scattered over the floor. From time to time a shovel struck the side of the thief-proof safe and it rang like a gong.

At last the tunnel was large enough to let Nancy slip in. She pushed up on the floor inside the safe. She sweated and strained and gasped and gurgled. At last there was a cracking sound and Nancy croaked, "Done it!"

She hammered at the broken boards with her fists and soon the gap was large enough to let her climb up into the safe. "Pass me a candle," she panted.

The flickering amber light shone on a wall of brass doors. Behind each door was a box and in most of the boxes lay someone's precious parcel of savings or something worth its weight in yellow gold.

Smiff was next through the tunnel. He looked at the brass. Each had a small label in a slot. "Here we are."

Property of
Mr Silas Sharkle
Only to be opened by
the authorised owner
of Key.
Safety deposit box
number
39

"Can you open it?" Nancy asked.

Smiff Smith nodded. "Yes. They just have simple locks on these boxes. Gordon Griggsby never expected thieves to get this far, did he?"

As Smiff set to work to pick the lock, Millie and Martin Mixly slipped through the opening. "Where's Bunty?" Nancy asked.

"Waiting on the other side to pull the treasure through," Millie explained.

"She said she'll be fine, waiting there alone," Martin said. "It would spook me!"

"Nothing can happen to her," Nancy said. "There's no one there."[26]

Alice White crossed the quiet High Street with a bundle over her shoulder.

She walked down the alley by the side of the bank. She stepped carefully past the wheelbarrow that stood there. She gently pushed the night-safe door open.

She looked through. A single candle lit the room. The massive thief-proof safe shone like polished silver.

A girl sat on a pile of sacks. She was looking at a hole in the floor that led under the wall of the safe. She had her back to Alice.

"Careless sort of look-out, Bunty McGurgle," Alice said softly to herself. "You haven't learned much from your time at Master Crook's Crime Academy. I will also show you how to get through an iron door without the sort of racket you lot made."

26 Hah! That's what you think, dear Nancy.

Alice moved so smoothly through the gap she was inside in a silent moment. She pulled the soft bundle after her. The bundle was fastened at the top with a thin rope. She tugged the knot and the rope came loose.

A bundle of blue tumbled on to the floor. Alice took the rope and held one end in each hand. Then she stepped softly over the soil-stained floor till she was standing behind the girl in the blue dress. "No more burgling McGurgling," she said with a fierce smile.

Constable Larch saw a sinister shape creeping along the quayside. "Halt or I will beat you with my truncheon till you are black and blue – well a nasty shade of pink anyway. Who goes there?"

"It's me, Liddle," his partner said.

"Evenin' all. Aren't you supposed to be guarding the bank?"

"New orders." Liddle explained quickly. "Wildpool will be blown away if we don't stop these plotters. *Boom!*"

"Better get to the *Guns of Boom* then," Larch croaked. "We could get hurt if Wildpool gets blown away."

The men marched down the quayside. The fish filleters had gone home to supper – fish pie with fried fish and fish pudding with fish custard. The dock workers had unloaded their last sacks of the day and the sailors were supping in the taverns. Only the ship-builders went on hammering to finish the mighty, the new, steel steam-ship that would be one of the first in the world. It was called *The Pride of Wildpool*.

The ship named *Guns of Doom* lay at the quay with a shaky gangplank to the shore. A man in a thick blue jumper and cap stood at the top of the plank.

"Evenin' all," the constables said. They placed themselves at the bottom of the plank and peered left and right along the quayside. Larch took a pie from his pocket and started to munch it. Gravy ran down his chin.

After a minute the sailor called, "Can I help you?"

"We've been sent to guard your ship," Liddle explained.

"Why?" the seaman asked.

"Our information says there may be an attack from Chinese enemies," Larch said. "But, fear not! We will make sure you're safe!"

"Does my captain know about this attack?" the seaman asked.

"Maybe not," Liddle said. "It's a secret."

"I'd better tell him," the seaman said.

"What's his name?"

"Hoo," the seaman replied.

"The *captain*. Who is he?"

"Yes," the seaman said.

Liddle muttered to Larch, "I think we are dealing with an idiot here."

"Oh, yes. I know an idiot when I meet one," Larch nodded.[27]

"What's your name?" Liddle asked the seaman.

"Watt," the man said.

"I said what's your name."

---

27 Of COURSE Larch knew an idiot when he saw one. Because he saw one every time he looked in the mirror.

"That's right. It is."

"What?"

"Yes."

Liddle sighed. "Yes. Mad as a March hare."

Larch frowned. "What? In April?"

Liddle looked at his partner and wondered if he was talking to TWO idiots. He turned back to the seaman. "I'm Liddle."

"Well . . . you're thin but you're quite tall. I wouldn't call you little."

Liddle went on, "And my partner is Larch."

"Maybe he shouldn't eat so many pies," the seaman said. "I'll go and report to my captain."

"What?"

"No, that's me. Hoo is the captain."

"I don't know . . . we've been asking you for ages."

"I'm a little confused," the sailor sighed.

"No. I'm not confused," Liddle said. The sailor disappeared. "Idiot. I'm surprised they don't crash their ship."

"Oh, but they do! I read in the *Wildpool Gazette* that Silas Sharkle lost a ship last month. The captain said he was lucky to escape alive."

"Well he couldn't escape dead, could he?" Liddle grumbled. "It was probably the same captain. What was his name?"

"Hoo."

"The captain."

Larch stared at the thin constable. He pushed the rest of his pie in his mouth. "Forget it."

"What?"

"I think that was the name of the lieutenant. Now keep your eyes open for Chinese villains," Larch said.

"What does a Chinese villain look like?" Liddle asked.

"I'm sorry you asked me that, Liddle."

"Why?"

"Because I don't know the answer. But if *anyone* comes down Low Street firing pistols just hit them with your truncheon."

"Here's one now!" Liddle cried. "Halt! Who goes there?"

"Blind beggar," the man said.

"Shouldn't you be in the workhouse?" Larch asked.

"Just dropping off a message for the captain, then I'll be on my way," the beggar explained.

"An odd time to be delivering messages," Liddle said.

"That's what I said to the bloke that gave me the message," the beggar agreed. "But he said it was important. Fella in a cloak."

"A cloak? Sounds like a plotter to me. Did he look Chinese?"

"I don't know, it was dark. Anyway, I'm blind."

"Better look at that note," Larch put in.

"Careful!" Liddle called. "It could be an exploding letter!"

"Is it an exploding letter?" Larch asked the beggar.

"Let's find out," the man said. He took the letter and placed it on the cobbles. Then he jumped on it with his heavy boots.

Nothing. No *boom*. Not a sound – well, maybe a little rustle.[28]

28 This is a foolish way to test for exploding letters, of course. If YOU ever get an exploding letter do NOT jump up and down on it. Place it on a gravestone in a churchyard, climb the church steeple and throw rocks down till you hit the letter. Duck out of the way of flying bones and you should be fine.

The beggar handed it over. "Safe as Withering's bank," he said.

Liddle read it in the dim light of the quayside lamps.

Captain Ping Hoo

If two police officers turn up at the ship tell them it's a trick. They must go straight to the police station, get their net guns and guard the bank. There is a robbery taking place. If the criminals are already inside the bank then they must capture them as they try to escape.

They must not net the girl in the blue dress. She is an insider.

A friend

"Ohhhh!" Liddle moaned. "We've been tricked! We could lose our medals if Withering's bank gets robbed."

"Ooooh! But that letter could be a trick to get us away from the ship we were sent to guard!" Larch cried. The two officers ran in small circles wondering what to do next.

Captain Hoo and seaman Watt came on deck to see what was going on.

"No!" Liddle said suddenly. "No, no, *no*! The letter is NOT a trick."

"How do you know?" Larch moaned.

"Because, Larch, it was signed by 'a friend' ... and a friend wouldn't try to trick us!"

"Brilliant, Liddle. You're right! Let's get to the bank before we lose our medals."

The officers shook their rattles to scare dogs and rats and cats out of the way as they hurried up Low Street towards the bank.

The captain of *Guns of Doom* shook his head. "What an idiot."

The seaman snapped, "How dare you!"

Chapter 12

BLUE DRESS
AND BAILIFFS

Tuesday 18th April 1837

"Hello, Charlotte," Alice said.

The girl in the blue dress gave a small scream and swung round. "Alice! You gave me a fright. What are you doing here? You've been expelled."

"Not exactly. I was sent away till I apologized to Bunty McGurgle," she said with a little sadness in her voice.

"If you are ready to apologize then I accept your apology. You can stay and help if you like."

Alice shook her head. "You are too kind. You would like that, wouldn't you?"

"Well," the girl said, "if you are truly sorry you are welcome to share in the robbery."

Alice nodded. "And share in the punishment when everyone is caught?"

"Why do you say that? I was just trying to show you are forgiven. You apologized..."

"To Bunty McGurgle, not to you," Alice said.

"But I am Bunty McGurgle!" the girl in the blue dress said.

"No, you are Charlotte Sharkle ... your father calls you Lottie. A friend in Darlham asked questions about you. Bunty McGurgle has red hair – yours is dark brown like your father's. I'm sure your beard will grow like your father's one day."

The girl turned fiercely on Alice. "You will pay for that you little slabberdegullion."

"Pay for it? When I'm caught by Wildpool police?" Alice asked. "The police your father sent for once we were all trapped inside the bank?"

"Yes," Charlotte Sharkle sneered. There was a rattle behind her and a sack marked "Swag" was pushed through the hole in the floor. Charlotte snatched it and threw it through the night-safe door so it landed next to the wheelbarrow in the side alley. She came back for the next sack. Alice smiled. "That's very kind of you. Loading the McGurgle fortune so we can wheel it away."

"You won't get away," the dark-haired girl said as the third heavy sack appeared from the safe. She carried it across the floor and sent it to join the others.

"Don't tell me – we will all be hanged while you wheel the treasure away."

"That's right," Charlotte Sharkle said.

The fourth and last bag marked "Swag" appeared and the girl carried it across to the door and threw it out.

Moments later Nancy wriggled out of the tunnel followed by the Mixly twins and finally Smiff.

"What are you doing here?" Smiff asked. "Don't tell me – you've betrayed us out of spite?"

"No," Nancy said quickly. "Alice is saving you." She looked around the group. "Alice got me to ask about the McGurgle and Sharkle families when I was visiting Uncle Rick in gaol. This girl here is Charlotte Sharkle – she's helping to steal her own father's money."

"Oh, so it was *you* that spied for Alice in Darlham, was it? I expect nothing less from a frumpy, ugly serving girl."

"It's not true, Bunty, is it?" Smiff cried. "Alice is lying because she's jealous of your pretty face."

Charlotte Sharkle sighed. "Of course it's true, you stupid little, weedy little gutter child."

"I thought you *liked* me!"

"Hah! Like a slum boy? I think not."

Smiff slumped against the shining safe. His hurting eyes turned to Alice. "Sorry, Alice," he muttered.

She shrugged. "Charlotte Sharkle is a good actress," she said. "She even fooled Mr Dreep. Nothing to be ashamed of, Smiff."

"The best actress in my school," Charlotte gloated.

Before anyone could answer there was a low whistle from the night-safe door. "The police!" Smiff cried. "That's the signal. The police are here! We're done for."

"Yes you are, slum boy," Charlotte said. "But I'll be fine."

"You're part of the robbery. You'll hang alongside us," Millie Mixly said angrily.

"I think not. You see, I have something you don't have," Charlotte Sharkle said.

"A rich father?" Nancy asked.

"No something much simpler. A blue dress." And she laughed.

Samuel Dreep had seen the two constables appear at the bottom of Low Street. They seemed to be hurrying as fast as their old legs would carry them.

The town hall clock struck one. Dreep knew what the notes said.

1:00 a.m. Millie and Martin empty the Sharkle box and pass the loot to Smiff and Nancy who place it in "Swag" sacks. Bunty loads the wheelbarrow with the sacks.

The class would be caught loading the loot from the bank. The policemen seemed to be carrying their net guns. Even if they only caught one pupil each it would be a disaster. The teacher ran ahead of the police and turned into the alley at the side of the bank. He stumbled over the sacks on the ground and heaved them into the wheelbarrow.

He placed his face to the night-safe door and whistled.

He waited.

Nothing happened. He could hear them talking. But no one was making a run for freedom.

Samuel Dreep looked back towards the gaslit street. The constables appeared. A half-moon made shadows in the alley. He shrank back into one of the shadows so the constables couldn't see him. Whichever pupil came out now they would be captured. He moaned. "Master Crook would know what to do – even *Alice* thinks quicker than me. I wish they were here!"[29]

---

29 Luckily one of them was...

Alice White, inside the bank, heard the whistle but did not panic. "Yes, Charlotte Sharkle, you have a blue dress. And, as it happens, I have another five blue dresses here," she said nodding to her bundle. "A good friend made them for me. Four small ones for the Mixlys, me and Smiff. And a ... er ... slightly larger one for Nancy. We will put them on and walk free."

Charlotte Sharkle's face twisted in rage. "Clever little slabberdegullion, aren't we? But even if you walk free with Papa's money he'll get it all back from the bank."

"Maybe," Alice said with a wide smile. She passed the dresses around the class.

"I'm not wearing a dress," Smiff Smith objected.

"That's fine, Smiff. Part of your dear Charlotte's plan is to bring the constables here to arrest us. You heard Mr Dreep whistle. They're waiting for you now. If you're not wearing a blue dress they'll arrest you."

"They won't catch me," the boy muttered. "I'll outrun two old coppers."

"We tried that, Smiff," Nancy said. "But we couldn't outrun the net-guns."

Martin Mixly said, "I don't mind wearing a dress if it saves me from the gallows," and he slipped one over his head.

"You look stupid," Smiff snapped.

"Yes, but at least he looks stupid on the streets of Wildpool ... at night where there's no one to see him," Millie said as she put her dress on. "*You'll* be looking stupid on the gallows outside Darlham Gaol!"

"But we'll all come along to watch, Smiff," Alice promised. "We'll wave to you!"

The thin boy snatched the dress from Alice and pulled it over his head. "Right. Can we go now?"

"Oh, no!" Alice cried. "There's one more thing we need to do. We need to let the constables arrest *someone* for the robbery. We want them to keep their jobs, don't we?"

"But we're *all* wearing blue dresses," Millie argued.

"I've thought of that," Alice said. "Martin and Millie, hold Charlotte Sharkle's arms so she can't move. Nancy, hold her legs so she can't kick out – that's right. Now what have we here at the bottom of my bundle? Why it's a pot of paint and a brush. Red paint. Now, Charlotte, hoity-toity, namby-pamby, simpery-whimpery, high and mighty, lardey-dardey, wishy-washy, snooty-snotty, goody-goody, burgling bungler – we'll have you red as a rose in no time!"

WILDPOOL POLICE FORCE

REPORT

DATE: 18th April 1837

Constables Larch and Liddle proceeded to Withering's bank, acting upon information received in a letter.

We proceeded to the night safe in the alley at the side of the bank.

The door was open. We observed
a wheelbarrow with sacks marked
"Swag" outside the safe door.
After a while the head of a boy
appeared from the safe. However we
were mistaken. He was wearing a
dress so he could not have been a
boy. We had been instructed not to
arrest a girl in a blue dress so we
did. That is to say we did un-arrest
her. The girl said, "Evening all,"
then walked towards the High Street.
A second boy who looked like a girl
emerged in a blue dress. We un-
arrested her as well.
Two thin girls in blue dresses (who
looked like girls) emerged. We un-
arrested them. Then a large girl in a
blue dress emerged. She took the heavy
wheelbarrow and wheeled it away.
Then a girl in a red dress emerged.
She said it was a blue dress but

Constables Larch and Liddle are not
easily fooled. We arrested her. She
screamed very loudly about being a
shark, but that is a fish and we are
not easily fooled. Fish don't wear
red dresses.
The girl in the red dress was locked
in the cell to cool off. We gave her no
blankets to help her do so. Inspector
Beadle will question the suspect.

Smiff Smith's mother had hair like a bird's nest. Some people in Low Street swear they saw the odd family of sparrows flying in and out of it.[30]

The Master Crook's Crime Academy students and Mr Dreep sat around Mrs Smith's kitchen table. They were silent.

30 This was a cruel lie made up by jealous people. Let me put the record straight. I was there and I know it wasn't true. Mrs Smith did NOT have a family of sparrows nesting in her hair. Definitely not. They were starlings.

The money from Silas Sharkle's safe-box was stacked on the table. Mrs Smith had made a list.

The Sharkle fortune	
Pennies	£10,00,00
Florins	£10,00,00
Half Crowns	£80,00,00
Sovereigns	£900,00,00
5 bank notes	£99,000,00,00
Bank draft	£10,000,00,00
TOTAL	£110,000,00,00

"One hundred and TEN thousand pounds," Smiff breathed.

"One hundred and *ten*?" Millie Mixly echoed. "I thought he robbed Mr McGurgle of just a hundred thousand."

"Where did the extra ten thousand come from?" Alice asked.

Mr Dreep spread his rippling fingers. "Who cares? We know where it is going *to*. That ten thousand pounds is going into the Master Crook's Crime Academy treasure chest to be shared out to the poor at Christmas."

"And the hundred thousand?" Martin said, his eyes fixed on the piles of money on the table.

"We have all agreed on where that will go," Samuel Dreep said.

None of the eyes left the shining pile. All of the heads nodded.

*

Bunty McGurgle sniffed back tears. "So, Daddy? I will have to leave Darlham Ladies College?" she asked in a voice like a mouse – a very unhappy mouse.[31]

"Yes, my little Bunty-wunty. Daddy lost all his money when the ship sank in the China Sea."

"Two sugars please," Bunty said.

"Pardon?"

"If you're making some China tea I'll have

---

31 I am talking about the real Bunty McGurgle here, not Charlotte Sharkle pretending to be Bunty McGurgle. Not Bunty McGurgle pretending to be Charlotte Sharkle ... though I don't know why she would want to do that. No, this is Bunty McGurgle being herself. Got that? Good.

a cup with two sugars, please," the girl sighed with a mousy sigh.

"China *Sea* … Silas Sharkle's sip shank … I mean ship sank. We are left with nothing."

"Nothing, Daddy? Not even a cup of China tea?"

"Not even a cup. Today the bailiff will arrive and take away our every possession. Darlham workhouse is a harsh place, Bunty, but it's what your foolish Daddy deserves."

"I thought a bay leaf was a herb you put in a stew, Daddy," Bunty said with a frown on her pale face.

"No, my little cherub, I said *bailiff*, not *bay leaf*. The bailiff is a man who takes our things and sells them to pay the people we owe money to. He can take everything we have except the clothes we are wearing."

"Will Charlotte Sharkle and her parents lose everything too?"

Mr McGurgle pushed back his thin hair … hair that was turning grey with worry.[32]

32 Hair does that you know. It turns grey with worry. But don't YOU worry about your hair turning grey. It can also turn blue, green, pink or black with hair dye. Buy some at your local apothecary shop as soon as you spot a grey hair.

"No. Mr Sharkle said his ship was insured – an insurance company paid him ten thousand pounds for the sunken ship. It was the weapons I bought that were not insured."

"Are the bay leafs very nasty men?" Bunty trembled.

There was a rattle on the door.

"We'll soon see," Mr McGurgle said. "That'll be them now."

Chapter 13

KNOCKING
AND NOTHING

Gordon Griggsby looked at the wrecked room where the thief-proof safe stood. His round face trembled with rage. "It was that man, Preed – he told me to build that night-safe door – and *he* had a key. It was all part of a cunning plot."

He looked at Constable Liddle who had broken the news of the robbery to him. "The bank will pay for posters of this man all over the country. Find *him* and we'll find our money."

By the end of morning those posters were printed.

Constable Liddle lifted his hat and scratched his head. "Strange that only the Sharkle box was opened. Maybe the gallant actions of me and Larch stopped her before she got away with more."

Gordon Griggsby peered up at the constable and spoke very slowly. "It is VERY strange that only the Sharkle box was touched. An interesting point, constable."

"It takes a wise dog to fool Wildpool Police, Mr Griggsby, sir. We have medals you know."

Griggsby frowned. "And you say you have one of the gang under arrest?"

"Yes, sir."

"But you didn't get the money?"

"No, sir."

"Then let's go and pay this bank robber a visit. See what he has to tell us before they hang him."

"She, sir. It's a young lady in a red dress."

"A girl, eh?" Griggsby said. "Very interesting. Inspector Beadle is known to me. He won't mind if I am in the room while you torture the villain and get her to confess."

Constable Liddle gasped. "Ooooh! Sir! We never torture no one! We sometimes makes them eat one of Mrs Bunton's meat pies. That's a bit cruel. But we never hurts them!"

"I'll hurt her if I don't get my money back," Griggsby growled. "Withering's bank trusts me. I will not let them down."

Charlotte Sharkle was shivering and smudged with red paint. "I am Charlotte Sharkle and I demand to be released," she said to Inspector Beadle. The large policeman sat at a desk ... in a very strong chair.

"So you say," the bald, round bank manager said. He sat alongside the inspector and glared at the girl through his spectacles.

Inspector Beadle nodded. "This is Mr Gordon Griggsby, manager of Withering's bank – the bank that you robbed last night."

"It wasn't me."

"The constables caught you coming out of the night-safe door," the inspector reminded her. "The Sharkle safe-box was empty. The box that contained over a hundred thousand pounds. Now you say you are Silas Sharkle's daughter."

"I *am*!" she cried. "Papa is staying with Mayor Twistle – go and ask him. He'll tell you."

"Tell us what? That you are his daughter? Or that *he* is part of the plot to rob Withering's bank?" Gordon Griggsby asked. "Because, if he *is*, then he'll hang beside you on Darlham gallows! No one robs my bank and gets away with it! Clever Constable Liddle *said* it was odd that only the Sharkle box was robbed. Now we know why."

Inspector Beadle held up a huge hand. "Let's send for Mr Sharkle and see what he has to say." The inspector sent the weary old Constable Liddle up to South Drive to bring Silas Sharkle to Wildpool police station. "Constable Larch can make us a pot of tea while we wait."

"Yes, that would be nice. Two sugars," Charlotte sighed.

"Water for the prisoner," Inspector Beadle said.

*

Bunty McGurgle – the real Bunty McGurgle – walked to the front door with her father.

She looked out to see the bailiff. Would he be as strong as an ox and as wild as a wasp? Or as wild as an ox and strong as a wasp.

Bunty stared. Bunty's little mouth flew open. A gasp flew out of it. "Look, Daddy! Look!"

"I'm looking. I see it. I don't believe it."

For there ... there on the McGurgle doorstep ... stood no one. No one at all.

"Is someone playing knocky-nine-doors with us?" Bunty asked.

"I don't think bailiffs do that," her father said. "I thought I saw two children running away."

"What are these bags on our doorstep? Someone left them there, knocked then ran away. Who would do such a thing? Daddy, oh Daddy!" Bunty cried in her mouse-squeak voice.

"Yes, Bunty-wunty. Who would do such a thing?"

"Daddy, oh Daddy ... I haven't a clue."

"Oh. Better go back inside and wait for the bailiff to arrive."

Mr McGurgle closed the door.

"Daddy?"

"Yes, Bunty-wunty?"

"Do you think we should open the sacks? They were marked 'Swag', is that like loot? Miss Meldrum said a lute is something the Ancient Greeks used to play. She told us a lovely story about Orpheus who played his lute for his girlfriend. And then she was poisoned by Charlotte Sharkle."

"Orpheus's girlfriend was poisoned by Charlotte Sharkle?"

"No, Daddy . . . Miss Meldrum was poisoned by Charlotte. Can we open them, Daddy? I've always wanted to see a real lute."[33]

Go ahead, Bunty," the man said and opened the door.

Bunty untied the first sack and sobbed. "Oh, no! Oh how disappointing!"

"No lute?"

"No, just a bag stuffed with money," Bunty McGurgle sighed. "Oh, I am sad."

33 Orpheus and his lute is a famous Greek myth – or maybe it was a "lyre". My teacher said Orpheus played a "lyre" – he played so beautifully he could turn iron soft and melt stones. But I think my teacher was a lyre.

"Money? How much?"

"Don't know, Daddy. About a hundred thousand pounds ... at a guess."

Inspector Beadle sat at the desk. Gordon Griggsby sat beside him.

At the other side of the desk sat the red-painted Charlotte Sharkle and her father.

For a long while the only sound in the room was the ticking of the clock. For every tick there was a tock of the clock. And so it went on. Finally Silas Sharkle spoke. His beard rustled against his hard, white collar.

"Withering's bank lost my hundred and ten thousand pounds," he said. "You owe me that money. You will pay me." He slapped a piece of paper on the table.

Withering's Bank

Your money is safe as houses.

Your valuables locked in the world's safest safe.

We guarantee that any money lost will be replaced in full.

Gordon Griggsby

Manager: Gordon Griggsby BBC, BARF, MONICA

"We didn't lose it," Griggsby said sourly. "It was stolen by an evil gang."

"It was stolen from your *thief-proof* safe," Silas Sharkle said and bared his teeth.

"It was stolen by your daughter," Griggsby said. "And I would not be surprised if you didn't put her up to it."

"You cannot prove that," Sharkle snarled.

Griggsby spread his hands. "I don't have to. We don't have your friend Preed – the one you sent to get the key – and we don't have the little gang your daughter worked with. But, we do have your daughter. Caught in the act!"

Inspector Beadle leaned forward. "Caught red-handed you could say!" He laughed till his bellies wobbled and made the desk shake.

Gordon Griggsby gave a faint smile. "Remember how we set up a fake robbery of the wagon? It was meant to teach the thieves of Wildpool a lesson – it was meant to show them they couldn't get away with it."

"Of course I remember. I drove the wagon," Sharkle snapped.

"Then we will give the thieves another

lesson," Gordon Griggsby said softly. "We will hang young Charlotte in front of Darlham Gaol and show those thieves what happens when they try to break into the bank."

"That's not fair!" Charlotte cried. "I was only doing what I was told..."

"Hush, Lottie," her father said quickly. "You were only playing a game, weren't you?"

Charlotte pouted. "If you say so, Papa."

"I think I can see a way out of this," Inspector Beadle said. All eyes turned to him. "Mr Griggsby has been taught an important lesson. The thieves have done him a favour – they have shown him a weakness he didn't know about."

"I am not paying over a hundred thousand pounds for that lesson," Griggsby snorted.

Inspector Beadle raised a hand. "Wait, let me finish. Now, Mr Sharkle plotted to steal his own money—"

"How dare you say that!" Sharkle roared. "You can't prove that."

Again the inspector raised a hand. "I don't have to. We have the thief here in front of us –

your daughter, caught by my trusty constables. A girl who steals that much money has to hang. It's the law."

"It's not fair," Charlotte wailed again.

Inspector Beadle ignored her. "What if Mr Sharkle's bank box was empty? What if Charlotte broke into the bank and stole exactly *nothing*, Mr Griggsby. Would you still want to see her hang?"

Griggsby's round eyes glittered behind his round glasses. Roundly. "No," he said.

Inspector Beadle stared hard at Silas Sharkle. "So, Mr Sharkle. How much did you have in Withering's safe?"

Sharkle's jaw moved from side to side so his beard moved like a brush. He breathed as harshly as a pig at a trough. Finally he whispered, "Nothing."

"And how much money do you want from Withering's bank?"

Sharkle swallowed hard. "Nothing."

Inspector Beadle turned to Gordon Griggsby. "Charlotte Sharkle broke into your bank and stole ... *nothing*."

"She damaged the floorboards!" Griggsby grumbled. "Someone can pay for that."

"Charlotte can pay," Sharkle snarled.

"I haven't any money, Papa!" the girl said.

"We'll sell your dolls' house," he told her.

"Oh," she sniffed. Then she got a cunning look in her eye. "I can tell you who helped me – give you their names and tell you where to find them."

Inspector Beadle shook his massive head. "There is no point. Nothing was stolen. Mr Griggsby does not want the police to charge anyone, do you Mr Griggsby?"

"I don't," the bank manager agreed.

Inspector Beadle rose to his feet. "So, that's it. Charlotte is free to go. The case is closed."

Gordon Griggsby smiled.

Silas Sharkle glared. He marched out of Wildpool police station and a girl in a red dress ran after him crying, "I suppose a golden dolls' palace is out of the question?"

He didn't reply.

Chapter 14

BANK AND THANK

Tuesday 18th April 1837

The pupils of Master Crook's Crime Academy stood at the window of their classroom and looked down on the High Street. They watched Silas Sharkle march from the police station towards the railway station.

He pushed past shoppers, he barged past the stalls where shopkeepers showed their clothes and vegetables, meat and fruit, boots and books, he stamped through puddles and splashed the poor blind beggar on the corner.

He brushed away the newspaper seller who was selling the *Wildpool Star*. He didn't want to read the news.

And he definitely wouldn't want to read the news the next day.

Wednesday 19th April 1837

19 April 1837

THE WILDPOOL STAR

CONSTABLE CLOWNS

On Monday night a daring attempt was made to raid Withering's bank on its first day. Thieves tried to enter through the night safe. Manager Gordon Griggsby told our reporter, "Nothing was taken because the thief-proof safe is thief-proof. People can leave their money safe with us . . . in the safe . . . safely."

Our reporter saw Norman Craggs, the safe builder, arrive very early with a new sheet of shining steel. It looked like a floor for the safe. Gordon Griggsby said, "Don't be ridiculous. As if we'd build a safe without a floor."

Mayor Twistle said he was shocked to hear of the raid. His police constables were aware that an attempt was being made. However, by the time they reached the bank they were only able to arrest a girl in a red dress.

The constable clowns were at the docks when they were told to guard the bank," the mayor said angrily. "As soon as I see them I will rip off the medals I gave them earlier this month."

N o arrests have been made. Inspector Beadle said, "The thieves probably came from Darlham. They escaped arrest by a whisker and got away with nothing. People of Wildpool can sleep easy. The bank robbers will not be back."

Smiff Smith looked out of the classroom window. He gave a sigh. "She won't be punished, then?" he asked.

"No," Alice said. "I never liked her, but I wouldn't want to see her hang."

"They don't hang rich people," Nancy muttered. "Only the poor."

A whistle sounded. It came from a speaking tube that hung on the wall. Martin ran over and blew down it to show someone was answering. Then he placed it to his ear. He listened. He looked at the class.

"Master Crook wants to see us," he said. "Now."

The pupils followed Samuel Dreep down the stairs and into the basement. The room was dim, no windows and only a single candle. The pupils and the teacher sat on green wooden chairs and faced a curtain that hung across a corner of the room.

The curtain stirred as a door behind it opened. Master Crook did not step through the curtain. He never did. His deep voice rumbled through the room.

"Mr Dreep and I are sorry," he said.

Silence. Alice said, "What you sorry about?"

"Sorry we were fooled by Charlotte Sharkle . . . we let a spy into your class. And she set a trap that could have caught you all. I'm sorry."

"But it didn't work," Millie Mixly said. "We got away with it."

"How did you get away?" Master Crook sighed.

"Alice saved us," Smiff muttered.

"Exactly. The girl that Mr Dreep threw out of his class . . . the girl that saw Charlotte Sharkle for what she truly is. We all owe Alice White a very large 'thank you'."

"Thanks, Alice," the pupils said.

"Oh stop it!" Alice cried. Even in the dim

light of the candle the class could see her blushing. "The others would have done the same ... wouldn't you? We're a team. We fight for each other. Look at rule eleven."

11 PUPILS OF MASTER CROOK'S CRIME ACADEMY LOOK OUT FOR ONE ANOTHER.

The class nodded silently.

"There are so many people out there who need our help," Alice cried. "We shouldn't be sitting here, moaning on about how we nearly got caught! We should be up in the classroom planning our next adventure. There are hundreds of rich people out there – people like the Sharkles – that make their money by stealing from other people. It's our job to get money to the right people!"

Her words rang off the walls of the basement room and died into silence. "Erm ... thank you, Alice ... that is *exactly* why I set up this academy."

"And you didn't set it up so we could sit down here talking, did you?"

"No I—"

"No, you didn't. One day someone is going to ask us to tell the story of Master Crook's Crime Academy. They won't ask us, 'Hey, what did you *talk* about?' No, they'll ask us, 'What did you *do*?' So let's go and do it!"[34]

The pupils jumped to their feet and ran to the door. "Come on, Mr Dreep, what are you waiting for?" Smiff laughed as he disappeared.

"Erm ... class dismissed," Master Crook said.

"I think they already have," Dreep said faintly.

In Wildpool police station, Constables Liddle and Larch stood in their red-smudged uniforms. The little mayor, Sir Oswald Twistle, stood in front of them and ranted. "One hundred and

34 You have to admit Alice was right! Here you are reading the adventures of the Master Crook's Crime Academy, just as she said ... over 60 years ago. No one will ever raise a statue to Alice White ... it's the rich villains that get the statues ... but at least she and her friends are not forgotten. Not as long as you read her story. Alice says thank you!

ten thousand pounds," he shouted. "You stood there and watched some villains wheel away one hundred and ten thousand pounds in a barrow and did nothing."

"Sorry, sir, were we supposed to help them? It did look a bit heavy," Larch said.

"Yes, we should have helped," Liddle nodded.

"You should have *stopped* them ... searched the barrow ... saved Mr Sharkle's money!" the mayor raged.

"Inspector Beadle said nothing was stolen," Liddle argued.

"Yes ... ah ... yes ... as far as the people of Wildpool know there was no money stolen. That's what Mr Sharkle and I are *saying*."

"So it's a lie then? You and Mr Sharkle are telling lies?"

"That's not the point!" the mayor snapped. "You let the thieves get away."

"With nothing," Larch pointed out.

"With ... nothing," the mayor said. "But you should have stopped them!"

"Ah! But we were told not to touch the girls

in the blue dresses," Larch said. "That was the message to Captain Hoo."

"Who?

"Hoo!"

"I don't *know*," the mayor cried. "I'm asking *you*. But that is not the point. If *I* wore a blue dress would you let *me* walk out of this police station with a sack full of cash?" the mayor cried.

"No sir. If you wore a blue dress we'd lock you up! For your own good, of course. The whole town would laugh at you if we let you walk out on to the High Street in a dress," Liddle said.

"Have you got a blue dress?" Larch asked the mayor.

"No I have *not*!" Mayor Twistle roared.

"That's all right then," the policeman smiled.

Mayor Twistle reached up and snatched at the medals on the front of the constables' uniforms. He tore them off. "You are a disgrace to the uniform," he said and stormed out of the door.

Liddle looked at Larch and sighed. "We're a disgrace to the uniform," he said.

"Yes but Mayor Twistle is a disgrace to the whole town!" Larch argued.

"How's that, Larch?"

"Coming in here, telling lies about money, and threatening to rob the police station wearing a blue dress. At least we're not as disgraceful as that."

"Very true, Larch, very true."

The two men wandered out into the sunny April morning. They breathed in the rotten air of Wildpool, looked up at the clouds as fluffy as dead sheep, and smiled. "Spring in the air," Larch said.

"Why should I?" Liddle asked.

The day after the robbery, Bunty McGurgle was tidying the money bags when she found a note that she had missed.

"There was a note with the money, Daddy!"

"Then read it, my little sweet-pea. Read it!"

Bunty, who always did as she was told, read it.

Dear Mr McGurgle,

Just before Mr Silas Sharkle's ship sank we managed to rescue some of the weapons. We sold them and made one hundred thousand pounds. Here is the money. Please do NOT sell weapons to China or anywhere else. They will only kill people.

Captain Hoo

P.S. Mr Sharkle doesn't know about this. Do not tell him or we will send a ship to take the money back.

Bunty McGurgle gasped. "That explains it ... sort of. The main thing, Daddy, is we are not poor after all."

"No bailiffs!" Mr McGurgle happily cried.

"I was looking forward to a beef stew with those bay leafs," Bunty sighed.

"Oh, Bunty, you are a silly girl," her father said.

"I know. But at least I didn't lose a hundred thousand pounds," she shrugged.

THE END

Look out for:

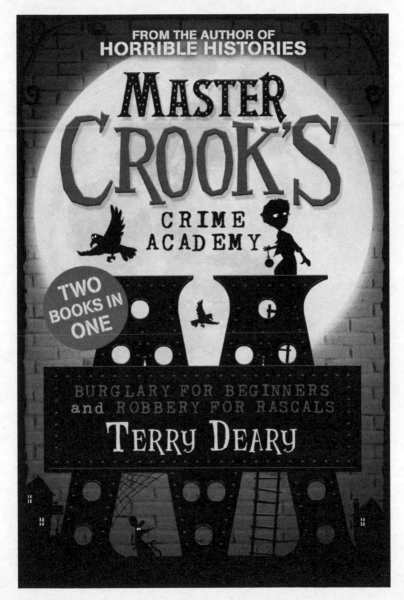

FROM THE AUTHOR OF
HORRIBLE HISTORIES

MASTER CROOK'S

CRIME ACADEMY

TWO BOOKS IN ONE

BURGLARY FOR BEGINNERS
and ROBBERY FOR RASCALS

TERRY DEARY